Earthquake

APRILYNNE PIKE

MIX

Paper from
responsible sources

FSC

FSC C007454

FSC is a non-profit international organisation established to promote
the responsible management of the world's forests. Products carrying
the FSC label are independently certified to assure consumers that they
come from forests that are managed to meet the social, economic and
ecological needs of present and future generations,
and other controlled sources.

To Ashley, because I miss you.

First published in hardback in the USA by Razorbill,
a division of the Penguin Group in 2014
First published in Great Britain by HarperCollins *Children's* Books in 2014
HarperCollins *Children's* Books is a division of HarperCollins *Publishers* Ltd,
77-85 Fulham Palace Road, Hammersmith, London, W6 8JB.

www.harpercollins.co.uk

ISBN 978-0-00-755306-8

Printed and bound in England by Clays Ltd, St Ives plc.

1

CHAPTER ONE

*M*y pulse throbs in my temples—a frantic rhythm that matches the pounding of my feet. I feel ridiculous stooping to something as primitive—as human—as running away, but I can't beat them in my natural way.

I should be able to. My sudden increase in strength terrifies even me. But that's the problem; I'm too afraid to unleash it. Afraid of what I might do. The people I might hurt. It's too much all at once.

It's not right. So I run.

But I'm not really a runner. Not the long-distance kind for sure. They're gaining on me. It was inevitable. It's not like I really thought I could get away; I just needed a few minutes to think. So I took off.

What are they going to do? Shoot me in the back? They need me alive and we all know it.

With my lungs aching, I gasp to a stop and they surround

me, all of us breathing hard. I'm not completely sure where I am. An overpass. No, one of those pedestrian bridges over a freeway. Cars zoom beneath me, the sound of roaring engines echoing in my ears as vibrations shake the cement under my feet. The people around me have drawn their guns. Obviously they don't care about creating a scene. They'll kill any witnesses without a second thought.

But I care.

I care, damn it!

I grasp at the gritty edge of the cement railing. As I lean back the rushing wind from cars and trucks bursts up, tossing my hair and ruffling my shirt. A semi passes beneath the already swaying walkway. The driver must have seen us because he lets loose the long bellow of his horn as though in warning, and I wonder if he's calling the cops even now.

Not that it matters. It's too late.

"It's over," the closest man says, edging even nearer. "Come with us. We don't want to hurt you."

It's a lie. We both know it.

My eyes scan their faces. Each and every one is a person I would once have called a friend. Not recently. Certainly not for a dozen lifetimes. But once.

I scrape my palms on the hot, crumbly concrete, using the pain to focus my mind. There's no barrier. I could jump. But they'd save me. They're already too close.

Think.

Think.

The answer hits me, and my breath catches in terror.

"Sonya, you're being ridiculous." Marianna's voice—belittling as always—strengthens my determination, even though my bones feel like water. I would rather die than let her have me. Than let her figure out how to become like me.

Because if that ever happened, gods help the entire world.

For the thousandth time I consider killing her. Killing them. But the delay would be momentary at best. There are dozens of them.

And only one of me.

Fortunately, there are also more than six billion people to hide among.

I close my eyes and a ripple of apprehension goes through the handful of operatives pointing weapons at me. I might have three seconds before they do something stupid. I picture my heart, beating so steadily, if way too fast. A sob catches in my throat, but I push it away.

And turn my heart to stone.

Literally.

The agony in my chest tries to force a scream from my lips, but it's too late. It takes only a moment, maybe two, before I know I've done it.

I've killed myself.

And I taste victory on my tongue as everything goes black.

CHAPTER TWO

I sit up with a muffled scream, my hands clutching my chest. Air is honey-sweet on my tongue as I suck in breaths—gripping my arm with my nails to feel the pain. To assure myself that I'm alive.

Three nights in a row it's been like this. Dreams of Sonya. Sonya running from what I can only assume are Reduciates: Earthbound bad guys. Sonya afraid of her own powers—afraid to protect herself.

And, of course, Sonya taking her own life. But in the dreams I'm not looking down at her. I'm not an observer. In the dreams I *am* her.

Am myself, I guess. In my past life. My most recent life.

But unlike true memories, this dream shifts every time it comes to me, the way I end my life changing with each passing night. I've pulled the trigger of a gun pressed to my head, thrown myself in front of a speeding semi.

4

But turning my heart to literal stone? This one was the worst. I don't know if that's how it happened. If *any* of them are how it happened. I don't understand why my mind is making me see her death over and over—and why I can't remember how it all actually went down.

Or better yet, *why*.

Well, I know why, *technically*. The secret. The one from way back in Rebecca's time—the girl I was in the early nineteenth century. The one I told no one, not even my partner, Quinn. I was silenced at the end of that life, silenced myself at the end of my life as Sonya. But I don't know what that secret is.

And I have a feeling the dreams won't end until I figure it out.

I *should* remember. I'm an Earthbound—a cursed goddess who lives life after life, seeking my perfect love. I should remember all my lives. But something about the injuries I received in a plane crash last year have made everything . . . difficult.

My body is covered with sweat, and it's not all from the harrowing dream. The Phoenix heat is sweltering even in the dusky hours of dawn, and the air conditioning is . . . less reliable than the hotel manager insinuated. I drag myself from sticky sheets to twist the tap on the sink that's inches from the foot of the tiny single bed.

The water dribbling from the tap is lukewarm at best, but I'm in no position to be picky.

The spring heat is too intense, topping 110 for several days even before I arrived. The temperature broke records every day last week. I wonder if it's part of the weather phenomenon my former guardian Mark was sure the virus was somehow causing. It seems like it must be. Everything in the world is crazy right now. The virus is spreading so quickly no one can get a truly accurate death count. Five thousand yesterday, one news channel said. Ten, claimed another.

Either way, it's out of control, and nature apparently isn't immune.

I don't know how the hell I can possibly stop this, but Mark and his wife, Sammi, were certain I held the key, if I could just resurge with Logan—the boy Quinn is in this life. I have to trust that. It's all I've got.

As I splash myself I consider again the braid of twine that Sammi gave me. The one Sonya made. Sammi kept it from when she encountered Sonya eighteen years ago. Sammi and her father were Curatoriates. They're supposed to be the good guys—the opposite of the Reduciates. I'm not convinced it's that simple. Neither was Rebecca. I have a feeling Sonya wasn't either.

I could find out. The little braid is still in my faded red backpack where Sammi put it last week. It'll give me my memories back. The memories that Sonya had.

Probably.

But considering the way the last awakening went, I'm not completely sure I'd survive a second round. Not without someone to help me. And I can't take *any* risks until I resurge with Logan.

Or we'll both be dead forever and the rest of the world will die with us.

That is the single truth that keeps me here. Trying.

I'm desperate. *That* is also a truth. More true than anything else in my life today. Besides, what I really need is to figure out how to wake Logan up before the Reduciates who are after me kill us both. And Sonya's memories won't help with that since she never found him during her life.

I turn on the leaky showerhead and duck into the tiny stall, sluicing away sweat as though I could somehow cleanse myself of the awful dream. Of this awful week. Everything is falling to pieces. I lean my head against the tiled wall and review the last few dismal days as water beats down on my back.

It started out so well a mere three days ago. After sleeping the whole night in a real bed for the first time in almost two weeks—not to mention getting my first shower in eight days—I woke up on Sunday morning ready to take on anything. I was in Phoenix, I'd located Logan, and I knew he was *the one*. The rest would be easy, I was certain. I didn't care that the hotel towels didn't look quite clean, or that the clerk had vastly under-reported how loud the train just outside my back window would be.

That first night I didn't even care about the lack of reliable AC. I had a home base that didn't require ID. And more importantly—thanks to getting his number on Saturday—I had a date with Logan. Quinn. Whatever anyone in my head wanted to call him, I had a date with the love of my life. The love of my many, many lives.

And it went fabulously. We talked, we laughed, the sun glinted off his golden hair, short now and a lighter blond thanks to bleaching from the desert sun. At one point he even reached out and touched the end of my nose. It was perfect.

At that moment it was easy to forget the entire reason I

was in Phoenix: because I'm being hunted by the Reduciata. Because *we're* being hunted, really.

If they can kill us before we resurge—before we both remember our past lives and regain our powers—we'll be gone permanently.

But none of that mattered as I sat there bantering with Logan. I knew, was *sure* I was only minutes away from reaching my goal. The Reduciata was way in the back of my head. As far as I was concerned, I'd practically won already.

Then it fell apart. *I* fell apart.

I'd told him I was a history buff, and right before dessert was served I pulled out what I said was a rare antique. A journal.

His journal.

This was the moment.

I'd realized that morning that I'd been stupid to think the necklace could bring his memories back. The necklace that initially brought *my* memories back. Some of my memories, anyway.

Of course, I thought it was Quinn who *made* the necklace. . . .

Anyway, that didn't matter—the journal, full of *his* handwriting, would give me back my destined lover. My Earthbound counterpart. The god to my goddess. I pulled it out, opened it, and wondered if he would recognize his own writing. Then I slid it across the table.

He laid his hands on the pages and . . . nothing.

I tried to smile. To act like everything was okay. But I could almost feel the shards of the world clattering down around me. On top of me.

In the previous weeks I'd run for my life, seen people die, had my entire view of reality revamped, and been betrayed deeper than I ever thought possible.

All to get me here to this boy. For him to remember me. To love me. And then for us to somehow save a world that's dying more and more quickly every day from a mysterious virus I have no idea how to fix.

I couldn't stay there at the restaurant with him. It was too hard. I threw down enough money to cover the bill, mumbled an apology, and took off without waiting for my sundae.

About ten feet from the table I stopped. I couldn't help it; I looked back.

And he was just staring at me. He called my name—a question, almost—but I ignored him. And even if he *had* run after me—thrown the doors open, tried to look for me—he wouldn't have found me. Because in that shadowed space between the two sets of doors, I changed.

Changed into my mother.

I do it every time I'm in public. Use my powers as an Earthbound to wear her face the way I desperately did on the bus in Portsmouth. I pretend it keeps me safe.

There's a chance it does.

I walked back to my hotel and—of course—the door had been kicked open. I didn't know if a Reduciate assassin was to blame or simply the fact that my hotel was so crappy, but it wasn't worth risking my life to stay to find out. In a fear-fueled panic I grabbed my stuff and got the hell out of there.

Five minutes later, with nothing but the belongings in my backpack and an already aching leg—it still hasn't fully healed from the plane crash that took everything from me—I moved to another cheap hotel. A less-than-pristine establishment that didn't ask questions when I laid an antique gold coin on the dingy counter, one of many from a collection Quinn and I had stored two hundred years ago. It was a win for both parties; they got to feel like they were ripping me off, and I got a bed and shower that didn't cost me anything I considered important.

The next day the bedbug welts showed up. Large, painfully itching bumps all over my arms and legs that make me look like I have a disease. Or, at the very least, cleanliness issues.

I hate them. And there is no lotion that takes that burning itch away.

If I'd been smart—no, not smart exactly, but slower and less desperate—I would have stopped at a store somewhere. Gotten a pretty, long-sleeved shirt to cover my scabby arms. After all, I have money. Plenty of money. I've been selling a little gold at slimy pawnshops in every city where the Greyhound gave us a break. Hoarding it. Just in case.

But I wasn't smart and I wasn't slow.

I was in love instead.

So I went to Logan's house early Monday morning, walked to school with him. Followed him all the way to the front doors. Stuck to him like glue, hoping something—something!—would click in his head. I suspect it wasn't any *one* thing that made him drop his eyes and lie to me when I asked if he had plans for dinner—it was everything all mixed together. The welts, the rumpled clothes, the stalker-ish behavior, the desperation emanating from me in waves.

I waited for him after school, but he must have seen me and gone another way. I should have camped out at his house instead. All I had to show for my two hours was a nasty sunburn.

Some goddess I'm turning out to be.

I'm ten minutes into my tepid shower—which actually feels pretty good on my reddened shoulders—when I realize I have one more item. One more shot at getting Logan to believe me. I shove my soggy head around the shower curtain to glance at the tiny clock. 7:04 A.M. Still time.

I get at least most of the suds out of my hair before half tripping out of the bathtub and drying off as fast as I can. Yesterday he left the house at 7:35. I can still make it. My hair is a mess, but it can't look much worse than it did the last time he saw me, so it'll have to suffice.

I grab a gold coin and clutch it in both hands, taking a moment to close my eyes and release my hopes into the universe. *Just let this work!* You'd think an Earthbound—a literal goddess—would be able to handle something as easy as restoring memories to her eternal partner. But none of my abilities can help with this.

My leg is throbbing as I approach his house, and I can't stop my heart from racing when Logan bursts out of his front door. He looks around warily—I guess I really got to him—but he doesn't notice me duck behind the bushes. I follow him from across the street and touch the heavy silver necklace for confidence. The one that brought me back my memories but failed to bring back Logan's.

The one he made for me two hundred years ago. He just doesn't know it.

Now.

I jog quietly up behind him before saying, "Logan?"

He whirls around, and I get a glimpse of real fear painted on his face before stubborn anger takes over.

"I have something to show you," I announce before he can speak.

"Listen, Tavia," Logan says, rubbing at his neck in what Rebecca-in-my-head instantly recognizes as his nervous twitch. "I don't really understand why you keep bringing me stuff. It's . . . it's kind of weirding me out."

"Will you at least look at it?" I beg. I have no pride left. Not anymore. None of my attempts have had any effect whatsoever, and everything I've sacrificed—everything others have *died* for—will mean nothing if I don't succeed.

Logan studies me for a long time, and I try to keep my face relaxed. "Fine," Logan finally replies after what feels like ages. "Whatever."

I hold out my hand and pray—to whom, I don't know; the God I was raised on, the other Earthbounds, whoever *made* the Earthbounds; I don't care anymore—that this will work. The coin falls from my palm into his with a barely audible smacking sound.

He lifts the gold circle close to his face—but not too close—and studies it. Then he sighs and hands it back to me. In a show of what I can only imagine is pity, he curls my fingers around the coin and then his hand around mine. "Tavia, I know someone must have told you this is gold, but you've got to stop believing everyone so easily. I—" He hesitates, and my heart sinks. I can sense the impending rejection. "I think you're a really nice person. And pretty," he blurts out and then looks like he surprised himself with those words. "But I *can't help you*."

He's talking again before I can latch onto the word *pretty* too hard. "I'm just a kid, and I think you seriously need some professional help."

My hands are so weak from disappointment that I can barely hang on to the coin. It *would* be my luck that when we split up supplies, I took the bag of gold coins *I* made as Rebecca, and Benson got the bag that Quinn made. Or maybe I made them all—I'm a little fuzzy on the details.

I swallow hard at the thought of Benson—the boy I thought I was in love with . . . until he betrayed me—but push it away just as I have innumerable times in the last week. It hurts too much to dwell on. To wonder where the Reduciates are keeping him. If he's being treated humanely. If . . . if . . .

I can't. Logan. *Focus on Logan.*

"You don't understand, Logan." I can hear the crazy-laced desperation in my voice, but I can't stop. I don't know what else to do. If I don't pull out something impressive I'm going to lose him.

"They're coming after you," I whisper, trying to sound so serious—and *so* sane. "They almost killed me last week and they're after *both* of us now and I have got to find some way to make you remember and I've tried everything and—" I force myself to stop; I'm just babbling. I plead with my eyes for him to believe me.

"Who's coming after me?" Logan asks after a second,

indulging me as one would a very young child telling an obvious lie.

"The . . ." I almost tell him everything—that it's the Reduciata who are on his trail. That they are going to kill him. Probably in a matter of days, if not sooner. Possibly the Curatoria too, considering Mark and Sammi were hiding me from them. But I know that the specifics will only make me sound even more like I have a couple of screws loose.

His face is a rumpled mess of emotions. Despite my failed attempts at subtlety, he obviously thinks I'm out of my mind.

But there's something else—that pull that made him ask if he knew me the first day we met. That attraction that makes him *want* to forget all logic and throw himself at something completely unexplainable.

I understand. I felt that way toward him.

We stand there, steeping in the silence, and for just a moment it looks like he'll believe me. Or at least that he'll listen. But good sense takes over, and he sets his lips in a hard, straight line. "Tavia, I—"

"I'll show you," I interrupt, my hair starting to fall across my eyes in damp strands as sweat rolls down my temples. Even at seven thirty in the morning the heat is so intense I know it can't be natural. "Watch." I glance in both directions and then open my hands to reveal a pencil.

I probably should have come up with something more original.

Logan just rolls his eyes and starts to push past me.

"Wait!" I gesture vaguely at the yard to my left and conjure a table and two chairs into existence. *Show* him what I can do:

14

create something from nothing. He doesn't know it'll disappear in five minutes.

It's not just any dining set. It's the hand-carved oak set we shared as Quinn and Rebecca two hundred years ago. Maybe . . . maybe seeing it will do something. Spark some memory. Maybe not enough for a full re-awakening, but enough that he'll take me seriously.

I turn back. "They're after us because we're *special*," I say with solid conviction, keeping my voice even. "You can do this too, you just don't remember. And you *have to* remember. At least *try!*" I wave again, and the table fills with "our" dishes. A rug that used to sit in front of the fireplace. His favorite coat draped over the chair. I'm ready to recreate the entire *house* if I have to.

Each time I make a new item appear, I glance back to check his reaction—to see if I'm stimulating any memories.

But he just looks confused.

Then angry.

Anger does not come naturally to him—never has. I'm not sure who that thought comes from in my tangled web of memories—which one of my predecessors felt compelled to share this tidbit of information—but I know it's true. Whatever I've done—whatever he thinks of me—this has pushed him over the edge.

"Stop!" he hisses very quietly, but with a harshness that swings me around to face him.

"Please," I whisper, and somehow I know it's the last word I'm going to get in.

"No," he says. "Take your hidden cameras and practical jokes somewhere else. I'm done."

"Logan—"

But he puts his hands on my shoulders—firmly, not roughly—and moves me out of his way. "Don't follow me anymore."

I'm gasping for breath as sobs of failure slam into me, overwhelming me like ocean breakers. I can't . . . I can't just—

An unseen force slaps my back and throws me against Logan as the world ripples beneath my feet. The motion tosses us to the sidewalk, splaying us both on the ground. My elbow stings, and blood drips from a cut across Logan's eyebrows. I'm staring disbelievingly at the vibrant red when a burst of sound reaches us, deafening me even as I scream at the top of my lungs. Logan's face contorts into a mask of horror, and I whip my head around to follow his line of sight.

All I see are flames.

Flames where Logan's house used to sit.

We both scramble up and run toward it, our mutual desperation to see what's happened so intense that I hardly feel the sharp pain jolting up my leg.

His house is *gone*.

A smoking pile of charred rubble sits in its place. Orange flames dance over its remains, staining the sky. If I didn't already know, I couldn't have guessed what sort of structure had previously stood there—everything has collapsed. The flames burn so hot that even from several hundred feet away the waves of heat feel like they might blister my skin.

This is a fire meant to kill.

Meant to kill *Logan*.

And I know who set it.

"We have to get out of here *now*," I say, whirling and grabbing Logan's arm, trying to drag him with me.

I might as well be trying to shove a boulder. He stares, dumbstruck, at the horrifying destruction.

A column of thick, murky smoke is already rising high. It's going to attract the attention of everyone for miles around. Reduciata handiwork for sure—subtle is not in their vocabulary. If I have any shot of hiding the fact that Logan survived, I have to get him out of here. "Logan, *please!*"

I don't hear the sound of tires screeching as a car pulls up beside us, but I smell the acrid scent of rubber a second before something comes down over my head, blocking my sight. I fight and tear against the suffocating material, but a sharp jab stings my arms, burns for a second, then blackness.

CHAPTER THREE

I'm not sure how much time elapses before I haze into consciousness. My head aches and my throat is painfully dry as pinpricks of light worm through my lashes. I throw my arm over my face—my eyes are so sensitive; I must have been out for a while—and struggle to remember where I am.

And how I got here.

The explosion, Logan's house, the bag over my head.

The stinging pain in my arm.

Drugs.

Logan! Where is he? My head whips around, making me dizzy even as I fight to focus. There's something on the floor—a dark lump in the corner, and as soon as I realize what—who—it is I fling myself over to it, to him.

"Logan. Logan!" I roll him over, my head spinning, and he emits a low groan but doesn't open his eyes. I curl my body protectively around him and throw my hands up to create something—*anything*—to protect us from whatever the Reduciata, or whoever, has in store. But a new bout of sharp pain thrusts through my arm, and again the world swirls in front of me.

I collapse onto the floor, and my cheek falls against chilly tile.

My eyelids close.

The next time I float back to reality I keep my eyes clamped shut and take a few minutes to think. I acted too quickly last time. That doesn't help anyone. No sudden movements—that's step one.

Slowly, I lift my eyelids just enough to peer through my lashes at my surroundings. I'm in a stark white room, and I can see a huge mirror on one side that throws my reflection back at me. A two-way mirror, no doubt.

I sniff and smell what I swear is fresh paint. Everything is so neat and new as to be almost sterile. The smooth white walls, squeaky-clean white tiled floor, even the grout between the tiles is scrubbed to a pristine cream color. Like they poured a huge bottle of bleach over this place before dumping us in here. I shudder, wondering just what they had to scrub away.

I'm lying on my side, curled against Logan, and the warmth from his body makes me feel a tiny bit better. Yes, we're obviously in some kind of prison, I guess, but at least I'm not alone. He's still unconscious. Last time I awoke I at least got him to groan, but now he doesn't respond to my touch at all. I wonder if at the same time they injected me they also got him with . . .

whatever was in the needle. I glance down at my arm, where I can see two red dots. They make me want to scream in anger, but I've got to keep my cool. I focus on Logan instead.

I pull his limp torso halfway upright across my lap and cradle his large frame against my chest. I tell myself it's because I don't want him to get too cold lying on the freezing tile floor, but the truth is, after three days of him not letting me get near, I just want to hold him. This is the first time I've really gotten a chance to look at him this close. His skin is so tan against the honey color of his hair. I run my fingers through the short strands, remembering when they were long. Remembering *Rebecca* remembering. I scrunch my eyebrows together at that. Close enough.

He has a smattering of freckles along his hairline and across his cheeks that didn't used to be there. Probably from living in the desert. There's dried blood from the cut over his eye. I prod it gingerly, but it doesn't seem too deep. My arms tremble as I attempt to check him for further injuries. I'm not sure where we are or how much longer they're going to let us live, but at least we're together.

As long as we're together, there's hope. Logan *is* my hope.

An icy spike of fear makes its way through my intense relief, and I force myself to peer around with what I hope is a degree of subtlety. Not that there's much to observe. The room is bare and small, and the only possible escape is beyond that mirror I can't see through.

Glancing at my reflection, I curl my shoulders, trying to look both harmless, which isn't too hard given my pathetic appearance—bad hair, bedbug welts, no makeup, a big red mark across my cheek—and ignorant. The latter is, of course, more challenging. What I *want* to do is scream and yell and demand they let us go, but I have a feeling I'll have better luck if I try to act submissive. That tranquilizer is nasty stuff. And I have no intention of staying a prisoner for long. Not after everything I've done. *We've* done. I just need to bide my time for a little while. First things first, I have to get Logan awake. There is no way on earth I'm leaving him.

While I'm waiting for Logan to open his eyes, I feel out the situation. "Hello?" I call quietly. My throat is so parched that only a hiss of a whisper comes out.

A bottle of water appears on the floor in front of me. *Appears.* It doesn't get pushed through a little door or anything. Just pops into existence. Now I know for sure that there are Earthbounds involved. But whether they're Reduciata—as I suspect—Curatoria, or something else entirely, I can't be sure.

I reach for the bottle tentatively and consider the risks. They'll want me to talk—so this water *probably* isn't poisoned.

Probably.

I could make my own, but it'll only disappear a few minutes later; and besides, I have a feeling that would bring about unhappy consequences.

I unscrew the cap and intend to sip—hoping to maintain some semblance of decorum despite my desperate thirst— but as soon as the cold water touches my cotton-dry tongue I'm gulping, and in seconds the whole thing is gone. Trying to cover my embarrassment, I resume my hunched posture of submission and screw the lid back on with as much dignity as I can muster. Then I set the empty bottle in front of me.

It vanishes only to be replaced by a new one.

This time I manage to drink the first few sips more slowly, considering this a test to make sure that this water is safe to ingest. It's too late for caution regarding the last one, but I'm not taking chances anymore. I begin counting to three hundred, deciding that if I make it through a full five minutes without croaking, then the water *most likely* hasn't been tampered with.

By the time I reach the 290s, I'm satisfied that the water isn't poisoned and start actively trying to rouse Logan. This bottle is for him.

"Logan?" I lift his eyelids, first one and then the other. I poke and pinch his arm, shake him back and forth, and pat his cheeks sharply, just shy of a slap. Finally he starts to groan again. I keep prodding, not willing to lose this progress. He rolls to the side and starts to raise himself up to a sitting position, his eyes eerily out of focus.

"Here," I say, proffering the nearly full water bottle. Even in his fuzzy haze he takes it and gulps it down about as quickly as I did. He shakes his head and rubs at his face as I set the water bottle down. "More," he murmurs, his lips chalky-white.

Looking up at what I still believe to be two-way glass, I echo Logan's request with my eyes and am rewarded with a cold bottle a few seconds later. Now that we're three bottles in, I hand the newest one directly over to Logan without testing it. I'm going to have to trust whoever is behind that mirror one more time. After all, if they *wanted* us dead they would have done it already. Right?

But I think of Logan's house, and doubt curls in my stomach.

Maybe it is the Curatoria after all. Don't the Reduciata just want to murder us? Sadly, the thought that we might be in the custody of the not-as-bad guys doesn't make me feel much better.

Logan is halfway through his second water when his eyes gain focus and zero in on me. "You!" he exclaims. Liquid spews from his mouth as he tosses the bottle down and crab walks backward away from me. His arms crumple beneath him, but he keeps scooting until his back is up against the corner, as far from me as the suddenly claustrophobic room will allow. "You stay away from me!" he shouts.

"Logan, I—"

"You did this!" he yells. "You made—you made all of this happen. Stay the *hell* away from me!"

"I didn't—"

"My house," he's almost talking to himself now, struggling to get to his feet. But his strength isn't back yet, and he leans against the wall, staggering to the side when he attempts to stand. He covers his face with one hand and lets out an inhuman sound halfway between a bark and a sob. "My family." He's nearly hyperventilating, and one arm splays against the wall as though grounding himself against everything.

Against me.

"They're dead, aren't they?" He sounds like a little boy. But all I can do is give him the honest answer I know in my gut is true. I nod.

His breath is labored, the sound filling my ears. "Oh no. I can't—they didn't . . . Did I do something wrong?"

"You didn't do anything," I blurt. "It's not your fault."

My voice finds its way through his devastation, and his eyes narrow. "You're right," his says, his lips curling into a terrible grimace. "It's *your* fault. Why couldn't you leave me alone!"

"I was trying to save you," I reply, my voice barely more than a whisper as I wilt beneath his accusations. My heart bleeds at his revulsion.

"Save me? The only reason I'm here is *because* of you." He limps but manages to get across the room to the mirror, having clearly also identified it as the place where our captors are hidden. He pounds on it with both fists so hard I'm sure it's going to shatter beneath his rage. "Please, get me away from her!"

"Logan, stop!" I shout, tears running down my face. I couldn't stop them if I wanted to.

He's right. I brought attention to him and in so doing I got his family killed.

I would hate me too.

There's nothing I can do but crouch there on the cold, tiled floor, the strength drained from my body. It's been eight months since my parents died, but watching Logan pound on the mirror, my mind flies back to the moment I realized our plane was crashing. Tears stream down my face in a torrent that splashes on the tile and joins the puddle of water that still drips out of Logan's discarded bottle. For an instant it almost seems like the entire pool could have been formed from my tears.

It feels like hours before Logan relents. Finally, he crumbles into a heap on the floor, his face pressed to his arms, his forehead dotted with sweat.

I can only imagine what the people watching us are thinking.

Are they amused? Satisfied? Is this what they wanted? To watch us be so helpless? So at each other's throats?

We've got to be in the hands of the Reduciata. Surely the Curatoria wouldn't kill Logan's family.

Surely.

But I can't muster up a great deal of confidence to back that up.

My head aches from crying, and my eyes feel like cotton balls. But none of that compares to how my heart feels. Broken, shattered. No, something else. Empty.

After a while I feel my eyelids droop, and I fall into an exhausted, desperate sleep. Logan must as well because when I open my eyes again he's calm. He's back in his corner, far away from me, but his eyes are dark and glittering when they meet mine. He's been waiting for me to wake up.

"Who are you?" he asks, his voice a little hoarse. Whether from screaming or disuse after sleeping I'm not sure. "And don't lie this time."

"I never lied," I say, massaging my aching leg and trying to clear my foggy head. "I'm Tavia, like I said."

"The whole truth."

I look him in the eyes. What can I say to make him trust me? "I'm your eternal lover. We've been together since the beginning of time—in every lifetime that we could find one another."

He lets out a harsh, mocking laugh. "Right. I should have known better than to even ask."

"Then *you* tell me why you feel like you know me," I say, my voice low. I've decided to focus on Logan and Logan alone, not the fact that we're trapped or that we're probably being watched by creeps who get their jollies from making us suffer; just Logan and getting through this conversation with him.

"Some people just seem familiar," he says, brushing off my words. But I can tell, from the tiny creases between his eyebrows, that it bothers him. He doesn't want to believe. He's *desperate* not to believe.

"You saw me make that furniture," I say, even as I wonder why I thought to make something so trivial.

He shakes his head. "A trick. Something to distract me while people were *blowing up my house*," he says, the words a savage growl.

Okay, he's right, *that* coincidence is not a happy one.

"Where did the water go?" I ask, and though a slight shake in my voice betrays me, I'm fighting not to let him know how much his mistrust is affecting me.

"What water?"

"The water bottle that spilled on the floor."

He looks away. "They came and cleaned it up while we were asleep," he says with total dismissal.

"Are you thirsty now?"

His eyes only dart toward me for a moment, but I can tell the answer is yes. I'm parched myself. And hungry. And I have to pee. But that'll have to wait.

I take a chance and look directly at the glass, then hold up two fingers like I might to order coffee at a diner. If I have to depend upon my kidnappers, at least I can be sarcastic about it.

Within seconds two water bottles pop into existence on

the floor. One within my reach and one within his. His jaw is shaking, and I wonder if I've just shoved him over that delicate precipice into insanity.

"I can't . . . I can't. No." He turns away from the water and curls his face against his knees, his whole body shuddering. I don't know if he's crying or trying to keep his mind from cracking.

But clearly I'm not going to get any help from him until he figures out who he is. And that likely won't happen unless I can get him out of here. Not that I don't empathize. I was pretty much a wreck when all this stuff started happening to me too.

But the timing is . . . less than ideal.

I stand and walk the perimeter of the room, giving Logan as wide a berth as I can. My fingers stray up to Rebecca's necklace and I fiddle with it as I consider the situation. I think about what happened when Logan pounded on the glass—how the surface rang with vibrations but never cracked. The material must be something stronger than glass. What can I create that could break it? And how could I do so without anyone noticing?

I take deep breaths, trying to keep my thoughts hidden. My shoulders slump as though in defeat but in my mind I see a heavy sledge hammer. In an instant my knuckles are white on a splintery wooden handle, and with a loud grunt I swing the newly formed hammer at the mirror. Shards of glass rain down like snow and my heart races for three beats, four, enjoying the sensation of success.

It doesn't last. A burning that feels like knives assaults my arm.

I can't move.

Every muscle in my body rebels and clenches tight, My tendons ache and twitch, and it's only when the sensation releases me that I look down at my arm and realize that I've been tased.

Shit.

I fight for consciousness, my body already overwhelmed from whatever tranquilizer they gave me earlier and today's lack of food.

Or has it been two days without food? I don't even know.

My knees give out, and I sprawl to the floor. My fuzzy brain grasps for daylight, and I manage to push back the darkness gathering at the edges of my vision. I will not succumb again. I suck in air, focusing on my breath until I'm certain I'm not going to lose it.

I glance about me.

It's as if my entire attempt never happened. The mirror is as it had been—whole and unbroken—the shards of glass I distinctly remember peppering my skin are gone. Even my bottle of water is sitting full and upright, just how it was when it first appeared.

"I suggest you don't try *that* again." A bored voice booms in from an unseen speaker, frightening me as much as anything. I know that voice. I just can't put my finger on it. "As you can see, you can be instantaneously subdued if you try anything."

I nod shortly—since it's clear they can see me—anger trickling through my body as a weary absence of energy replaces the fierce tension of the electricity from the Taser. *No using my powers. In any way, shape, or form. Got it.*

I glare at the mirror, knowing that even though all I can see is my own scowling face—a red mark across my cheek—there *must* be people on the other side watching me. The familiar voice, for one. I stare at the mirror, willing my expression to travel through the thick glass the way my vision can't, and all of a sudden the surface almost seems to turn transparent. At first I think it's my imagination, but then something clicks and the lights on our side dim, and I know it's not my tired body playing tricks on me; I can actually see through.

A man in a dark suit is standing at what appears to be a long counter. His hands are planted on the surface, and he's leaning forward in a manner so menacing it can't possibly be accidental.

I would have recognized him in an instant, even without his signature shades.

Sunglasses Guy. The guy who followed me for two weeks in Portsmouth. Who shot at me, and terrified me, and dragged Benson away on that terrible night.

And just over his shoulders, painted on a gray wall so obvious I can't miss it, is a black symbol, at least four feet high. An ankh, with one side of the loop curled up like a shepherd's crook.

The symbol of the Reduciata.

CHAPTER FOUR

I mean, I guess I knew. But seeing those two things in a jux-
taposed tableau like that—utter proof that I'm in the jaws
of the enemy—makes me understand how helpless my situation truly is. I'm certain of one thing though: when I leave this
place it will either be through my own powers—and not a small
amount of luck—or I'll be dead.

Three other faces join Sunglasses Guy, and they study me
the way I would a strange bug or mold in the fridge. Like I'm
inferior, something there only because they allow it to be.

Which, admittedly, might be true.

The anger inside me changes to a simmering rage as they
observe me with amusement, as if I'm some kind of joke. I'm
already planning an—admittedly childish—revenge when a
beep starts to sound.

"That's the sign that your heart rate is rising," a woman
says, leaning down to speak into a small mounted microphone.

"If you don't want us to sedate you again, you're going to have to calm down."

I take three seconds to hate them with every fiber of my being before I close my eyes and count to ten, taking long, deep breaths as I do. After about a minute the beeping stops.

I haven't given up. I've just reached a dead end in this maze, and the first step to finding another route is to pretend to abandon the search entirely.

I raise my eyes; the woman is sitting in front of the microphone with a pen in hand.

"Your name?" she asks.

What am I supposed to say? I know they know who I am. I consider giving a fake name anyway. Maybe they're not 100 percent sure.

"Don't kid yourself," the woman says. The smile that curls across her face makes vicious butterflies take flight in my stomach. "We already know the answers to all the questions we're going to ask. We're just testing you. Seeing if you're going to be honest with us." An interested gleam flashes in the woman's eyes. "And I hope you'll play nice." I'm not sure how, but she manages to be even more terrifying than Sunglasses Guy. "Name?" she repeats, leaning forward.

"Tavia," I finally say. I guess I have nothing to lose. If I answer, maybe they'll give me some degree of freedom. If I don't . . . well, the rest of my life might not be very long one way or another. It's probably worth the risk. "Michaels," I add, just to prove I really am trying.

"*Sum Terrobligatus; declarare fidem.*"

My eyes widen, and I stare at her. Those are the same words

I shouted at Elizabeth two weeks ago—has it really been two weeks since I demanded answers from my former therapist? It feels like forever.

But this woman isn't screaming; she isn't out of control the way I was. She's calm; her voice is soft. Sinister.

And I know what the words mean this time. *Sum Terrobligatus*: I am an Earthbound. Simple concept; you give information before you demand it back. *Declarare fidem*: Declare your loyalty, Reduciata or Curatoria.

I remain silent. How can the woman claim to know the answers to all the questions they're going to ask when this is one that even *I* don't know? She breathes in slowly, and just as she opens her mouth to say something—probably to repeat herself—I say, "I don't have one."

A single blink is the only response I get.

"And I don't *intend* to have one either," I continue, forcing back the urge to cross my arms over my chest. I don't need to look petulant right at this moment. "I've had bad experiences with both brotherhoods, and I don't want to be a part of either."

"Are you hungry?"

The question catches me off-guard. It seems silly that they would even care. I look up at the woman, and for a moment I think she's staring off into space, but then I realize her gaze is focused over my shoulder.

On Logan.

He's looking up at her with a strange expression that I vaguely recognize as *hope*, and it sickens me. That the Reduciates behind a plane of glass can inspire any sort of positive emotion

32

in him while I instill nothing but fear makes me equal parts angry and sad.

He tries to speak, clears his throat when he fails, and starts again. "Maybe." There's a rebellious lilt to his voice, and I allow myself a slow blink of relief. I certainly haven't won him over, but at least they haven't either.

Yet.

"Are you the ones who destroyed my house?" He sounds tentative, even weak, but I can hear him getting to his feet behind me. He's not broken. Thank goodness.

"I'm afraid it was necessary."

"My *family*?" He's trying so hard to be strong—to be brave. I don't dare look back at him at the risk that seeing me would make him change his mind. Or snap his last thread.

"I'm afraid it was necessary," she repeats.

Now I glance back. I can't help myself. His jaw is clenched so hard I can see the muscles standing out like marbles beneath his skin. His eyes glimmer—just a sheen—as they tell him what he already knew. And in that moment, I see a glimpse of Rebecca's Quinn—*my* Quinn. Quinn, who was so strong and could handle anything. He's *in there*. I know it!

"Why was it necessary?" I say, when I sense he's not ready to speak. Part of me is curious how the Reduciata will attempt to justify their actions. A larger part knows that if I can't get Logan to remember—the chances of which are basically non-existent in here—I'll need to make sure that it's *me* he sides with.

"To keep everything clean. The authorities will assume you died with them." She addresses Logan brusquely, as though she weren't speaking of the murder of four people, two of them Logan's siblings, just children. "They'll be looking for an arsonist, for sure, but not a missing person."

"You killed four people to cover up a *kidnapping*?" he says, throwing the words at her as though they were a weapon. I wish they were.

"We killed 255 people to get to Tavia."

Logan turns to look at me in shock and horror. I suck in a breath and hold very still as a wave of mourning washes over me. My parents were two of those 255. "Is that true?" he asks.

All my work. Undone. But I nod. I have to.

"None of that matters now." The woman's amplified voice cuts through me.

"How can you say it doesn't matter?" Logan says hoarsely.

"Because once you remember, they *won't* matter."

I crinkle my brows. I don't understand why remembering should change any of this, but I dismiss it as a vain attempt to pacify us. "So what now?" I ask. I want to rise gracefully to my feet, but I'm too weak. My hands slip on the smooth white walls as I drag myself up, but I manage to stand and plant my fists on my hips.

"*Now* you both need to eat."

A veritable picnic appears—complete with a red-checkered blanket, which I don't find amusing in the least—on the floor between us.

Logan snorts even as his eyes glitter. "Like we'd eat anything *you* gave us."

At that, she laughs. She could have hidden it—not turned on the intercom—but she wants us to hear the easy, carefree sound. "Please, we could have added poison to your water and you didn't mind drinking that, did you? We won't kill you. You're too important. Well, *she* is. But she needs you. So we need you too." I close my eyes, frustration and mortification making me feel beyond weary. She would confirm that this really *is* all my fault. The Reduciates want my stupid secret. I hate myself for not knowing what it is.

"Why you?" Logan asks, barely over a whisper. He's looking straight at me, but the hellish woman answers anyway.

"Maybe you should have listened to everything Tavia has been trying to tell you for the last few days." Then there's an audible click, and the microphone is off. The window is a mirror again.

And Logan and I again have the illusion of being alone.

He eyes the food. His face is pale, but I doubt it's from hunger. Still, he's going to need energy.

Hating my own frail human needs, I lower myself shakily to the blanket and begin sorting through the pile of food.

"Are you sure they won't poison us?" Logan asks from far above me.

"Not until they've gotten whatever the hell it is they need from us," I grumble. I say us, but we both know I mean me.

My stomach protests as I lay the food out slowly. Who knows how long they'll wait before feeding us again? We might need to ration.

Of course, they could just make the leftovers disappear. I don't know what to do. I'm so hungry, I'm sure that it's got to have been a full two days since we were brought here. At least. I briefly wonder how many more people have died of the virus while these Reduciates have been toying with us, but I tamp that thought down and file it away. It's not something I can do anything about right now.

Logan drops down to join me on the blanket when I hold out a piece of cheese, though he still looks nervous. "What *do* they want?" he asks, his voice so quiet I practically have to read his lips to understand him.

"I'm not sure," I reply in that same hushed tone. "It's . . . a little hard to explain. There's some kind of secret that I know—except that I don't. I used to—ugh!" I rub at my temples, the aftereffects of the tranquilizers making my entire skull ache and buzz like someone's playing the timpani inside it. I take a few calming breaths and try to will the pain away.

"What kind of secret?" he asks, his eyes darting to the again-opaque glass.

I shake my head no, hoping that we still have enough of a connection that he'll understand that I'm telling him that they're listening no matter how quietly we talk. "It doesn't matter," I say in a whisper, even though that effort feels pointless. "The thing I *need* you to understand is that if we're going to survive this, we have to be a team. I need to be able to depend on you."

He looks wary, and I know I'm pushing him to his mortal limit. But like me, there's a hidden core of strength in there. The strength of an Earthbound. Of a god. And I'm counting on it.

"They will do anything—kill *anyone*—to get to this secret that I have. . . ." I hesitate, not wanting them to know I don't *know* what the secret is. "The key to that secret is you," I finally settle on. Nebulous, but enough. "So as long as we work together, we can keep each other safe."

"How am I the key?"

I can't answer that. Not even cryptically. "I'll tell you when I can," I say, my voice raspy around the near lie.

The food is gone quickly and I'm feeling better—even a little overfull. I have to wonder why they fed us at all. Food is the fuel for my powers—if I were them, I'd have starved me.

But I'm certainly not going to question my advantages.

I rise and resume stalking the perimeter of the room, feeling much like a tiger in a zoo. What can I make to get us out of here? I lay my hand against the wall and wonder if I know enough about bombs to make one. Excitement zings through me as I add, *make one* inside *the wall*, to my thought. I try to remember the chemistry class last year in Michigan when my teacher taught us how to make gunpowder. Sulfur, charcoal, saltpeter. A metal casing. A fuse. *I can do this!*

I'm so wrapped up in the thoughts whizzing through my head that I hardly notice when a beeping begins to sound, then speeds up. Logan is calling my name, but as the beeping gets louder, faster, two sharp pains prick the skin on my arm and my knees buckle as I sink into unconsciousness.

Again.

CHAPTER FIVE

I smell him before I open my eyes. It's Quinn's smell. Unique. My head is lying against something soft and warm; it must be him. Without conscious thought, Rebecca's arms reach out, pull him close. She buries her face in that perfect smell that means safety and love and *home*.

A groan escapes my mouth as I nuzzle against Quinn's warm, soft shirt and the yielding skin beneath. My hand is searching for a way to get under his clothing when a sharp "Tavia!" pulls me all the way out of unconsciousness.

I open my eyes and see his face—*Logan's* face. Worry and disgust color his features.

I yank myself up and away from him, fire filling my cheeks. "Sorry," I mutter, though my skin burns where I pressed against him—tingling with want and need and other emotions I should *not* be feeling in a Reduciata prison.

"What happened?" My voice is hoarse. Again. I wonder just how much of that tranquilizer stuff I've had. How bad the after-effects are going to be this time.

"I'm not sure what you were planning." We both jump as a voice comes over the loudspeaker. It sounds like Sunglasses Guy. I spin toward the mirror, but it's still just a mirror. They're not interested in letting us see them this time. "But it was something exciting enough to raise your heart rate."

I remember the beeping that got faster and faster right before they shot me. *Damn it!*

"We're not stupid," the guy continues calmly. "You're not getting out until we let you. Until we've gotten what we want." A low chuckle. "And I guess at that point we'll probably just kill you."

My jaw is shaking with fury, and I roll my shoulders to attempt to calm down before the stupid beeping starts again. As I move, the left joint sends out a sharp stab of pain. "Ow," I say in surprise and look down at my arm. The shirt I'm wearing has short sleeves, and when I push it up, I see that my entire shoulder is reddened and starting to turn purple.

"You fell against the wall pretty hard when they took you out," Logan explains sheepishly. "I managed to get to you before you hit your head, but I wasn't fast enough to stop that." He points at the darkening bruise.

A tingly feeling zips up my spine, and I barely manage to hide the sappy grin that threatens to reveal itself. He helped me. He *tried*. "Thanks." I clear my throat and look away, trying not to show him how pleased I am. It's not the time.

"So what now?" Logan asks. It's something just less than a whisper. He practically breathes the words.

I glance at the mirror, but it looks no different than before I got knocked out. Again. I incline my head at Logan and start scooting backward until I'm leaning against the wall. He joins me and I curl closer so my lips are right next to his ear. "Do you trust me?"

His nod is just enough of a motion for me to feel it.

"Rub my back, softly. Help me stay calm." Then, before he can argue, I shift so my legs lay across his lap and I let my head rest against his shoulder, my face turned toward him so it can't be seen. I breathe in the scent of his shirt—fabric softener, a light aura of sweat, the clean kind that smells earthy—and close my eyes when his arms drape over me, his fingers gingerly kneading along my spine. I'm surprised at his soft touch, but in my head, Rebecca clearly isn't. I let myself listen to her and slump against Logan, breathing steadily.

My heartbeat speeds again at his nearness, but I'm counting on that. They're watching, analyzing, but now they'll think this is my baseline. I try to lose myself in the hypnotic massage, pretending it's my mom, or even Sammi. Anyone but Logan. Once I've detached the feeling of those soothing hands from their owner, I start to let myself think of science again. Of my teacher Mr. Peterson lecturing in his boring fashion. Even explosives were tedious when *he* was trying to explain them.

I hold the image of his crisp shirt and tie in my mind, recalling the nasal sound of Mr. Peterson's voice as he dryly listed off ingredients. Sulfur, charcoal, saltpeter. Sulfur, charcoal, saltpeter. Over and over in my head until it doesn't feel exciting anymore. I let out a heavy breath like I'm *really* enjoying this backrub and stare out from beneath my eyelids. I glare at the wall and then, as I let the air out like I'm breathing through a straw, I create a metal casing. *Inside* the wall.

I don't see anything.

Nothing cracks.

That was the risky part.

The ingredients of gunpowder float along in my consciousness, and I remember mixing a small amount in class. I double, triple, quadruple that in my head and—again, as I breathe out—I fill the metal canister.

I'm so close, adrenaline tingles in my fingers. I toss my head back and pull closer to Logan, turning the simple backrub into something sensual—I need to hide my increased excitement. Logan's body clenches up beneath me, but he doesn't fight as I pull him close and rest my lips against his neck. I can sense the Reduciates watching my every move and nearly gag at the thought of actually being romantic in front of them.

Like. I. Would.

But apparently they don't know me *that* well because they don't do anything to stop me. I'm all the way on Logan's lap now, and I can feel sweat start to trickle down his back as he grows more and more uncomfortable with the intimacy I'm forcing on him. But we're almost done. I pull his head down, close to my chest—not sure just what *that* is going to look like. Then, as I set my head down on his back, my arms wrapped around him—covering him, protecting him—I create a spark.

Debris shatters out of the wall, ricocheting off the other walls and pelting Logan and me. "Come on!" I say, staggering to my feet as I try to pull him with me. "Run!"

I clench my fingers around his and dive into the smoke, hoping there's actually a hole all the way through the wall. I can't see—I can barely hear after the blast—but I keep moving forward, one hand stretched out in front of me, the other hanging on to Logan for dear life.

I bounce off something warm and squishy enough that it must have been a person, but I keep running. I pivot to my left and run toward light. What I think is light. I trip over something and go sprawling, but because I refuse to let go of Logan, he follows my trajectory and lands on top of me, pushing the air from my lungs. I landed badly on my wrist, but I can't let that stop me. I don't need my arms to run.

Pushing the pain away, I yank Logan to his feet. I'm desperately thinking of what I can make to help us escape when something hard hits me across the stomach and I double over, gasping for breath yet again. Arms wrap around me, and I try to scream but I have no air yet, and I fight against my own muscles as my lungs burn. Finally I get out an enraged shriek that's way higher pitched than I intended it to be.

I slam into a wall, and the back of my head clangs against something. A sob of fiery pain escapes my mouth and blackness invades my periphery as my cries reverberate in my aching head. My knees have no chance, and I collapse onto the floor, my whole body quaking in fear and agony.

A blurry face invades my fading sight, but I can't even raise my hand to block the view of Sunglasses Guy, two inches from my nose.

"Sit," he says, and I dimly feel a fleck of spit from the *T* at the end of the harsh word. "Stay."

He rises to his feet and he looks even taller from where I lie crumpled on the floor. As he walks away I fight to stay conscious, but the pain is overwhelming and it's a relief when I slip away.

I have no idea how long it is before I wake, but the pain is even sharper than last time. My ears are ringing—probably from the noise of the bomb exploding—and my entire body is sore and achy. I try to take stock while cradling my head in my hands. Throbbing, puffy lip; I probably bit it. My shoulder is still tender. But the worst is my wrist—it's swollen twice its normal size and purple bruises are starting to form. I move it and cringe. It's either broken or very badly sprained. I'm stiff from sleeping—well, lying unconscious on the ground—but that particular discomfort is so minor in comparison that it barely registers.

I push up onto my knees with my one good arm and peer blearily around. I don't care what I look like to them. Not this time.

I've been relocated into a much, much smaller room. The walls are the same glaring white, same bleachy tiled floor, but probably half the size. Worse, the tiny box is lined with an even smaller cage of bars. That's what I must have hit when I was literally thrown in here. There's another two-way mirror, but it's on the other side of the bars, where I can't even attempt to reach it.

My mind is having trouble thinking clearly, but I know I'm missing something. Something is wrong. Something big. I close my eyes and rub hard at them before I remember.

Logan.

He's not here.

I have a feeling I've just been put in Reduciata solitary confinement.

CHAPTER SIX

The hum of the air conditioning unit kicking on pulls me from my stupor. *Ah, new tactic then.* They're going to keep me cold, stiff, and devoid of energy.

Sunglasses Guy did warn me they weren't stupid.

The Reduciates seem to want me alive, but the state I'm in is apparently unimportant.

I push myself off the hard floor and start pacing to keep myself warm. I'm guessing it's been about an hour since they separated me from Logan. I rub at my temples, willing the throbbing to go away. The stark halogen lights hurt my eyes and make it hard to think. But thinking's all I've got at the moment. I reflect on what I've figured out thus far.

They want something—something in my head. A secret.

The memories of whatever the secret is come from Rebecca. *She* knew. And if my dreams can be believed, Sonya knew too.

45

But for some reason it remains locked inside my brain, dancing away like shadows from a flickering candle whenever I think about it. How do the Reduciates think they're going to get it out of me when I can't get it out of myself?

I had assumed they were trying to get Logan and me to re-surge—even Mark had said that was the key. But why? I'm certain Logan doesn't know. That it was too dangerous to tell him. I'm *sure* of that. But since they've separated us apparently our re-awakening is no longer a priority for them.

Here's the thing, though: it *is* a priority for me. I'm officially done playing their games. I'm not going to get less tired or hungry as time progresses.

It's now or never.

For the first time, I wish I were a Destroyer. I could simply make the prison around me disappear.

My mind latches on to that idea. It seems like I should be able to do *something* like that. I consider how I change my face into my mother's when I'm in public. I mean, her nose was longer than mine, so I guess you could argue that I'm creating cartilage there? But my eyes change color too.

Maybe it's simply a matter of creating one thing that replaces what was there previously.

Could I *replace* a wall with created air? Is it all about the way you think about it?

I certainly have nothing to lose by trying. And *everything* to gain.

I pull in as much oxygen as my lungs can hold and clench my eyes shut as I push the air out. When I open my eyes, the walls on three sides of me are gone.

That's Step One.

I nearly faint with relief when I leap to my feet and see Logan sitting on the ground a mere ten feet away, staring at where the walls used to be. At a glance I see he's in the same room we were both in an hour ago. Two? Yesterday? I have no freaking clue.

I expect the sting of tranquilizer to hit me at any moment, but I still feel nothing as I scramble to Logan. I guess I'm just harder to hit when I'm moving.

So I better keep doing that.

"Come on!" I grab his arms and yank him to his feet. "Don't you dare let go of my hand," I say, ignoring the throbbing pain in my leg and shoulder. Without waiting for a response, I start to run.

Get Logan: Step Two.

"Tavia!"

The voice startles me into absolute stillness. It almost sounded like—

I can hear noise—shuffling, shouting, something that certainly could be a weapon—behind me, and I race forward, clenching my teeth as I drag Logan along. I create a dense cloud of smoke behind me, checking off Step Three in my head as I do so. My hands shake, but I'm already committed to Step Four as a fully loaded handgun fills my palm, making my injured wrist sear in pain. I grit my teeth against the agony and create more smoke behind me, trying not to cough as it tickles my throat.

The smoke is for the people behind me; the gun is for the people in front of me.

Time for Step Five. I pick a hallway and start running, re-placing every obstruction in my path with harmless puffs of air.

My plan works for twenty seconds.

The hallway dead-ends.

No problem.

I replace the wall with air, and the innards of a large build-ing are revealed. More replacing, more layers peel away. I can see light. One more layer vanishes and sun pierces through, and I have to throw my arm—still holding the gun—over my eyes to block the blinding rays.

But I keep running.

And hit a solid wall of cinderblock.

My elbow burns, and I can feel blood trickling. I make the wall go away again, but it returns in an instant. I wonder if I should make more walls disappear, but I'm risking this un-known structure collapsing in on me as it is.

I don't have a Step Six.

Whirling, I realize the Reduciates are so close even smoke isn't going to work. Logan has staggered to his knees, but I clamp my arms around his chest to keep him with me.

It's going to have to be the gun.

I hold it out in front of me and brace my shoulders against the wall, pointing it wildly at the shadowy figures surrounding us, my eyes darting too fast to make out any features in the smoky air.

Can I do it? Can I pull the trigger? For myself?

For Logan?

For Logan.

48

I scrunch my eyes shut and start to flex my finger, but the wall behind my back suddenly disintegrates and something snakes around my neck, catching me before I can fall and cutting off half my air. The chilled edge of something metal touches my temple.

So much for *my* gun.

The circle around me stills, their eyes wide, and for a moment I remember the identical scene in my dream about Sonya.

"Hold on to that boy," the voice whispers to me, and though I certainly didn't need anyone to tell me that, I do, gripping Logan so tightly I swear I can feel the bones in my wrist scraping against each other from the pressure.

Then, to the others, in a loud, scratchy voice, "One move—a single Earthbound trick—and her brains splatter the wall."

Oh. Good.

He drags me backward, and I pull Logan, my wrist screaming in pain. A mere foot or two and the wall reappears—hiding the Reduciates from sight but not thick enough to completely muffle their cries of outrage.

"Help!" the man calls as his arm falls from my neck and he reaches for Logan.

"No!" I scream, not willing to let him go.

"Hurry," the man says to the black-clad masked figures that surround both Logan and me. They shuffle us toward a loud noise that I finally take note of. A helicopter! There's a small feather and flame emblem near the nose of the helicopter. Curatoria. Is that good news or bad news? I'm paralyzed by indecision, but the helicopter blades spin so fast the wind threatens to knock me over until a person I can't see pushes me forward, toward the ramp, despite my resistance.

The same one they're dragging Logan up.

I give up my struggle. At least I'll be with Logan. If we've gone from one dangerous situation to another, I'll have to decide what to do about that later. For now, I reach out my hand for Logan, and with my fingers gripping his, I follow them up the ramp.

Inside the helicopter is chaos, and I'm shoved down into a seat that—though cushiony—jars my shoulder and thumps the back of my head. A small groan sounds in my ears.

My own.

Then there's a woman in my face, her cheeks red and flushed, probably from the mask now pushed up on her forehead.

"I'm sorry," she says. "It's just a precaution."

Something covers my face, and I gasp in a surprised breath of something strong and sweet. I think briefly to hold my breath, but whatever I've inhaled has already made my head fuzzy and my eyes roll strangely as I continue to breathe, my eyelids going heavy. I get one last look of Logan sprawled over two seats, surrounded by people in black clothing. I'm not sure whether I imagined the feeling of the helicopter leaving the ground, but sleep is too tempting, and I let my eyes close.

"You're safe now," a low voice whispers, just before I fall asleep. "Both of you, you're safe."

I try to open my mouth, but my jaw feels like a heavy steel trap and I can't even mumble, "I don't believe you."

CHAPTER SEVEN

"You can wake up now," a calm voice says. "We're out of danger."

A warm cloth rubs softly across my face, moistening my eyelids and making me feel clean and refreshed. I'm ready to smile until I remember what just happened. My eyes fly open and I try to jerk to a sitting position, but there's a heavy strap across my chest that holds me in place.

"Stop, please." The same voice. Soft hands on my shoulder. "Let me unhook you. You were only restrained to keep you from rolling while you were asleep."

Asleep. She says it like I just dozed off. But I hold still while she unbuckles the strap and helps me to sit up. She then props up the bed behind me so I can recline.

"Logan?"

"He's right there. Look. He's fine." I see him almost near enough to touch, on a tiny stretcher that looks just like mine. I slowly register the noise around me, the rhythmic pulsing that fills the tiny, cramped space. We're still in the helicopter.

"I'm Audra," the voice says, pulling my eyes back to her.

I startle at the sight. She's . . . she's a girl. Younger than me. *Maybe* fifteen.

"And this is Glenn and Christina. We're doctors with the Curatoria."

Doctors. Curatoria. I don't know what to think. I notice now that they're wearing light-colored scrubs, and I vaguely remember seeing the feather and flame. *Doctors. Curatoria.* What have I done?

I'm still considering whether we may have jumped from the frying pan into the proverbial fire when I glance again at Audra. "Doctor?" I say, the question popping from my lips in a scratchy croak.

She catches the look of skepticism I can't hide and laughs. "Yes, I'm a doctor," she says. "And yes, I'm fifteen. I actually have been a doctor for several lifetimes now and was lucky enough to have my memories restored almost three years ago."

An Earthbound then. "That's amazing," I say, still staring at her and trying to comprehend that this girl—younger than I am—could already have the knowledge and maturity of a long-practicing physician.

"We can talk later. They wanted you patched up by the time we reach Curatoria headquarters."

"How long will that take?" I ask. They're all crowded close around me because of the tiny space, and the rhythmic beat of the helicopter blades makes everything feel a little ominous.

Maybe it's just because I'm in the air again for the first time since the plane crash.

Oh gods, don't think about that.

Audra peeks at her watch. "Oh, uh, probably within the next fifteen minutes or so." She looks up at the other two doctors for confirmation, and they give her a tight-lipped nod. "Your partner's not yet awake, so we'll start with you."

"He hasn't remembered," I warn. "The name 'Curatoria' won't mean anything to him. He'll be panicked and terrified." I don't know why I'm telling them that. Because I'm afraid he'll freak out? Because I don't want them to throw a whole bunch of *new* information at him before the two of us have had a chance to talk? Maybe some of both.

Audra gives me a wan smile. "At least he's here. We'll find a spark for him. Now, where are you hurt? We didn't want to invade your privacy without your consent by doing a full-body examination." She gingerly lifts my swollen wrist that is now one huge purple bruise. "This looks pretty bad though."

"Is it broken?" I ask.

"Let's see." She smears my wrist with jelly and slides some kind of plastic piece of machinery over it. The other two doctors—a middle-aged woman and a man sporting gray hair and thick glasses—set their fingers on the side of my wrist. They all look at a screen flashing weird black and white images.

"This shouldn't hurt," the man says. "But it will feel strange."

I brace myself—after surviving major brain surgery, I've learned never to trust doctors when they say it won't hurt—but he's right. I suck in a breath as I feel like everything in my wrist is collapsing in on itself. Then, like a gear slipping into place, everything returns to normal.

Like *normal* normal. All the pain is gone.

"What did you do?" I ask as they release my arm. I flex it back and forth. The bruising isn't totally gone, but almost— merely a few smudges of purple here and there. The swelling, meanwhile, has disappeared completely. "It feels better than it did before I injured it."

"That was the intention," Audra replies, a hint of fifteen-year-old smugness coming through.

The woman called Christina tilts her head at her colleague. "It was broken," she explains matter-of-factly. "Though not badly. We—well, Glenn—removed the damaged cells, the inflammation, the blood that leaked from your veins and made the bruises, and then I replaced the bones cells with new."

"You can do that?" I say with wonder.

"Oh yes," she says. "We used to have to cut into you to do it, but with our EB scanner—"

"Earthbound scanner," Audra interrupts with a smirk. "Although we'll make up something else when we release it to the public. Like the CAT scan. I'll give you one guess at what the *C originally* stood for, and it rhymes with Muratoria."

"Thank you for that," Christina says dryly. "Anyway, with this scanner we can see what needs to be done and make the switch without doing anything invasive."

"It's basically a combination ultrasound and X-ray, with some MRI functions," Audra says.

And is apparently small enough to take on a freaking helicopter.

Audra gives me another once-over. "What else?" she asks, as though she hadn't just told me about a completely revolutionary piece of medical equipment.

"My shoulder."

I spend the next few minutes in awe as my injuries are quite literally erased.

"What about your leg?" Audra asks as I'm fingering my lip made whole again.

"My leg is fine." I'm half distracted as I swing my shoulder around, stretching it. I'd gotten so used to the ache I almost forgot what it was like not to have it.

"I was told you were limping quite badly when they rescued you."

"Oh." I understand. "That . . . that's an old injury."

"No reason we can't fix it," she says. She glances over at Logan and shares a silent message with the person watching over him. "Your partner is just starting to stir. We have a few more minutes."

"I guess," I say, not certain why I'm so nervous.

I'm wearing jeans, but the fabric across my thigh disappears with a glance from Glenn. More jelly and then Audra is sliding the probe over my leg and peering at the screen.

"Titanium plates," Glenn says. "Those'll have to go."

Go?

"And extensive scar tissue in the muscles here and here," Audra says, pointing. "No wonder it's not healing well."

I close my eyes. I don't want to watch.

The same weird feelings take over my thigh, but this time it *is* a little uncomfortable. "Sorry," Glenn says. I must have grimaced. "Christina will fix it in a moment."

No titles, not calling each other "Dr. So-and-So." As though we are all equals here. "We're finished," Christina says softly, rubbing goop off her hands.

I look down, and it's like the plane wreck never happened. The staple marks are gone; the skin on my thigh is smooth and new and . . . looks rather exfoliated to boot.

"Good?" Christina asks.

I nod dumbly, and right before my eyes the missing piece of my jeans reappears as though it had never vanished. I'm not sure why this all makes me so uncomfortable. I mean, it's a good thing, but it's like they erased not only my scar but an entire section of my life. I force myself not to touch the scar on my head. I've had enough supernatural medicine for today.

"Let's get you up," Audra says. "No reason for you to be in bed any longer."

I swing my legs to the side and gingerly get to my feet, holding on to a strap connected to the low ceiling for balance in the tiny square of space between my and Logan's little beds. They hand me a large pouch of juice, and as they fold the travel-sized stretcher away I test my weight on my right leg and almost laugh in glee.

No pain.

Not a twinge or jolt. Nothing. Not even when the chopper hits a brief patch of turbulence.

I can't remember the last time I could walk without at least a throb of discomfort.

"Get off me!"

I'm shaken from my wonderment by Logan's voice.

"It's okay!" I take two steps—still in awe that there's no pain when I do so—and lay my hands on his chest, pushing my face into his line of sight. "It's okay," I repeat, softer now as his focus hones in on me. He stops struggling, and as soon as he does the guy watching him unfastens the chest strap, just like they did with me. Logan's hand immediately clamps onto mine, and he continues to hold my fingers in a death grip as the very basics of the situation are explained to him. I can't help but be pleased by that—even if it's only during the panic of this moment, he's clinging to me instead of pushing me away.

The doctors question and then examine him, but all he has is the cut over his eye from the explosion at his house, and Audra doesn't even need her ultrasound for Glenn and Christina to put that right.

When they touch him, Logan tightens his already iron grip on my hand, only loosening it when Christina backs away. "Pretty amazing, right?" I ask. He looks over at me with wide eyes, and I give him a little nod and squeeze his hand with numb, tingly fingers. I know he's feeling the same cessation of pain that I did.

We're both given a bag of dried fruit and more juice, and it's all so welcome that I almost feel normal again. We're shooed out of the way to a padded bench along the back of the chopper, and Logan and I sit together, thighs touching. I'm closing my eyes in silent gratitude that I've managed to at least get him to tolerate me, when I feel the warmth of his fingers creep across my hand, hesitate, and then twine through mine.

I don't dare look. Like I might break the spell. I've proved something to him and I don't want to question it. Certainly don't want *him* to question it. I just squeeze lightly and pretend there's nothing out of the ordinary about two people who couldn't coexist in the same room a couple days ago holding hands.

As I munch on my fruit, a shadow crosses the floor, and Audra hurries to confer with a man who has just emerged from the cockpit. A moment later she returns with a little smile and says, "We're going in now. You guys should see this."

Confused, I scoot over to the window and bring Logan with me. We sit, hand in hand, peering out through the glass at . . . nothing.

Endless dunes of desert sand stretch as far as I can see, with a bright orange sunset starting to paint its way across the horizon.

Except . . .

Yes, there's a glimmer. I can barely make it out at first, but as the chopper gets closer I realize it's a silvery triangle. Just like I saw in Portsmouth.

And yet this one is nothing like those triangles. It shines so brightly it almost hurts my eyes.

It's got to be at least a hundred yards on each side. An enormous triangle glinting in the sand. I know I must have a look of pure shock on my face when Audra giggles and says, "Oh, that's nothing."

Seconds later, a huge circle inside the triangle splits like pie slices and begins to pull back, revealing a cavernous space with a cement floor. On the perimeter I count six other helicopters parked and at least a dozen figures scurrying around beneath us.

I can't come up with words as we lower into the shadowy space, landing with a bump on the ground, the whine of the chopper blades immediately quieting.

As soon as the helicopter has touched down there's an entirely new low rumbling, and only when the light starts to dim do I realize that it's the opening above us closing. My chest is tight as the panels come together and block out all the sunlight, but when I look back at the space we've landed in, I see it's well lit. We haven't been plunged into darkness.

A great boom sounds as the gates above us close completely, and then the doors on both sides of the helicopter open and people are there ready to help us out. Logan is still clinging to one of my hands, but with the other he reaches out and pulls on Audra's sleeve.

"Audra?" Logan asks, and I can hear the fear in his voice. "Where are we?"

"Oh," she says with a light smile, as though this detail was entirely unimportant. "I guess you wouldn't know. This is the headquarters of the Curatoria."

CHAPTER EIGHT

Terror and relief both run through me so strongly I have trouble even breathing. The headquarters of the Curatoria. A place that has taken on a level of intrigue so high, it's hard to believe it exists at all.

I reach up to touch my silver necklace for courage and feel a warm hand cover my shoulder. Logan's. He lowers his head close to my ear and whispers, "Whatever this is, I'm here. I mean, I don't feel very useful right now, but if you need me, you just say so."

I can't speak as I stare at him. Does he . . . remember? Or have I actually won his trust?

But he looks as worried as I feel, and I know he would understand his true usefulness if he had remembered.

And wouldn't *I* know if he had? If we had resurged? I'm still baffled about what I would have to do to make that happen, but the first step is definitely keeping Logan with me.

He gives me a very small smile and slips his hand into mine as we follow the team of doctors down a ramp and out of the helicopter, leaving the rest of the crew behind. I take a moment to covertly glance around at the huge but dim space, surrounded by the other helicopters I saw from the air, all quiet and still along the perimeter of what looks like an enormous landing pad. The area is hexagonal, and a bunch of bright lines are painted on the floor. Tools line two of the six sides, and the next wall over is covered by some kind of radar-looking thing, with ropes and other supplies mounted on the fourth.

A huge feather and flame symbol is painted across the entire fifth wall, and my stomach twists at the similarity to the Reduciata symbol in the prison we were just in.

We're not exactly prisoners here—at least I don't think so. They're letting us walk together without our hands tied or any weapons pointed at us, but still, I don't feel *free*.

In the center of the sixth side is a set of gray double doors that look thick and soundproof. A woman in the lead—not one from the helicopter, a new one who was waiting for us when we landed—stops and turns, her eyes seeking me out. "When we walk through those doors you will enter the headquarters of the Curatoria. It's a privilege we never allow Earthbounds who have not sworn themselves to our cause." I'm about to tell her that I have no intention of swearing anything to anyone when she continues, "But you two will be an exception." She eyes us both carefully, her attention lingering on me. It's clear that she's not a fan of this idea. "While you're here," she adds, "we ask that you remain entirely peaceful, that you don't interfere with our work, and"—she hesitates—"that you have no communication with the outside world whatsoever."

Like I have anyone to communicate *with*. My parents, Sammi, Mark, Elizabeth—all dead.

Benson . . . good as dead.

And Logan, but he's here with me now. I feel a shiver of pleasure ripple down my spine at that thought and squeeze his hand.

I fix my gaze on the stern-looking woman and ask, "Why?"

"For our safety. It's not something we ask of our sworn members. But we have extra restrictions on you."

"Why let me in at all then?"

"Because Daniel wants to see you."

Every cell in my body freezes at the name.

Daniel: the leader of the Curatoria. He's here.

Not merely here, *expecting* me.

I don't know whether I just became exponentially safer or more at risk. But I'm pretty sure it's one or the other.

I shoot Logan what I hope is a meaningful glance, but he obviously doesn't understand *any* of this. Regardless, we're led into a space that feels more . . . domestic, for lack of a better word. Once the doors close behind us, the noise of the helicopter engine, the slowing blades, the crew shouting instructions to each other are all gone. I hadn't realized until now how loud they were. Now, even the noise of our footsteps is muffled by thick, soft carpet that feels absolutely luxurious on my tired feet.

I take a few quick steps to follow the still-nameless woman as she heads down a dimly lit, long hallway that reminds me of one from a hotel, albeit a nicer hotel than the type I've been staying at lately. Doors line each side, and pretty little tables abut the walls, which themselves are covered in pleasant—if generic—pastel paintings. I glance back and see that everyone else has peeled off and disappeared, and part of me wishes Audra were still here. Although I only just met her, she seemed to genuinely care about our well-being.

The woman before us evidently does not, however. "It won't be today that you meet him, of course," she says without turning to face us, and I have to strain my ears to hear. "He wants you to rest. To sleep. We reported the condition you were held under for the last three days—"

"Three days?" Apparently, I spent more time unconscious than I'd thought. "What day is it now?"

"Thursday," she responds automatically, not missing a beat. "As I was saying, Daniel insisted you be fed and rested before he meets with you." The tone of her voice tells me just how ridiculous she finds all of this. "Now, we'll house you here—where all of our Earthbounds-in-Residence live—and you can simply pick up the phone if you need anything." She pauses, then sneers, "Daniel has ordered us to be at your service."

"Really?" Logan pipes up. "Why would he—"

"This is you," she says, cutting him off. She raps sharply on a door with a silver number seven on it and then hands us each a key. "We have duplicates," she warns, and I wonder just where the hell she thinks we might go. What we might do in this classy, but nonetheless clearly fortified, underground fortress. One of us powerless, the other with abilities that last for five minutes. Maybe we could rip those sconces from the wall and stage an incredible escape. Right.

I mumble a quiet *thank you*, not wanting to get even more on this woman's bad side. Logan says nothing, just pockets his key and squeezes my hand.

"Daniel left you a gift on the table," she says as she pushes the door open, which swings silently on well-oiled hinges. "He says you'll know what to do with it."

Curiouser and curiouser, I think wryly. But I'm anxious to get out of this woman's sight and be able to talk to Logan without overly attentive eavesdroppers. "We'll be fine," I say aloud.

"Food," Logan blurts, then looks at me apologetically. "I'm starving."

The truth is I am too, so I can hardly blame him. The dried fruit only went so far in making up for three days with only one meal.

"I'll have something sent up." She looks Logan up and down and adds, "Something substantial," in a tone that makes me want to smack her.

Whatever. As soon as she's through the doorway I close it behind her, just inches shy of knocking her over. "Finally," I say, my back to the door.

We're in a very large room that seems to be part kitchenette, part bedroom. Like a studio apartment, really, with a sitting room around the corner on one side and what looks like a doorway to the bathroom on the left.

Logan is standing a few feet from an elegantly made king-size bed, and he runs his fingers through his hair awkwardly. Trusting me, even holding my hand, is one thing; being shoved

64

into a bedroom with only one bed after being told to "get some rest" is another.

I look away, giving him a few seconds to get his bearings, scoping out the room instead. The hallway was elegant and nice, but this room is a completely different *kind* of elegance. It's sparse and a bit artsy, with silver and black trim on pretty much everything. In place of paintings, black and white photos of buildings and cityscapes dot the walls. Here and there a touch of maroon breaks up the color palette: a throw on the back of a plushy chair, a vase that stands empty on a high shelf, one pillow in a pile of several on the bed.

I remember the woman's cryptic comment about a gift from Daniel and look around for the table—seems like it would be easy to find, but it turns out that it's a semicircular, bar-height table that's mounted below a mirror, and so I miss it at first glance, thinking that it's just part of the decor.

Still trying to avoid awkwardness with Logan, I walk over and pick up the cardboard tube sitting atop it. "No note," I muse. But whatever. I pop the top off the tube and start to shake it out, but as soon as I realize what's inside I yank my fingers back like they've been burned.

It's from the dugout back in Camden that Quinn took me to. The painting that messed me up so badly. My breathing is sharp and noisy and Logan is walking toward me, but I hold up a hand to stop him and force myself to calm down.

A little.

This canvas was in Benson's backpack the night I found out what he was. Why does the Curatoria have it?

"What is it?" Logan asks tentatively.

"It's just a painting," I respond absentmindedly. I'm too caught up in the sight before me to attempt to act like less of a total weirdo.

"If it's just a painting, then why did it make you jump out of your skin?"

He's right. It did make me jump out of my skin. But that was nothing compared to what happened the last time I touched it.

I'll never forget the sensation. It was like I was a radio set to the wrong frequency.

"Tavia?" Logan says.

I look up at him with what I'm sure is a nearly manic expression. If it was the wrong frequency for me, then there's only one person who it could be right for.

And in a bright flash of light, I remember. I *remember*! Quinn and I knew our artifacts were too obvious. Him a jewelry maker, me an artist. Of course a necklace and a painting would be obvious creations, with obvious owners. So we reversed them. I created a replica of a necklace he made me; he created a copy of a painting of our home. That way someone looking to destroy all of *Rebecca's* memories would miss one. Then we packed them away in the dugout.

That's why the necklace worked on me and not him.

I didn't *paint* this painting; Quinn *created* it.

My whole body trembles now as I realize what a treasure I'm holding in my hands. "Logan," my voice is too quiet and too high-pitched all at the same time. "You should see this."

His eyes are hooded, fearful, and I realize that in a world that has literally turned upside down on him in the last three days, anything might happen. Any paranoid fear might become a reality.

"It's a good thing," I say quickly, hating that expression of terror cast in my direction. "Just . . . here, take it."

I hold out the painting and he obliges. The second his fingers come in contact with the canvas, everything changes.

His hands tighten around it, crushing the edge of the painting, and he takes two stumbling steps backward until his shoulders meet the door. His eyes widen and then focus on me.

"Tavia," he murmurs. And it's clear, he *knows* me.

He takes one step—not even a proper step, half a step—and his hand rises as though of its own accord. I'm still, stunned into paralysis even as my lungs force air in and out with a gasping, hissing sound, and adrenaline fills my veins in a rush that deafens me.

His fingertips brush my face so gently, as though I'll break into a million pieces if he presses too hard. His eyes scan me, taking in every detail, until I feel like I've been stripped naked in front of him.

And I don't mind.

Logan stands like a man transformed, even though his appearance hasn't technically changed. His shoulders are straighter, his eyes more knowing. That *face*—suddenly it understands unspeakable wonders of the universe that normal humans simply can't comprehend.

Then the world hits Play and his lips are on mine, his hands clutching, until I feel every part of him pressed against me. Hands, chest, hips, lips, teeth. With a growl he pushes my back against the wall and grabs at my hips, pulling me to him like he needs me closer *now*. "Becca," he breathes in my ear, whispering my old name like a sacred memory before attacking my mouth again.

My brain is full of the chorus of women in my other lives singing with joy. Their strange music fills me, making every inch of my body tingle and glow. I know tomorrow I'll have bruises from Logan's rough, desperate handling, but I don't care. I want it—all of it.

"I'm so sorry," he whispers between kisses that trail down my neck, over my shoulder. He lifts my fingers to his mouth and kisses every fingertip, then rubs his face against my palms. "For everything I said. The way I treated you. I didn't know," he says, his voice gravelly now as his hands grip the waistband of my jeans.

I groan as his hands can't resist and slip under the back of my shirt, his fingers skimming bare skin. Everything I ever wanted with anyone explodes into this one moment. "It's okay," I manage, as I lean against him, his mouth back on my neck. He rolls his hips against me. It's like an ocean wave we can't stop, crashing into us, sweeping us away with it.

We walk unsteadily backward—in the direction I hazily remember the bed sitting—we're grasping at each other as our worlds collide in the most blissful crash I could ever imagine.

Logan lifts me, wraps my legs around his waist, and carries me the last few feet. He tosses me on the bed and kneels over me, reaching for the buttons on my jeans. Impatient with his fruitless fumbling, he tears his T-shirt up and over his head, and my whole body shakes at the sight of the familiar yet brand-new bare skin of his chest. He reaches for the bottom of my blouse, and as I raise my arms it suddenly seems to me that everything, every terrible, awful thing that has happened in the last month, was worth it.

The next few minutes are a blur of desperation as we learn each other all over again. It has that brilliant excitement of newness wrapped in the comfort of the commonplace. We say nothing as our bodies speak their own language; and even though I feel like I should savor this moment—take time to renew our friendship, our love—I can't.

I look up into his leaf-green eyes above me, my hand clenching at his shoulders, and for the first time since the plane wreck, I feel free. I let go of everything. Of every fear and doubt, of tension and pain.

And in that moment I let my entire body fill with pure, unadulterated joy.

CHAPTER NINE

I'm so wrapped up in Logan I scarcely notice when the lights
flicker and then die, plunging us into total darkness.

For a moment there's silence, and then we both start to
laugh. "Did we do that?" I ask, finally getting some control.

"I didn't do it. Did you do it?"

"Bad timing, I guess."

"Or extremely good timing," Logan says, his lips brushing
my neck.

A moment later there's the glow of a candle that wasn't
there before.

"You made that!" I say with a gasp.

He raises one eyebrow, the expression somehow sultry in
the dim light. "Of course I did," he says, pressing a kiss against
my brow. "I still want to look at you," he says, a hint of a growl
in his throat. "And kiss you, and touch you, and hold you." I

pull his face back down to mine, and it's like the weird power outage never happened.

It's only hours later, when exhaustion overtakes us both, that we slow down. Logan helps me into his discarded T-shirt and kisses my forehead one more time before blowing out the candle. Then he pulls me against him and breathes a long sigh, the kind that sounds like it's been waiting two centuries to be released.

"We found each other," I marvel, and even now I hardly believe it.

"You found me," Logan whispers, kissing my forehead. "Fate needed a little help."

It's mere seconds before I hear Logan's breathing slow, and he falls asleep, his arm draped over me. I'm near sleep myself, but I take a moment to revel in the last few hours in this silent, dark room. Every part of my body feels tender and new, like a butterfly emerging from its chrysalis for the first time. New, and perfect.

As perfect as I will ever be.

He's looking at me when I wake up, and for half a second I wonder why his eyes aren't blue.

Guilt stabs my chest as the memory of last night comes flooding back. I push visions of sky-blue eyes aside and smile at Logan.

My lover. My *diligo*.

"Good morning, I think. Lights finally came back on," he whispers in his rough morning voice.

A voice I last heard over two hundred years ago. My mouth curls up at the thought.

"What?" he asks, running the tip of his nose up my cheek and making me feel very awake indeed.

"I haven't seen you in a long time."

He tosses his head back and laughs, and I realize I miss his long hair. It's not a big deal. Hair grows. I, of all people, know *that*. He kisses me soundly and then leans on one elbow and looks down at me, my head still buried in the pillows. "So, Tavia? That's a funny name."

A giggle busts out in more of a snort. "My mom came up with it," I say, a tiny pang making its way into my heart. "No one ever says it right."

His eyes soften and he kisses me again, and we waste another half hour or so kissing and rolling about on the bed before Logan's eyes grow serious. "We should probably talk," he says.

I nod and sober up. I guess the honeymoon is over.

For a little while anyway.

Logan pulls the sheet off me, and I fight the urge to grab it back. Or at least cover the fact that all I'm wearing is underwear and his shirt. But he's not looking at me that way. His eyes are serious—maybe even sad—as he pushes his T-shirt up around my ribs and looks at the scars from my surgeries. The huge staple-marked scar on my thigh is gone—compliments of the Curatoria med team—but there are plenty others to see. My trach scar, several small marks where ribs broke the skin, the remains of a lesion across my hips from the seat belt on the plane, that sort of thing. Enough that even in the darkness last night, he would have felt them.

72

"What happened to you?" he whispers, his voice so full of sympathy and anguish it makes tears of joy come to my eyes.

Joy that I found the person who feels this way about me. That we're together now and can be forever.

Literally, *forever*.

I swallow hard and then take his hand and move it to my head. I angle my neck and sweep my hair away and let him see that scar too. Feel it. Other than doctors, nurses, people I *had* to let feel it, no one else has ever touched my scar.

Except Benson.

He doesn't count anymore.

"Tavia," he says, touching the scar very softly. He doesn't say anything else, but after a few seconds he drops his hand and looks at me. Waiting.

It takes a long time, but I tell him everything that has happened in the last eight months: the plane wreck, the slow manifestation of my powers, Sammi and Mark, the Reduciates, Marie, the virus. *Especially* the virus since we couldn't really talk about it in the prison.

I don't mention Benson.

I should. But I can't. He's too raw a wound, and I don't want Logan to know about him at all.

Maybe someday.

I get to the part of my story where I arrive in Phoenix, and we both laugh at how stupid we were.

"Mostly how stupid *you* were," I say in mock defense.

"*So* stupid," Logan agrees. "I could have been doing this days ago."

I sober. "Maybe if I'd found a way your family wouldn't

have died," I whisper, needing to get that out. To let him know he can talk about it with me. That, having lost my own parents, I'm especially suited to understand.

But he only shrugs. "Maybe. But that doesn't matter anymore. You're my family now."

My eyebrows scrunch together as I stare at him and try to keep the horror out of my eyes as he—likely unknowingly—repeats the phrase the Reduciate woman used. His little siblings, his mother, his father; they just don't *matter* anymore? I remember very distinctly the months of feeling as though part of my physical body had been cut away when my parents died. How can he act like I could replace his family?

Maybe he's in denial. I can be patient. Especially with so much going on with us. Later. It takes time—I know that.

He stares off into space, and I take a moment to love the sight of him, the overhead lights reflecting off his tousled golden hair. Between it and his tan skin he looks just like a god should.

"We have to go soon, don't we?" His voice is full of mourning.

"Yeah." I choke out that tiny word.

"Meet Daniel. Find out what he wants with us."

"*From* us."

"No one ever lets us just be happy," he says, turning to look at me again with those eyes that paralyze me with wanting. "At least we'll get to see each other afterward." He casts his eyes downward, and I understand what he's not saying—that this time, it won't be like the night the hooded horsemen came for us two hundred years ago. I nod and he rolls over onto his stomach. "Hungry?"

"Starving," I admit. "We never did get food last night."

"Probably because of that power outage. Here." He snaps his fingers and a wooden breakfast tray appears on the bed between us with a hot French press full of coffee, croissants, steaming eggs perfectly over easy, crispy bacon, and two glasses of cold orange juice.

That's right. We have *powers*.

And unlike me, he remembered that little fact.

But . . . have we actually resurged? I don't know exactly what that means—what it requires. Just that it makes our creations permanent and gives us seven more reincarnations. I'm about to say something when I catch sight of the melted nub of candle on the bedside table.

Logan created that last night. It's still here. Does that mean that we've done it, that the clock on our lifetimes has been reset?

A warmth of happiness and accomplishment starts to fill my chest, when I remember Sammi wondering if I was too damaged to resurge. Not Logan, me. All the permanence of Logan's candle means is that *he's* safe. And although that fact makes me gloriously happy, I can't help but fear I've saved him only to damn him to seven lifetimes without me.

"Think that's enough?" Logan asks, looking down at the heaping tray. "Do you want to add anything?"

I force a smile when what I really feel is a rush of fear. "It looks great," I say. And no, I most certainly do *not* want to add anything. If it disappears—if I'm not good enough—I . . . I don't want him to know.

As Logan is browsing the tray, I clench my fist, peer at my

bedside table—just outside of Logan's line of sight—and create the first thing I think of.

Now I just have to wait five minutes.

Trying to hide my nerves, I dig into a croissant, only now remembering how famished I am. I was a little . . . distracted before. As I chew, it occurs to me that, at least as long as I'm with Logan, I'm never going to have to worry about not getting enough to eat again. I'll never wonder if I'm going to pass out before Benson can get me food.

I swallow that thought away along with the bread that suddenly feels dry and wash both down with a long sip of searing-hot coffee.

The pile of food is completely gone in five minutes. Logan pats his bare stomach. "I'm stuffed."

"You're a good cook," I say with a laugh.

"It's so weird that I could just forget that I literally can have anything I want with a simple thought," Logan says, and I have to struggle to pay attention. "But boy am I glad I remembered! Serious perks." He stands, stretching, and all my worries flee at the sight of his bare skin spread out before me with such casual confidence. I don't think he had that yesterday.

I like it.

"I'm going to go shower," he says with utter nonchalance. Then he raises one eyebrow. "Join me?"

"Soon as I'm done," I say, gesturing to the nearly finished croissant in my hand. But it's just an excuse. As soon as I hear the water turn on, I toss the croissant onto the tray, close my eyes, count to three, and turn and look at the bedside table.

At a tube of ChapStick.

I pick up the tube and rub it with my thumb, then sink back down onto the bed. My hands tremble so badly I can barely keep a hold of the ChapStick.

"I did it," I whisper.

I'm not broken. I created something permanent.

A glow of victory accompanies that thought.

But how am I supposed to feel about the fact that, even after spending the night with Logan, the first thing I thought to make was a memento of Benson?

CHAPTER TEN

It's strange to suddenly start *making* everything I need. Soap, towels, clothing, hairbrush. I just think of it, and it appears. And even though I've known I could do this for a couple weeks now, my creations never felt exactly *real* before because I knew they would only disappear a few minutes later.

Now? Everything is permanent. There are consequences. I mean, advantages too, obviously. But let's just say I've spent a lot of this morning thinking about the butterfly effect.

Honestly, I still don't *like* using my powers, but I've had to sort of come to terms with it. It's who I am. *What* I am.

Logan, meanwhile, doesn't have any of my hang-ups. The candle last night and breakfast this morning were just the start of his creations. Since then, he's made a garbage can, a shoe rack, an entirely new *wall* to set the kitchenette off from the rest of the room, and a full set of some kind of expensive soap plus cologne and deodorant. And he's done so completely casually. Like it's his right and he's been missing out on it for the last eighteen years. Like he has to make up for lost time.

"So, do you think we're supposed to simply wait here until they come fetch us?" Logan asks.

Fetch? He speaks just a little differently now. I think it's a hybrid of modern Logan and his past selves. Rather like his clothes. Which he also made. He's wearing cargo pants and a T-shirt, but those are definitely Quinn's comfy riding boots peeping out from beneath, and he just pulled out a gold *pocket watch* to check the time.

And his hair is longer. Not as long as when he was Quinn, but not the short—probably mother-mandated—cut he was sporting before. He has taken to his abilities so easily. Easier than I did.

Easier than I *do*.

I'm still wearing my jeans from yesterday. New underwear was a must, and my shirt was seriously sweaty, so I replaced that too, but it just feels weird.

Elizabeth—my therapist in Portsmouth—did say my memory process would be more difficult. I was worried it would be painful for Logan too, but it didn't seem to be at all. Watching him awaken was incredible! I could *see* the changes—could see in his eyes how much information was suddenly inside his brain! But it didn't hurt him. I still cringe at the memory of how agonizing my own awakening was.

I guess that's not the only difference though. Maybe getting used to my powers is one of the side effects. Thinking of *how* to use them.

Like those doctors. Seriously, wow.

"Yeah, I guess we have to wait," I finally answer, folding my arms over my chest like I'm cold. "I don't think I have to tell you that I don't like being here."

"I know," Logan says softly. "But it's better than being in Reduciata custody."

"Is it?" I ask. I don't feel like we have enough information to judge.

"Slightly. I guess it's the lesser of the two evils."

I open my mouth to say something like, "Cheerful," when a pounding on the door interrupts me. We share a long look and then go together to the door and pull it open.

"Morning!" An excited and overly loud voice echoes in our room, shattering my momentary relaxed state. A woman, probably somewhere in her twenties, is holding a tray of something—food, I assume—and she shoves her way through the doorway and sets it on the floor. "I saw this by the door and figured they just left it there once the lights went out. Gave me an excuse to come in and say hi!"

I've hardly taken a breath when she straightens and is suddenly standing with her nose about two inches from mine. I stagger and almost fall getting away from her, but Logan manages to wrap a hand around my upper arm and hold me steady.

"Are you *her*?" the woman asks, her eyes childishly wide. To my horror she lifts the hair on the right side of my head to expose my scar, her fingers feeling as hot as fire as they brush across the sensitive skin. I clamp my hand down over my scalp and jerk my body away, but I'm too late. Gods, I wish my hair were longer.

"You are!" she says, letting loose a high-pitched squeal

80

again, and all I can think is that I want to get away from this person no matter what it takes. "Everyone here has been hoping we would find you," the woman continues, her almost black eyes dark and wide, reminding me very much of Bambi. "Welcome. If there's ever anything you need . . . oh, look at me, offering my services to someone like *you*," she says with a laugh, her hands gesturing at me from head to toe as though I were some physical specimen on auction.

"I'm sorry, do I know—"

But the woman interrupts. "Oh, silly of me. I'm Alanna, and this is Thomas." A very tall man—probably in his early forties—with slightly wavy brown hair whom I had hardly even noticed steps forward and silently offers his hand.

Names are murmured, hands shaken, but inside I'm desperate to get them out of my space. Alanna links her arm with mine before I can protest and turns to view our room. Logan is stuck behind me with Thomas, which I think is the better of the available options. Thomas seems reserved, quiet.

I wonder how he stands Alanna. She looks like she's quite a bit younger than him anyway, but she *acts* like a ten-year-old. It's not just that she's annoying; she's tainting our space. This is the first real home that Logan and I will share—no matter how temporary—and she's violating it with her intrusion.

"Oh, it still has the old décor," Alanna says, studying our neat, elegant room that, oddly, reminds me of Sammi's room back in Portsmouth.

"You're both Creators, right? You'll need some help clearing things out then. Here we go." Looking more like a little girl than a full-grown woman, Alanna stands on her tip toes and points at the bed. "Poof!" she says, and the bed winks out of sight. "Poof, poof, poof," and the armchairs are gone.

I've never seen destroying in action except for Marie. So watching Alanna make something go away with so little thought makes my stomach sour. I have to remind myself: Destroying is not inherently bad. Both Curatoriates and Reduciates can be Destroyers. It's just the other side of the coin.

Still.

I stand there with my mouth open at Alanna's odd, childish enthusiasm as she clears the room of all its furnishings with that silly pointing of her finger.

"There," she says, hands on her hips. "Now you can set everything up yourselves. Not sad to see it go," she continues before I can even think about getting a word in edgewise. "A couple of human Curatoriates lived here before. Snooty. Didn't like to mix much. Mark, I think his name was." Alanna turns to me, eyes sparkling, "Her name—this is hilarious—her name was Sammi and she was super short and cute with blond hair and all, but she was a hard-ass. All business, no play. I laughed every time someone called her Sammi. Totally didn't fit."

I can't breathe. I look at Logan, silently begging him to help, to remove the woman who just zapped all my former guardians' belongings out of existence. Fortunately, Logan catches my drift and starts to bodily shove Alanna from the room. "Thank you. You were very helpful. But we're waiting for someone to come get us."

"Ooh, are you going to Daniel today?"

How the *hell* does she know all of this?

"Yes, they are," says a dry voice from the still-open

doorway. "And I don't think he'd be happy to find out you delayed them."

I never thought I'd be so happy to see the cheerless woman who brought us here last night, but at this moment I could kiss her.

"Run along, you two," the woman says dryly, and we share a look that tells me this couple is *not* popular around here.

Like I needed an insider to tell me *that*.

The two scurry away much like puppies who have just been caught peeing on the carpet, and the woman looks us up and down to judge our *readiness*. Then she simply says, "He's ready for you."

Instantly, the terror is back. Maybe "terror" isn't the right word. I guess I'm not entirely afraid of Daniel—if the last few weeks have taught me anything, it's that I truly am a goddess and—when I keep my wits about me—I can survive just about anything.

But Sammi and Mark didn't trust him. Went to great lengths to keep information about me from him. Which apparently didn't work.

And yet, he gave me the painting. And judging by all the stalling after that, he knew what would happen when he did. He gave me the one thing I wanted more than anything else in my life.

Or any other life.

He gave me Logan.

I glance over at my *diligo*, somber and silent beside me. It's hard not to feel grateful.

Nervously, I run my fingers through my hair and pull my

hand back in shock. My hair is down to my shoulders. When did that happen? Wait . . . I remember. When Alanna exposed my scar, I wished my hair were longer.

Did that tiny thought make this happen? That's more than a little terrifying. I vaguely remember the fear Sonya had of *herself* in my dreams. The surge of power that frightened her. Do I have it too, or is this normal? I hate that I honestly have no idea. I shove my hands in my pocket, pretending nothing's wrong. I'm going to have to give this some serious thought later.

After locking the door, we follow the woman—who still hasn't bothered to introduce herself—down the hallway full of doors, in the opposite direction from where we came in last night. A glow of light is beaming from the end of the hall, and as we round the corner my mouth drops as a cavernous space—bigger than any lobby I've ever seen—greets me.

But it's not just the space—everything is filled with color and beauty and décor all reminiscent of ancient Rome. Plaster frescoes cover domes of alcoves, and pillars line the walls. Pillow-laden chaises and low tables are spread about, and a large buffet holds gold plates full of fruits, olives, and nuts as well as pitchers of honey and marble palettes of cheese.

And the paintings! Everywhere are paintings of such exquisite artistry I can hardly breathe as I stare down at them.

My fingers itch for a paintbrush as I take in the gilded frames of oils and watercolors, photographs and lithographs. I see, here and there, familiar paintings, and I can't help but wonder if *these* are the real ones and if those displayed in museums such as the Met and the Louvre are actually Earthbound-created replicas.

I can barely drag my eyes away from the walls to take in the furnishings resting on intricately woven rugs of every shape and color I could possibly imagine. It's like a Roman museum. Each enormous alcove is decorated, perfect attention given to details I wouldn't even think of. Beautiful tables and china hutches and credenzas are placed just so on intricately threaded carpets. Even the landing we're standing on boasts a mezzanine with gorgeously carved rails. A navy blue stair runner invites me down the eight-foot-wide winding staircase.

"This is wonderful," Logan whispers. I nod in agreement but find that I'm afraid to go forward.

Afraid to enter this bustling world that feels too big, too advanced, too incredible for someone like me.

Too godlike.

"This way," the woman says, pointing us through the crowd.

That's right. We're going to see Daniel.

I never got a chance to tell Logan about how Sammi and Mark didn't trust their illustrious leader. How, as Elizabeth explained, they'd found signs of *corruption*. It was something I'd intended to address before we were *summoned*. But then Alanna shoved her way in and then the woman was there and . . . I wish I could tell Logan *now* so that he'd know that I'm not ready to show all my cards to this man who may or may not be on the same side as us.

But now isn't the time. Maybe it won't ever be the time as long as we're here. Do they bug rooms? Are they always listening? Or is that only the kind of thing the Reduciates do?

"Come on," Logan gently urges, squeezing my hand. The woman is a good twenty feet from us now, and I hadn't realized I was still glued to the floor. I force myself to nod, then lift my feet, clinging to Logan's hand like a security blanket.

We traverse the lobby, and though I expect people to turn and stare at us, they mostly keep to themselves. Small wonder—we may actually be the least interesting people here. Within one hundred feet I've spotted people in kilts, a woman in a long, sweeping gown, a man in a toga, and another in what looks like Indian robes. There are individuals in familiar modern dress as well, but they're far outnumbered by their more diverse counterparts.

"Are they all Earthbound?" I whisper.

"Certainly not," the woman sternly replies. "I would say that at any given time roughly ten percent of our occupants here are Earthbound. Many, *many* humans work with us. Support our cause. But then," she says, and her intense eyes swing toward me as we wait for an elevator, "you know that, don't you?"

My thoughts immediately turn to Sammi and Mark, and I wonder again just how much these people know about me. How much they *think* they know about me.

"The daily staff, however, are dressed to match the theme of the main hall."

Okay, I do see lots of people in multicolored togas. They look . . . busier than the others. So just what are the

Earthbounds here doing? A bubble of anger rises inside me. Don't they know humans are dying by the thousands—maybe tens of thousands now—while they're buried all safe and secure out here in the desert?

"Easier that way," the woman continues as I swallow down my anger. "You know who to ask if you need help. Togas on Friday, Baroque costumes on Saturday, Chinese dress jackets on Sunday, et cetera."

"Does the hall change too?" I ask, and chide myself for the wonderment in my voice. Logan seems to be taking it all in stride—I'm the only one pestering her with questions.

"Of course," the woman says.

Of course. I narrow my eyes at her back. I don't like her, but I have no one else to ask. "Why are there so many people here?" I ask, trying to keep my voice down. I still don't get it.

"Working," she says, as though that were all the explanation necessary.

"On what?" I press, annoyed at being evaded, especially when the fate of the world is literally at stake. They certainly don't look like they're working to me. More like being served by subservient humans. From literal silver platters, in some cases.

"Lots of things. Developing technology, searching for other Earthbounds, teaching newly found Earthbounds about the time they've missed. We're always busy here trying to protect our own and make the world a better place. The same thing we've been doing for thousands of years."

I think of Audra and the other doctors and the special scanner they invented. That makes me feel a little better. *Something* is getting done. Maybe half of these people here are just on break.

Break. Sure.

I try to make myself reserve judgment. After all, if I remembered more of my past lives, maybe I would understand more.

"Ah, here we go. Off to Daniel." The elevator doors open, and she herds us inside.

Instead of taking us up, as I assumed it would, the elevator begins to move downward as soon as the doors close. For some reason, I have the impression that we're in a small box descending into hell. I try not to squeeze Logan's hand too hard, but with each foot we go deeper into the earth, my fear grows and I grasp Rebecca's necklace like a talisman.

Who is this man that Sammi and Mark—such loyal Curatoriates—were willing to lie to? To sneak behind his back? The thought inspires very little confidence.

But then . . .

It's only seconds later that we're exiting the elevator. I expect a hallway to greet us, but we step out into a tiny eight-by-eight-foot space, one wall almost entirely taken up by a beautiful and massive carved mahogany door. I hear a sound from behind me, and when I look, the elevator has closed and the woman is gone.

Logan gives my hand another squeeze, but it doesn't do much to inspire confidence. My breathing is unsteady as we stand and wait.

And wait.

And then the enormous door begins to swing open.

CHAPTER ELEVEN

I'm not sure just what I was expecting, but the slightly short man with graying hair and soft blue eyes wasn't it.

Of course, surely the great *Daniel* wouldn't answer his own door—this is a . . . a secretary, an aide, something. But when he sees us his mouth tips up in a smile that crinkles the sides of his eyes.

"Tavia. At last."

I stare at him in confusion, but the man doesn't seem to notice.

"Logan. Nick of time, eh?"

The sheer absurdity of his statement-that-might-be-a-joke catches Logan off-guard, and he gives out a strange sort of cough-laugh.

"Please, please, come in," the man says, holding the door wide. "I'm Daniel."

My heartbeat speeds up at the now-certain revelation that

the man before us is in the fact the leader of the Curatoria, and I half expect to hear the beeping sound that plagued me while trapped inside the Reduciate prison.

I'm somewhere else. I'm safe.

To distract myself, I glance around the office. It's huge—like everything else in this place, apparently—with half-open doors leading to rooms unknown. But unlike the foyer we just left, this space lacks opulence.

Which, strangely, doesn't make it any less beautiful.

It has a simple hominess, and I have to bite the inside of my cheek when I realize it reminds me of the way my mother used to decorate.

Soft watercolors fill the walls, mostly of landscapes that are definitely *not* deserts. It makes me wonder if he misses green, housed here beneath the sand. The wood that makes the desk, the chairs, the tables, is a medium brown—probably maple or oak—instead of the stark but elegant espresso shade that practically filled the atrium. Pastel throws and pillows complement beige and sage-green upholstery, and potted plants dot the walls and corners, lending the only brilliant colors in the whole room.

Comfortable, I finally settle on as the word to describe this space. Everything about it makes me want to sink down onto a couch or chair and read a book.

Or nap.

Or some of both.

I look back at Daniel and wonder just how much of it is a facade. I mean, he could remake this room a hundred times a day, couldn't he?

I suddenly wonder if it's all just a trap. The spider's parlor.

As though sensing the dreary turn my thoughts have just taken, Daniel invites us to sit on a couch and takes his own seat in a cushy armchair across a low table. As I sit, I look up and catch Daniel studying me. His eyes glitter with interest and something else I can't read. I wonder how much of what I'm seeing of him is real.

But he doesn't look away when he catches me staring. Instead his eyes soften and he continues to stare, as though inviting me to study him as well.

I'm not sure what to think of that.

A strange feeling twists in my stomach as his face turns starkly serious.

"Tavia," Daniel says, leaning forward with his elbows balanced on his knees, "though I've gone to great lengths to try to make you as comfortable as possible, we both know we're not here to have a casual conversation."

I nod, accepting the inevitable.

"I'm told you won't join us," he says in that same light tone, but I hear the bitter edge of rejection hovering just beneath the surface.

"I won't," I confirm, refusing to let my voice quaver.

He hesitates, then says, "But I hope you *will* be willing to work with us to put an end to all these deaths from this terrible virus." Bitterness replaced by hope. This man changes so quickly I can hardly keep up.

"I don't know why you think I'm so special," I say, a hint of belligerence creeping into my tone, "but *if* I am, I will consider working with you." I fix him with a hard gaze and add,

"*Temporarily* and with the understanding that I am not one of you. I am *not* a Curatoriate."

Daniel nods, and although I see disappointment in his eyes, he doesn't appear surprised. Then, he turns to Logan. "Logan, even though it's Tavia we need, you're welcome to stay for as long as you like."

Logan's eyes look nervous, but he winds his fingers through mine and squeezes. "And am I free to leave when she does?" he asks, directing his question more at the table than at Daniel.

"Of course," Daniel says. He sounds neither offended nor surprised that Logan would inquire as much.

Which doesn't make me feel any more secure. I get the feeling Daniel knows us. Knows *me*. And considering how little I know myself, I'm not a fan of the sensation.

"Now, Miss Tavia," Daniel says, sitting back against his chair. "I know that Mark and Sammi didn't trust me. That they tried to remove you from Portsmouth without informing the Curatoria and, particularly, without informing me, and that likely you carry the same mistrust. Am I right so far?"

I gape at him and hear the sound of shattering in my head.

He chuckles. "Answer enough. Just wanted to get that out of the way. The fewer secrets, the better, in my opinion."

Before I can even begin to contemplate a response to *that* bombshell, he continues, his tone much more dire now. "I also know that your brain injury has . . . proven more extensive than anyone wants to admit. If you had the same perfect memory that most of us do, I think you would have figured out a while ago why you're so special."

I have no idea what to say as facts I didn't think he could

possibly know continue to come spilling from his mouth. Thoughts and doubts I'd considered only my own. Some I haven't even had a chance to share with Logan yet.

Although I would have. Soon.

And what does he mean, that I would have figured it out? Is he referring to Sonya and the secret she was willing to kill herself to protect? Or the secret Rebecca spent her life hiding from the Reduciata? Or are they same thing? And how could he know?

"Logan," Daniel says, still in the same tone. "You were literally plucked from the brink of eternal death-by-fire a few days ago."

Logan forces a hard swallow down his throat, nodding.

"Truth is, you're a very weak Earthbound. And that's not an insult," Daniel says, his hands lifted in a placating gesture. "It's simply *fact*. And Tavia should be just like you. But she's not."

"I am—" I start to protest, but a look from Daniel cuts my words off.

"Logan, would you please create a book for me? Your favorite novel."

Logan's jaw is tight, but he tips his fingers toward the table, and Charles Dickens's *A Tale of Two Cities* appears.

"Now you, Tavia. Your favorite book."

I have no idea where he's going with this, but I think of my dog-eared copy of *The Giver*, the one I left in Michigan when I boarded that fateful plane. The one I never considered asking Sammi to retrieve for me back when I thought she was my aunt Reese. I wonder where it is now.

With a deep breath I tilt my hand toward the table like Logan did, and my book appears beside his.

"Good," Daniel says as he leans forward and picks up Logan's book. He doesn't look at it; he looks at *me* as he flips through the pages, showing me Logan's creation. The beginning looks normal, but as the book continues, there are large sections of blank pages. Chapters that are nothing but short synopses. And then the end begins to fill in a bit more.

I glance at Logan, and he's leaning back with his arms folded over his chest, looking grumpy for reasons I don't understand.

"Now let's look at yours," Daniel says softly, and he opens my book and flips the pages the same way he did with Logan's.

My book is complete.

More than complete. The typed text is there, word for word. But also the notes I've made over the years, tiny sketches in the margins, even the page I accidentally tore one day and then taped back together is there.

Still torn.

Still taped.

"I don't understand," I say, staring at the two books. "Why is mine . . . ?" I hesitate, looking for a word besides *better*. Whatever is happening here, it doesn't make Logan happy, and I don't want to add to it. "More complete," I settle on.

"Because you're stronger than him," Daniel says, unapologetically. "And not *a little bit*—exponentially. Knowledge and creativity are the driving force of the Earthbound. Especially Creators. And how strong you are determines how much knowledge you need to create something. To create a book as

94

complete as yours, Logan would have to have memorized every word. An Earthbound as strong as you could recreate any book you've ever read. In *any* of your lives that you remember. And possibly even those you don't," he adds, looking at me with such intensity—such awe, bordering on reverence—that I have to turn away.

Without thinking, I turn toward Logan, which may have been a mistake.

He sits there with his lips in a hard line—he's obviously angry. Is it because he's weak—or because I'm not?

"But why?" I ask. "We lived our maximum seven lifetimes before resurging last night. We should both be weak. That's why Sammi and Mark were so worried about me."

Daniel nods but doesn't answer my question. "Logan," he says, and I hear sympathy in his voice this time. Not pity, exactly, but understanding. *Wanting* to understand, maybe. "What's your next favorite book? One from this life, perhaps."

Logan mumbles, "*American Gods*," and Daniel smiles. The irony of that admission isn't lost on either of them.

"Excellent. Would you please turn your book into this *American Gods*?"

Logan sits up now. "That's not how it works," he sputters. "I *make* things. I can't just *change* things."

"Try," Daniel says, utterly unruffled. "And Tavia, you as well. Change your book into your next favorite."

Logan and I look at each other, and with my eyes I try to tell him that he doesn't have to do this. But he shakes his head and flutters his fingers at the table with an almost dismissive gesture.

I smile in relief. As far as I can tell, he's done it. *A Tale of Two Cities* has turned into *American Gods*.

"Your turn, Tavia" Daniel says.

Still confused, I move my fingers and replace *The Giver* with *Sense and Sensibility*, the same way I replaced the walls with air in the Reduciata base.

Again, Daniel's hands go to Logan's book, and he begins to flip the pages.

The blood drains from my face, and I force myself not to show my dismay. The book hasn't changed at all.

The cover of Charles Dickens's story simply has an additional dust jacket on it, and as Daniel thumbs through, loose-leaf pages fall out, covered in what must be snippets of Neil Gaiman's book.

"Now yours, Tavia," Daniel says, and that strange reverence is back, this time in the warmth of his voice. He reaches for my book, and something inside me wants to bolt. To run from this room and from whatever it is I'm about to learn.

I want to hide from it, to go back to normal life.

I can't drag my eyes from Daniel's hands as he opens the book. He pulls back the dust jacket of my special edition hardcover to reveal . . . the deep green casing—*Sense and Sensibility* stamped in gold foil. He flips the pages, and I see Jane Austen's story flowing by, word-for-word, just like when it was *The Giver*.

I lean back and fold my arms, noting for half a second that Logan and I are now mirrors of each other. "So I'm strong and Logan's not," I say, not caring that I sound snippy. "I think you've proven that."

"Where did *The Giver* go, Tavia?" Daniel says, ignoring my words. "*A Tale of Two Cities* didn't disappear. All Logan could do was add to what was already there."

"No, no, it's just a different way of thinking of it. It's *replacing*," I argue. "You just create one thing *in place of* another. It's nothing special." I look to Logan, pleading. I want to be like him, I realize. I want us to be the *same*.

Daniel returns the book to the table and looks up at me with a depth of knowledge in his eyes that stretches down like a deep mine. "Creating is often considered the more powerful of the two abilities, for reasons we don't need to go into at the moment. But I've never been convinced of that. Perhaps as a Destroyer I'm biased. But regardless, creating something out of nothing is a much-coveted ability, as I'm sure you can understand." He leans forward, and the intensity in his eyes pins me to my seat. "But there is one limitation and one alone. You can only create. You can only add to what is already there. Creators are the masters of *more*. Not different, only more. You cannot *change*, you cannot *replace*, only *add*." He leans back and clasps his fingers over his slightly rounded belly. "So again, Tavia, I ask you, where did *The Giver* go? Where did the walls of your cell go?"

I have nothing to say. Nothing I *can* say. The silence stretches long, and no one wants to break it.

After interminable minutes, Daniel rises, strides to his desk, and retrieves a folder. He walks back to the low coffee table and lays three pictures on it.

Even as my eyes fix on them I feel the urge to retch build up in my throat.

It's my plane.

The wreckage.

My seat.

"We lost two Earthbounds and three human Curatoriates obtaining these photos a few months ago," Daniel says. "All we knew is that *these* were what made the Reduciates stop trying to kill you and start attempting to capture you instead. It took weeks and weeks before we finally saw what they saw." He points to the walls of the fuselage surrounding my seat.

They're already burned into my brain from months of reading news stories. I don't need to see them—don't *want* to see them—and yet I can't look away.

"Perfect," Daniel says. "As though your section of the plane weren't in the crash at all." He sighs. "A few weeks ago one of my top researchers finally came up with a theory that, even as recently as this morning, I wasn't convinced was possible. Not even after reports of what happened in your most recent escape from the Reduciates. But now I've seen it with my own eyes; I have no doubt. He was right."

He leans forward so close our noses are mere inches apart, but I can't move. Can't back away.

"You did not *create* something to save yourself in those fateful moments, Tavia. You transformed the entire section of the plane around you into something else. And because you had not yet resurged with Logan," he says, inclining his head to my lover, who sits silent and pale-faced, "a few minutes after the crash, that section of the plane reverted to its original form. As though it had never been in the crash at all. *Because it hadn't.*"

I look into Daniel's eyes as the truth of everything he's saying slams into me like a boulder. "How is that even possible?" I whisper. I've accepted so many impossible things in the last few weeks.

But this?

"Sometime in your past lives between when you were Rebecca and now, something happened. It turned you into something that is neither a Destroyer nor a Creator, but a hybrid of the two. A Transformist, I'm calling you, since such a phenomenon has never happened before."

Daniel stands now, his face finally leaving mine, and I gasp for air that isn't shared by him.

"Not only that, it appears to have returned you to your original level of power. Possibly even the level you possessed as an Earthmaker."

He looks down at me, and despite his next words, I feel very, very small.

"Tavia, you are the most unique, the most *powerful* of any Earthbound in the world, and that is why the Reduciata will stop at *nothing* to have you."

CHAPTER TWELVE

Nausea takes hold of me, and my heart feels like it's fallen into my stomach. I sense Logan rising, and though my mind registers that he's walked a few feet away, I hear nothing, see nothing, as my brain spins and tries to take all of this in.

Again. Because now I see why Sonya was so afraid. The huge increase in power that I didn't recognize. The unexplainable abilities I assumed were normal.

She understood. I didn't. But I do now.

"But . . . but what does this have to do with the virus?" I ask as the tiniest stream of logic works its way through the storm in my head. "Sammi and Mark said the Reduciates needed me because of the virus."

Daniel sits again and pulls out a large cotton handkerchief, dabbing at his forehead. "My team wasn't fast enough to prevent the fiasco that happened in Camden when the Reduciates found you, but we were able to retrieve the bodies of our Curatoriates afterward."

Bodies. Mark, Sammi, and . . . "Elizabeth?" I whisper.

His lips press into a hard line. "I'm afraid there wasn't much left of her, but yes, we did retrieve some remains."

I didn't realize until that moment that I'd been holding on to the tiniest thread of hope that she was alive. I choke back tears—I will *not* cry in front of this man.

"We . . ." he hesitates, and I know I'm not going to like whatever he's going to say next. "We were able to retrieve tissue samples from Mark that still had active virus specimens in them and—"

"Oh gods," I say, letting my head fall into my hands, pretty certain I *am* going to be sick after all.

"I know it's hard to think scientifically about this, Tavia. But I promise you that using his body to save others is what he would have wanted."

People use that phrase all the time. It's easy to say when the person in question isn't there to contradict you. Will never be there again.

"And in the last two weeks we've made some tremendous discoveries."

Daniel's voice slowly begins to register again, and I try to focus on what he's saying and not the image of Mark throwing his charred body over his wife as he hopelessly tried to protect her in their last moments.

"As far as we can tell, the virus was intended not only to kill off the majority of the human population, but also most of the

Earthbounds." He laces his fingers together, and a wrinkle appears between his brows. "The Reduciates have this theory—"

"That they can get their power back if the Earthbounds die forever," I interrupt rudely. "I know all this. How do *I* fit in?" Because that's the crux of it. How does my having become a Transformist help the Curatoria? And threaten the Reduciata enough to send assassins after me in my former life?

Lives. They killed Rebecca too.

"The virus mutated immediately after being released into water sources," Daniel says calmly, ignoring my current attitude. "It's creating the chaos you see now. The crazy weather, the rapid deaths. Over four *thousand* people died of the virus yesterday alone. Which wouldn't be so bad for the Reduciates, except that now the vaccine they created to inoculate themselves against their own disease is useless."

"Can't they just get an Earthbound scientist to study the new virus and *create* a new vaccine?"

"No. All a creator can do is make *more* of the current vaccine. The one they have now took them many lifetimes to develop. Coming up with a new one would take so long that by the time it was ready, it would be worthless; there would simply be no one left. What they *need* is someone who's extremely powerful to study both the virus and the old vaccine and transform the useless strands of genetic material within the current vaccine into something that can effectively fight the mutation."

I stare at him with wide eyes. "It sounds impossible."

"It almost is," Daniel says. "You would need to have broken

into the most top-secret vault in the Reduciata headquarters and stolen a vial of their vaccine, for starters. Then you would have to find an extremely powerful Transformist and pair her with a state-of-the-art lab including a few pieces of technology that haven't even been invented yet." He stares at me unblinkingly for several long seconds. "Luckily," he says in barely more than a whisper, "I have all of those things."

I feel cold and alone sitting on this couch and being stared at by a stranger. Ignoring any semblance of social acceptability, I rise from the couch without a word and walk over to Logan. I bury my face in his chest, and after a half second's hesitation, he wraps his arms around me and rocks me very slowly back and forth.

Is this it? The secret I've literally been killed for? Something . . . something about it feels wrong. But this has got to be it.

With my ear pressed against Logan's chest I can hear his heart; it's pounding. I don't know how to read him right now, and even trying to listen to Rebecca's voice in my head isn't helping. What I do know is that he makes me feel stronger, and that I can't do this—any of this—without him.

Mark was right. I can save the world.

No, I can *possibly* save the world. No pressure, right?

After a while—when I know I'm back in control of myself— I turn and cross my arms over my chest. I lean very slightly against Logan—not enough for Daniel to notice, but enough to draw courage from him.

Goodness knows my own reserves are empty.

I try to think clearly—look at this rationally. Is it such a big deal to just help him? I mean, look how much he's helped me. Us. That reminds me . . .

"Where did you get the painting, Daniel?"

He raises an eyebrow, and I can tell that he thinks he knows what I'm talking about but doesn't want to say anything until he's sure.

"The painting that awakened Logan."

"Ah," he says with a smile. "The painting that turned our lights off."

I know he's trying to bait me—to distract me—but *that* assertion is too much. "Why would that have anything to do with the power outage?"

"The moment of resurging is . . . quite extraordinary. While it generally accompanies both parties remembering each other, it is, in fact, a separate thing. It's a moment of total acceptance in both Earthbounds' minds. When that moment happens there is often a manifestation of power—our powers overflowing as they recharge, I suppose is the best way to say it. But you, Tavia, are so much stronger than any Earthbound we've seen in centuries. I suspect that in that moment you unconsciously created a flow of pure energy that transferred to the electrical conduits of our building, and let's just say they were not equipped to handle such a large surge." He chuckles and shakes his head. "Blew every fuse in the place. A price we're most happy to pay, mind you."

I think of the way I accidentally made my hair grow, and his explanation makes a horrendous kind of sense. But I'm not so easily put off. "The painting, Daniel. I know where it was last. How did *you* come to have it?"

His laugh breaks off. "I have spies everywhere, Tavia. Even in the heart of the Reduciata. I *have* to. How else would I have known you were captured?"

"So you took it?"

"I sent for it."

He's being cryptic. But do I want a full explanation in front of Logan? Do I want him to say he got it from the Reduciate boy I was in love with?

"Did you get anything else from the Reduciata? When you rescued us, I mean?" I ask, remembering for the first time that there's something else they have that I desperately want.

"Besides the two of you, with your limbs all attached?" he asks dryly.

"I'm not saying I'm ungrateful," I say quickly. "But, did you . . . I had a backpack, and it was—"

Before I can get the words "kind of important" out, Daniel is already shaking his head. "We barely made it out with the two of you. Besides, I suspect you can replace anything you need. Can't you?"

"It—" I don't dare reveal the braid's existence. Not even after all this. "There was a journal," I settle on. "And some files."

His forehead wrinkles in concern. "I admit, I'm not pleased things like that fell into Reduciate hands. But I suppose if we had to make a trade, we got the better end of the bargain. Anything else important that you were carrying?"

Nothing important, nothing that can't be replaced—except

my memories, the ones contained in Sonya's braid. The Reduciates wouldn't know what the braid was. They probably threw it away. The thought makes me want to cry.

I change the subject instead.

"Sammi and Mark didn't trust you," I say. "Why not, and why should *I*?"

Daniel's face crumples, and I try to hide my surprise at his reaction. "I suspect you'll understand this better now that you've reunited with Logan, but contrary to what many Earthbounds think, even with the entire force of the Curatoria behind me, finding an Earthbound's *diligo* is hardly an easy task." He pauses and seems to be pushing away a grief that doesn't match the cheerful, if businesslike, man we've seen thus far. "I haven't found mine in two lifetimes," he finally chokes out. "I don't know where she is, how old she is, how many times she's died." He looks up at me, and his eyes are no longer the sparkling, friendly eyes I was surprised to see when we first walked in. They're hollow and dull. "If we don't stop this virus, my beautiful angel could run through all seven of her lives in a matter of *months*. Before this one, I lived two lifetimes alone, running the Curatoria because that's what we agreed long ago that we should do. But I don't want to live another *four* that same way, knowing that nothing but lonely centuries and endless death await me."

My breathing is ragged, but I try to hide it—try to act like I wasn't facing similar thoughts only days ago. "Why would that make them not trust you?"

His eyes drop and he looks guilty. "I'm afraid desperation

has led me to make some choices I would not have a hundred years ago. I've risked lives on ventures that had a sadly low chance of success, and I've done it in the name of the Curatoria when in truth it was all very personal. I'm not saying I don't have regrets, or that I was never wrong," he adds as he once again lifts his chin and meets my eyes. "But maybe you'll understand that in a way Sammi and Mark never could. They simply don't comprehend the depth of love between two Earthbounds. Technically, the risks I took, the rules I broke, were for *everyone's* benefit. Everyone will be facing this same dilemma in a very short amount of time. But I won't lie to you and say I was thinking of everyone. I was only thinking of her."

He resumes his seat on the couch and looks almost sheepish as he raises his hand to gesture at me. "And now I've brought you into my headquarters. An immensely powerful young Transformist who refuses to take our oaths. Many would say *that* is the stupidest thing of all. But Tavia, you are our last hope, and I'm tired of lying to everyone and saying there are things we can do. There is *nothing* we can do. There is only what *you* can do."

I'm still not convinced. "How did you even know the Reduciata captured us? It seems to me that it would have been easier to nab us from Phoenix rather than infiltrate a secret Reduciate holding facility."

"The opposite, actually," Daniel says, a touch sheepish.

I stare silently, waiting for him to explain himself.

He glances around him, as though expecting to see someone. "This is extremely confidential information, but I want you to be able to trust me." He hesitates. Then, "It has taken several years, but I have a spy who lives right in the Reduciata headquarters. A compound, really. He's not senior enough to get much of the information I *wish* I had, but I'm trying to be patient. He wasn't able to find out where you had run away to, but he did discover that *they* knew. I made one of the hardest decisions I have ever made as the leader of the Curatoria. To sit back and do nothing. To let them do my work for me. I was all but certain they wouldn't kill you—that they needed you as badly as I do."

"You gambled with my life."

"I had to," Daniel says, and it's the sharpest tone he has used thus far. He takes an unsteady breath. "Somehow, they knew where you would go. They knew where Logan was. I let them do my work for me, essentially. And then, as soon as I could, I sent a team and got you both out of there. I'm afraid it was the best I could do. The best *we* could do."

I'm silent for long seconds, trying to sort everything out in my head. Finally, I settle on the true heart of the matter. "Would you have killed Sammi and Mark and Elizabeth yourself just to get me here?"

"Yes," Daniel says without hesitation.

"And Logan?"

"You were useless to me without him."

"Because my ability to transform the vaccine wouldn't have been permanent," I reply, not letting myself cringe at the word *useless*.

"Exactly."

I pause, then with my heart in my throat I ask, "Would you have taken down an entire plane full of people to get me here?"

He pauses and then looks up at me. "I believe I would have," he whispers.

"Then how are you any better than them?"

"Because they want you to save their elite. I want you to save *everyone*."

CHAPTER THIRTEEN

His gaze is so fixed, so intense, I can't look at it for very long, and I shift my focus to my shoes and simply say, "I need some time to think about it."

"Of course you do," Daniel says, and as though there were an audible *snap*, his face returns to the pleasant man who greeted us at the door. "While you are deciding, may I ask that you both go to our medical wing and have full-body scans?"

"Why would we do that?" The hairs on my arms rise at the thought of going back to what is essentially a hospital. To let them look at my brain.

"I don't like the conditions you were kept in at the Reduciata base," he says calmly, as though I hadn't just snapped at him. "You have bruising on your head—Audra told me," he says, raising his hands before I have a chance to accuse him. "Everyone here reports to me, and I'm afraid you're just going to have to get used to my, shall we say, *protective* governing style."

I bite my tongue and think of Audra. She's okay. I don't think I would mind *her* checking me out.

"I ask it of everyone," he says. "There's a reason our Earthbounds generally live at least into their nineties despite their human bodies. Constant medical evaluation and preventive care that only the Earthbound can give."

It makes sense but . . .

"I got you out of there," Daniel says, pinning me with a gaze that says, *you owe me one.* "The least you can do is give me the peace of mind that you were rescued unscathed. Or, at least, without permanent damage. The basic care our doctors were able to give you on the helicopter was only for obvious damage. But I'd like to be sure you both are in as perfect health as we can get you."

He's right. And I did hit my head pretty hard. Would it really hurt anything?

"I guess that would be fine," I say, looking at Logan for confirmation, but he clearly doesn't feel the same hesitation I do.

"I think it's a good idea." He places a hand at my waist, and I feel better. "I fell pretty hard when the explosion happened at my old house. A checkup can't hurt, right?" he says, but this question is only for me.

"Guess not," I say, squirming with guilt over the arson that killed his family. Not that it was my fault, but if I had only . . . that's a road I just can't go down.

"Great! Let's get this over with then," Daniel says in a surprisingly chipper tone.

"So, you have a whole medical *department*?" I ask as we all stand and turn toward the door.

"Where do you think all the very best doctors in the world come from?" Daniel asks, casually grabbing a set of keys from a hook on the wall and depositing them in his pocket.

"You just keep a bunch of doctors around?"

"About half the ones we have. And of course, we have an exceptionally advanced medical facility as well."

"Why?"

Daniel looks up at me now. "Research, mostly. Studying Earthbound anatomy. Finding cures for incurable diseases. Figuring out a way to introduce these treatments to the medical world without being discovered for who we really are. A doctor with the powers of an Earthbound can do so much more than any human doctor, you understand?"

I do now.

"So, Daniel?" I pause when he turns back to look at me. "I need to know the truth. Am I a guest or a prisoner?"

He holds his hands out to the side. "Do you see any bars?"

"Do you think I'm stupid enough to believe that's what matters?" I say in the same even tone.

He's silent for a few seconds, and then a sheepish smile emerges. "All right, it's only fair I be straight. We're in a remote location. For our security. It's not like you can walk out a front door to some main street in a town somewhere. But beyond the inherent complication of our location, yes, you are free to go at any time. But I hope you won't." Daniel escorts us out of his office back to the tiny entryway, and I expect the solemn woman to return to lead us upstairs, but when the elevator doors open, Daniel steps in with us.

"Oh. I—I assumed—"

"That I don't go out among the masses?" he says with a chuckle. "I do enjoy my privacy sometimes, thus the apartment on the lowest floor, but I think it's important that the Curatoriates see me, *know* me. I'm no better than them; I simply do more paperwork," he says with a grin.

As the elevator begins to rise I realize something I missed only a minute ago.

He told me I'm free to go, but he didn't show me the way out.

Before I can consider that thought further, the elevator doors open to the atrium. I'm instantly surprised to see that it's not the semi-chaotic milling of people we saw only an hour ago. Everyone—and I'm pretty sure by the sheer numbers that it *is* everyone—is gathered around a bank of enormous flat-screen televisions that weren't there earlier.

The bristly woman from before is wading through the crowd, and her eyes look frantic until they light upon Daniel. I glance at Logan, and we speed our steps until we're close enough to hear the words of the reporter as the screen switches to a satellite image of . . . the ocean? I don't see anything unusual until the man's nearly frantic words finally worm their way into my consciousness.

"As you can see, there is nothing, *nothing*, where only yesterday over a million people lived. It's hard to comprehend how something this extreme could be anything but a hoax, but a written statement from the president confirms that these satellite images are real and accurately portray what can only be described as the most devastating natural disaster in recorded history. We're being told that the loss of life is expected to be nearly total in a radius that best estimates suggest is many thousands of miles. There's hope that some survivors will be found among the literally *tons* of wreckage and debris floating free in the water, but even if rescue vessels find them, they're unsure they can reach them in time."

"What happened?" Daniel asks a middle-aged woman beside him with tears streaking down her face.

"The Pacific Islands," she says, gesturing at the television. "They're *gone*."

"Gone?" I ask. "What do you mean gone?" Surely even the most powerful Destroyer in the world couldn't do something like this. It's too big, too vast.

Too deadly.

"Shh," the woman says, as the camera goes back to the reporter.

"Scientists are at a loss to explain this incident as ships filled with research technology are even now making their way across the Pacific Ocean to the place where Fiji, Samoa, Tonga, Tahiti, and dozens of smaller islands once were. At the moment the only speculation that has been reported is a massive settling of the tectonic plates beneath these island paradises. The north and east coasts of Australia have been put on tsunami watch and ocean wildlife is also expected to suffer from this massive disruption. Even now, no one can be certain what the secondary consequences of this incident will be."

"This isn't right," I say, staring as the screen goes back to the empty ocean. "There's nothing *natural* about this at all. There can't be."

"Reduciates?" Logan whispers.

But I shake my head. "It's too big. It's more than that,

114

it's—" But my words cut off as Daniel pushes by me, through the crowd. Toward the grand staircase. He climbs about four steps and lifts his arms in the air for attention.

"Curatoriates, let's not panic. Obviously this is a tragedy we need to examine and research to figure out how we can help. What we can do." He lists some names and points into the crowd. "Please join me in our computer lab; we need to find the facts they aren't releasing to the public." More names. "Make a rescue team. Get out there as fast as possible and do whatever you can. Whatever they need. Go."

The word is a command, but it's so quiet. So devastated. Nevertheless, it works, and the people around us start to move away.

"Come on," I say, taking Logan's hand and weaving my way through the crowd to get closer. It's like wedging myself through a garden of statues placed too close together. Everyone is utterly unaware as I tap shoulders, whispering, "Excuse me," over and over again.

Finally, I reach the staircase. Logan and I continue to clasp hands as we climb up the steps toward Daniel. "What *actually* happened here?" I ask him the second we arrive at his side. Demand, really. Daniel must know. He *has* to know.

His eyes are a hurricane of emotions that whirl so fast I can't even begin to read them. "The first Earthbound has been permanently killed by the virus," he whispers.

I stand silently, waiting for him to continue, not understanding.

"Whoever created those islands—the surface of the land beneath the ocean—they're dead. Forever."

I gasp and whirl to face the television again. Then I shake my head. "No, that doesn't make sense. Other Earthbounds have died forever. That's why you know about the seven lifetimes thing." I stretch out an arm, pointing at the awful image on the television. "And *this* did not happen."

He nods. "In those cases the Earthbounds slowly faded from existence in an entirely natural process. But when the life of an Earthbound is ripped away—there's nothing natural about that. It's too extreme, and so it has violent consequences." He takes a shuddering breath. "It's something I only considered in my darkest dreams."

Anger tingles in my fingertips. "So you *knew* this might happen? And you didn't warn anyone?"

"No, no. Far from," Daniel says, his eyes still fixed on the television and looking very tired. "It was a tiny suspicion." He turns to me, a small light of frustration shining in his eyes. "And what *should* I have done? Warned everyone in the world that their home *might* disappear at any moment? Take a survey and try to figure out who shaped which parts of the earth?"

I open my mouth to say that might have been a good place to start, but Daniel doesn't give me a chance.

"Everyone's memories of being Earthmakers back before the curse are so shady they may as well not exist. Do *you* remember what you made?"

I clamp my mouth shut. I'm not ready to tell him that I know I made the Grand Canyon. That Marie told me.

But *remember*? No. I remember nothing.

"And all of this for a dark fear? A worst-possible-case scenario I didn't actually expect to happen?" Daniel shakes his

116

head. "I thought the earth was in enough turmoil with the more obvious aspects of the virus."

We turn as a new voice—with the tinny sound indicating a weak satellite connection—comes in extra loud over the newscast, the chop of helicopter blades in the background. "We've been out here for hours now, and I know you can't see much with the sun down, but what you don't see are lights. Homes. The cities. Amy, there is *nothing* left here in the place where the bustling city of Suva—the capital of Fiji—sat only yesterday. Rescue ships are on their way, but even so, we're estimating the death count to be over 1.5 million lives. A number so tragic as to be almost incomprehensible."

My knees feel weak as I make myself consider over a million people suddenly dumped into the middle of the sea. In their beds. In their houses. Trapped and drowning in the middle of massive apartment buildings. I almost feel the water filling my own lungs at the agonizing thought. The reporters are right—the death rate has got to be almost complete. Even those who had boats would likely have been trapped in their homes under roofs meant to protect them, that instead held them under. My throat closes. *Schools. Daycares.* It's nighttime in the Southern Hemisphere *now*, but what time did this happen? Were people awake? Asleep?

Children, infants, elderly, and everything in-between. Just . . . gone.

My voice cracks as I say, "At this point the destruction of the earth will kill people faster than individual cases of the virus."

Daniel nods. "Unless we find a way to safeguard all the known Earthbounds," he says with a significant look at me.

"Because remember, it's also the virus that's causing the destruction of the earth." He stretches out his hand to point back at the television.

He may as well have said it outright: help me or the next one's on *your* head.

But he doesn't have to say it.

I know.

And he's right. There's no question now. My doubts are still there—as strong as ever, but I could never live with myself if I didn't do something.

I should have started yesterday.

"Tell me what to do," I whisper.

CHAPTER FOURTEEN

But we still end up in the medical wing. I tried to convince Daniel we should start working on the vaccine right away, but he shook his head and insisted that he had to "handle this first."

"I could help with the fallout," I said.

"*We* could help," Logan amended, holding my hand as he and I stepped forward as one.

"What I really need is for you to be rested and ready to start tomorrow with focus. And healed of any damage that might have been done to you in that hellhole," he added. "Then we have work to do."

And so I'm here. Waiting for Audra to come in and tell me what they've found. Or haven't found. Hell if I know.

I don't know where Logan is other than *in the medical wing somewhere*. They separated us. Logan argued. I didn't.

Even though he knows—even though it's not a secret—explaining exactly how your brain is *damaged* is still . . . just difficult. Awkward.

But even with that looming my thoughts are still buzzing from *the incident*. The incident. It sounds too tame to describe something that killed over a million people and completely erased a section of the world.

But is there a word so vast? I don't think so.

All my doubts are gone. Well, perhaps not the doubts, but the hesitation. I *have* to help. However I got these new abilities, this strength, I have to use it to save people. I can't run away like Sonya did. I have to face it. What happens after that is a bridge I'm going to have to cross later.

A light knock on the open door makes my head jerk up, but it's just Audra with a tablet computer in her hand. "I'm waiting for one of our specialists to e-mail me one more report, but I didn't want to leave you sitting alone. Not after—" She swallows hard. "After today."

We both nod, and a heavy somberness settles between us.

Finally I take a shaky breath and break the silence. "So was it weird, suddenly becoming a thirteen-year-old doctor?" I ask.

She gives me a weak smile but seems happy to change the subject. "That part wasn't all that weird. What *is* weird is being in a teenage body, going through all this teenage physical shit—hormones, sweaty feet, massive deodorant needs—but feeling like a fully grown woman in every other way. Not just fully grown—elderly. I was eighty-four when I passed in my last life." She gives me a shrug and a *what-can-you-do?* smile, as though she expects me to understand.

Why? Because I'm a teenager too? I *don't* really understand. I've had the same kind of re-awakening she has—sort of—but I don't feel ancient, or even grown and mature. If anything, I feel younger and smaller.

A beep sounds, and Audra tilts the screen. "Here we go." Her eyes go rapidly back and forth, and after a few seconds she's nodding. "As I expected." She swipes her fingers across the screen a few times then scoots a little closer and turns the tablet so I can see.

They're MRI pictures. Of *my* brain. The organ that literally makes me who I am. Like my personality splayed out for all to see. My heart speeds up. I'm not sure why—despite their high-tech facility, I don't expect them to find anything my previous doctors didn't discover.

"I'm going to get right to the crux of the issue, Tavia," Audra says, gesturing to the black and white images on the screen. "The damage to your brain is considerable. There are signs of what we call nerve shearing in *three* places." She points to different spots on the MRI. "In addition, your frontal lobe—right under your scar—was all but crushed. That's what the doctors tried to repair when they took you into surgery." She returns to the scans and shows me the scars from where my blood vessels exploded and they put them back together.

"What this all means," Audra says, "is that your ability to process memory is exceptionally damaged—especially long-term memory. I suspect your human med team was completely and utterly amazed by your level of healing."

"They called it a miracle, you know, all that stuff," I mumble.

121

"As well they should. If you weren't an Earthbound, you should have basically wandered around, nearly incapable of reasoning beyond about a three-, maybe four-year-old level. And on top of that you probably would have remembered little to nothing about your life before the plane crash."

I'm sure horror is splashed all over my face as I stare at her. This is *not* something my doctors told me. "Why does it matter that I'm an Earthbound? I essentially have a human body, right? Why is my brain different? Is it . . . stronger?"

But Audra is already shaking her head. "Actually, the human brain is very different from an Earthbound brain, but in ways that a microscope doesn't show." She hesitates, and I can tell she's trying to find the right words. "It's just *more*. And for your sake, thank the gods it is. Have you had memory problems since you first awakened your memories?"

"I think so," I say very slowly. Elizabeth had suggested as much, but until I watched Logan's awakening process, I didn't fully comprehend that my own remembering wasn't quite as smooth as it should have been. "I don't actually have memories of all my past lives. The clearest one is the last time I was with Logan. Quinn then. All the others are either a blur or not there at all."

I wonder if I should tell her about my dreams of Sonya, but they're not quite the same thing as memories. I better keep them to myself. For now.

As I look up, I see Audra's expression change. *Pity.* Is it really so bad?

"The brain cells of a human contain their entire life," Audra says. "The brain cells of an Earthbound contain the

122

entire life of the *earth*. As a human, when you lose your long-term memory you forget everything earlier than maybe a few months. Tavia, you've forgotten everything from before this life. Because a single life *is* short-term for an Earthbound."

"But I remember *some* things from before," I protest.

"Was your awakening object something from the life you remember best?"

"Yes," I say hesitantly, feeling like I've fallen into a trap.

"How to explain this?" Audra asks herself, pinching the bridge of her nose. "Whenever you do anything in life, your brain makes it happen through connected synapses. When your brain gets disrupted you have to create all those synaptic pathways all over again. So while your awakening *should* have brought to life every synaptic pathway associated with memories of your past lives, because of the damage, it could only process that one. And even then, only because there was such a direct stimulation to do so. To be truthful," she says, leaning forward to touch my hand, "the few memories you have of other lives are probably nothing more than shadow memories from *that one* life."

"But . . ." I think of the way that Marie touched me and invoked a memory of yet another life. The brief seconds that I lived after re-awakening under a cold park bench in England. Despite my misgivings, I go ahead and tell Audra about that—though I keep the details to myself. To my surprise, she's smiling when I finish.

"That's very encouraging," she says, but I can't figure out how the hell that awful story could be *encouraging*. "It means that you can collect artifacts from your other past lives and use them to force new synaptic pathways into your stored memories. It's incredible, really."

Like the braid. The one I don't have anymore. Another wave of disappointment flows through me at the thought of that loss. "So, if I did find something—another thing I made in my past lives—it wouldn't . . . damage my brain more?"

"Oh no. If I had examined you before your initial awakening I would have suspected that you might not live through it," she says calmly. Exactly what Elizabeth was worried about. "But you did, and no other awakenings should be nearly so powerful. Similar, but not as extreme."

Similar. I remember the horrible pain in my head both with the necklace and Marie touching me—though, as Audra suggested, not as bad the second time—and don't even have to ask if it will always hurt.

It will.

"Can you . . ." I pause and take a deep breath and push back the desperate sob in my voice. "Can you fix it?" I ask in a whisper.

The room is silent, and I know the answer from the disappointment that hangs in the air like a thick fog. "You have to understand, Tavia, we're not miracle workers, as much as people would like to think since we're, well . . . former gods. In order to fix your brain we would have to go in and destroy your damaged cells and then recreate them from scratch. And even if we could study your individual, unique brain cell structure well enough to do that—it wouldn't be *you*. You would be a blank slate. Because no one, not even Christina, who you met on the helicopter and who is immensely strong—can rewrite all of your lifetimes' experiences onto your cells. Only actual experiences can do that."

"What about . . . specific memories?" I ask, thinking about my dangerous secret. The one even I don't know, the one that must have to do with my being a "Transformist," as Daniel called me. "Is there any way to target specific memories, or people, or . . . secrets?"

"At this point I think artifacts from individual lives are your best shot. But this is all new territory for me," she admits.

"So, I really am stuck like this forever?" I ask. I'm not embarrassed when a tear slides down my cheek.

"For this life," Audra says, as though it's a comfort. "The memories of your former lives will still exist in your soul when it travels to a new body. The next time you're reborn, you should awaken as normal." Her eyes dart up to mine, then away. "Almost."

"There's more?" I ask, terrified.

"Just one more piece," she says, and though there's a sad smile on her face, I know she's trying to brace herself. "Your brain's ability to store memories is . . . it's very compromised because of the damage to your frontal lobe. Not only does your brain have trouble retrieving long-term memories, it also has only a limited ability to *store* more memories."

"But I remember things just fine since the crash."

"Remember the *big* picture," Audra says patiently. "You may go your whole life remembering things okay, because one life is very short-term for an Earthbound. But your brain may never get your current life into long-term memory storage."

"I still don't understand what you're getting at."

"If your brain can't get this life stored in its long-term bank, next time you're reborn you'll remember all of your other lives, but you won't remember this one."

The significance of her words finally hits me. My life as Tavia, *this* life, will be erased from my memory. My eternal memory. Whatever I do, whatever I choose, I won't remember it at all. The joys, the pains, all washed away like they never happened.

Like I spent an entire lifetime truly being human.

"And you can't do anything about that?" I ask in a whisper.

She shakes her head. "It's all really quite fascinating." But her forced cheerfulness doesn't penetrate my cloud of gloom. In the end, all an Earthbound truly possesses is their memories.

So once I die, even though my soul will be reborn, Tavia will be dead.

Forever.

CHAPTER FIFTEEN

Before I leave I go into their bathroom and stand in front of the mirror, studying myself. I take a shaky breath and then begin finger-combing my hair, thinking of it being longer as I do. I stop when it's halfway down my back, and then I start to braid. I have to swallow down a strange flutter of fear when I realize that I'm nervous braiding. Just like Sonya must have—thus the reason I have the twine braid. Used to have it. What other characteristics might I possess that belong to long-dead people?

Pushing that thought away, I focus on finishing the intricate braids. When I'm done, I scrutinize my work in the mirror, tilting my head this way and that. I feel like a little girl wearing my hair in two Dutch braids, but at least the style securely covers my scar.

Covers it so completely that no annoying woman could lift my loose hair to see it.

It's *protected*.

I squint and realize that with my bangs pulled back I can still see just a touch of the scrape I got when I ran into the realtor's office in Portsmouth.

When I was trying to chase Quinn. Or really, my mind's hallucination of Quinn.

I snort now at the humor of the whole thing and touch the small spot that's slightly pinker than the skin around it. I rub my fingers across it as though I could simply paint it away, and gasp when I look again and the discoloration is gone.

My hands tremble. I just transformed my skin *permanently* with a single, almost unconscious, thought.

I close my eyes and count to ten very slowly, making myself calm down. I'm sure if I remembered my other lives more clearly, I would realize how easy it is to invoke my abilities.

Or maybe this is a result of the odd increase in power that Daniel told me about this morning.

I grit my teeth and look back in the mirror. I don't want things to be that easy—it scares me. But then, it scared Sonya too—what makes me think I'm braver than her?

I glare at my reflection—at the small spot on my forehead where my little mark—not even truly a s*car*—used to be, and I picture using a very light touch of a fan brush to apply the lightest stroke of paint.

And the mark is back.

I raise my chin in satisfaction and turn away from the mirror before I can question why this matters to me so much.

Logan is slouched on a chair in the waiting room, and I feel weak with relief when I see him."Hey," he says when I appear. "You look cute," he adds, wrapping his arms around me. "You just need one more thing." His mouth is close to my cheek, and I can feel his breath as he speaks.

"What?" I ask, not caring that my voice shakes.

"This." I nearly melt at the touch of his fingers on my ear and the scent of gardenias. I raise my fingers and feel silky petals tucked behind my ear. "Flowers every day," Logan promises. He twines his fingers through mine and points me toward the door.

"You didn't have to wait," I say once the doors close behind us.

He snorts. "Where else would I go?"

"True," I say with a grin. But it's a little bit forced. My mind is focused on what I've just heard from Audra.

I'm broken.

I mean, I guess I've known that for a long time, but I'm so broken I may never remember this life. What does that mean for me? For *us*? I'm not sure I know. I guess I should just be happy that I managed to resurge.

Too bad I took out the power in the Curatoria headquarters at the same time.

"Clean bill of health?" Logan asks, giving my hand a squeeze.

My throat is suddenly tight. "As clean as it ever could be," I mumble.

"What do you mean?"

"I still . . . I have . . ." I point at the right side of my head. "You know."

"They can't fix it?" he asks, and I realize that he was hoping they could too.

I shake my head.

"That's okay."

I turn to him. "Really?"

"Of course." He shrugs. "Why wouldn't it be? Every lifetime we deal with something. This is just another thing."

Tears glisten in my eyes instantly, and I'm having trouble breathing. He's so accepting, so casual even, that I can't tell him that *this* thing might have eternal consequences. "Whoa, whoa, whoa," Logan says, stopping and smudging a tear away with his thumb. "You okay?"

I make myself smile through my tears. He doesn't understand how different everything is now. How hard it is to focus, to find all the right words, to think as clearly as I used to. "It's just been a long day," I answer. "Meeting Daniel, the horrible thing in the South Pacific, this." I gesture at the etched-glass doors to the medical wing still just in sight down the hallway.

He threads his fingers through mine, and we walk quietly for a while.

"So you're going to do it," Logan says more than asks. "Work with Daniel."

"What other option is there? Leave here, hole up somewhere, and *hope* we don't catch the virus?" I ask. "It's in the water cycle; it's affecting the *weather*, Logan. How long do you think it will be before you can catch it simply by walking out in the rain?"

"I guess it's better to give the Curatoria what they want instead of the Reduciata."

"Is this what they want?" I ask, more to myself than to Logan. "The super powerful Transformist in their lab?"

"Don't you think so?" he asks. "I mean, this is it, right? Your secret?"

I hesitate, then back into a corner slightly protected by a pillar along the hallway and pull him close. I figure this is as close as we'll get to a truly safe place to talk. "It seems like it must be, doesn't it?" I ask.

"Does the whole Transforming thing spark any memories?" Logan matches my barely audible whisper.

"No, but seriously, my memories are so screwed up anyway." I feel tears prick my eyes at that but force them back.

"What do you think?" His head is so close to mine that all I want to do is lean in and forget everything.

But that's not an option.

I consider all the information I have. Which isn't much. "I think this *must* be it. What else could it be? Something bigger?"

He grins, though there's an odd edge to it. "What could be bigger than the fact that you are literally the strongest Earthbound in the world and the only Transformist in existence?"

I laugh at the sheer absurdity of it all. "It sounds ridiculous when you say it that way," I agree. But I sober. "I couldn't transform when I was Rebecca, though." I poke his stomach, "Right?"

The poke is supposed to inject a bit of levity into the discussion, but Logan's face turns stony. "You're right. You couldn't."

"So there must be something else. Maybe just something in *addition* to transforming. Complementing it, maybe."

He sighs and lowers his lips to the skin right where my neck and shoulder meet. "You are indeed a mystery."

A smile takes over my face, and I want to laugh in pure bliss.

"I don't want to let you go tomorrow, even for the day," Logan says, pulling me close and twisting his arm around my waist.

"We can stay together while I work," I promise him, slipping my hands into his back pockets and lifting my face for a light kiss. "You can sit on a stool and . . . watch," I say, realizing how lame and boring that sounds.

His brow furrows. "Actually, I thought I would explore the headquarters while you were doing lab stuff."

I raise my eyebrow in question, and Logan's eyes dart to one side then the other, as though someone might be listening . . . which might very well be the case. "You know, check things out, report back to you. Find out what the Curatoriates are up to."

"Spy?" I said with a half grin.

"If you want to put it that way."

"You don't trust them?"

He purses his lips then says, "I'm not sure I trust anyone anymore. Now that . . . that I know who I am, everything's different."

I nod, even though it doesn't feel that different to me.

"We've never trusted them entirely. I'm not saying you shouldn't work with Daniel, because after . . . after this morning I think it's clear that you need to. But when you're finished, if it's okay, I'd like to leave."

A bark of laughter escapes me. "Trust me. It is okay." I can't point out any one thing that's suspect here. In fact, everything has been amazing. But I can't help but feel like we shouldn't be here any longer than necessary.

"And if we can take some solid evidence with us, that helps everyone."

I consider this for a few seconds and then smile and nod, feeling a new sense of solidarity between us.

Solidarity in rebellion, I guess.

We go back to walking hand-in-hand down the softly lit hallway. As the buzz from the atrium grows louder I feel the calmness and security that surrounded us in the deserted hallway start to break away. Once again, we're strangers among people who might be friends or enemies, and once again, it's him and me against the world.

A world we're both desperate to save even though it might turn on us at any moment.

I gasp in surprise when we open the door to our room and find it completely empty. It takes a second to remember that Alanna literally eviscerated all the furniture.

"Cheery," Logan says in a flat tone.

"I forgot."

"I think we both had reason to."

We stand for a long time just staring at the bare room. A trickle of an idea begins to take root in my head, and I shove Logan back out the door, grinning the whole time. "Give me sec," I say, shutting the door on him before he can protest.

For me it's more than just the emptiness of the room; I can't bear the sight of the stripped walls, imagining what they were like when Sammi and Mark lived here.

What they were like just this morning.

Elizabeth once told me that one of the most effective ways to heal from bad memories was to replace them with good ones. So I cover Mark and Sammi's bare walls with wooden paneling and replace the vacant spot where their bed was with a feather mattress on a rough wooden frame. Next, I conjure red gingham curtains to cover the faux windows and install a fireplace up against one wall. In less than five minutes our room is a perfect replica of the home we shared when we were Rebecca and Quinn.

I turn to the door, but one more thought hits me. I look down at myself and transform my jeans and tank top to a long-skirted dress like the one I saw Rebecca wearing in my vision. I pat my braids one more time, take a deep breath, and swing the door open.

Logan enters slowly, his eyes wide. He stares at each wall, one by one, taking in the details with an expression I can't quite fathom.

"I hope it's okay," I say quietly, suddenly second-guessing my plan.

"It's *perfect*," he whispers, but he's not looking at the room now; he's looking at me.

He takes a few more steps forward and slides his arm behind my neck, pulling my face to his. With a sigh that gives my entire body permission to finally relax, I kiss him back. The feel of his touch on my skin lets me forget everything.

Not forever.

Not even completely.

But for a few minutes the world is a dull roar hiding behind the shivers that ripple up my spine as he runs his nose along the bare skin on the side of my neck.

"I love it," Logan says into my skin, his mouth pressed against my neck so hard I almost can't understand him. "I feel like we're back in that life before everything went wrong." He raises his head and leans forward to touch the tip of my nose with his. "I wish we could go back sometimes. Don't you?"

"Sometimes," I agree, but it's without much commitment. Being *me* feels so much more real than being Rebecca.

"You okay?" he asks, his fingers finding the sore muscles along my spine.

I let out a little moan as he massages away knots that have been there for weeks. I make a little note to myself to make a deep—modern—tub in the bathroom later. "Tired," I confess. "I don't think I've stopped being tired since my plane went down."

I close my eyes, tempted to surrender as Logan unfastens a few buttons and lays tickling kisses across the top of my back. "Logan?" I ask, and even I can hear the breathy touch in my voice. "Am I different?"

His hands slide up my ribs. "It's been two hundred years—of course you're different." He kisses me hard, clearly wanting more. "I'm different too, aren't I?"

A shrug is the only answer I can give. "I couldn't transform things when I was Rebecca, but I had my secret, right?" I manage to say when his hands slip higher and nothing but the feelings he's invoking seem important.

"Yep. That's all you told me," he says, his tone dismissive. He's not interested in this right now.

"Because it was too dangerous for you to know as well."

"Mm-hmmm."

But I need answers. Before the black hole of despair opening beneath me swallows me. "So I'm suddenly a Transformist, and super strong, and it's all because of something that happened in the last two hundred years that I can't remember, that may or may not be related to what I knew as Rebecca. Which I didn't tell you." I look over at him and can't keep myself from pushing a golden lock of hair off his sharp cheekbone. "Doesn't that *bother* you?"

Something sure as hell bothered him down in Daniel's office.

Logan pulls his hands away, and even though I've managed to get his attention, I wish he was still touching me. He's silent for a long time, then, thankfully, his hands return to my hips, gripping them tightly as though for balance. "It *is* strange," he finally says. "And I don't like that we're different now. We've always been the same, more or less." He moves closer, looking serious, but a tic at the corner of his mouth gives him away an instant before he bends low and scoops me against his chest. I let out a gasp and twine my arms around his neck, my heart pounding in both surprise and delight. "Plus, I'm a guy; I'll always hate that I'm weak and you're strong. But I guess it's a taste of my own medicine. Probably good for me," he adds with a grimace that I can't help but giggle at.

"But it doesn't *change* things," he says, angling himself over me again. "And it certainly doesn't change how I feel about *you*. I love you." He pauses, and he's practically sitting on my thighs as he looks down at me with a devotion that almost—*almost*—makes me uncomfortable. "I love you so much it almost hurts to be in a different room. Like earlier today, when they separated us for our exams. It was like my life just paused because you weren't with me. So, yes, you're different—the problems with your brain make you more . . . more human, I guess, but this new transforming thing makes you all the more godlike."

After a pause that may have been broken by several kisses down the side of my neck, he whispers, "It gives you a chance to do really cool things." He smiles now, and it's like the sun rose in our room. "And if I'm a little jealous, well, can you blame me?" And then he's kissing me again, his hands fumbling at my buttons with an urgency that tells me he's ready to be finished *talking*. "I bet you could use a nice long bath," he says in a whisper. "You took care of this room; I don't mind being in charge of the bathroom." He rises from the bed, letting his hands run over my entire body, from shoulders to toes. "You still like the water super hot?" he asks with a boyish grin.

I nod, then watch as he lifts his arms over his head and strips off his T-shirt.

Will that ever get old? I hope not.

My eyes follow his bare back all the way through the bathroom doorway. Then my brow wrinkles. Even in familiar surroundings, everything I do with Logan has the odd feel of being an actress in a play. I want him, I love *being with* him, I know the women in my head love him. But do *I* love him? I must.

I certainly feel *something*! And what other word could describe this immense, overwhelming feeling?

It seems strange to even question it after everything we've done in the last few days. After everything he just said to me. And it's not that I regret anything we've done together—not a single moment of it. It's just that I sense there should be *more*. I wonder why I don't seem to feel as deeply as Logan does.

But then, is it me he loves, or the woman I've been for thousands and thousands of years? And is that person really all that different from who I am now?

I hate that I can't remember. It's like I'm a thousand-piece puzzle, but as Tavia, only ten of the pieces are there.

I try to shake away my doubt-filled thoughts. If he loves even this broken, all-too-human version of me, isn't that proof that he loves *all* of me? And how foolish would I have to be to turn away the most eternal, *perfect* love in the world?

With a smile and a new spurt of cheer, I pad barefoot across the smooth wooden floor to the sound of running water.

And the soft scent of Rebecca's favorite soap.

CHAPTER SIXTEEN

"You hungry?" I call as I towel my damp hair, sitting cross-legged on our bed in a newly created pair of yoga pants and tank top that do *not* match the decor. But please, corsets and woolen undies? Let's just say ladies' wear has come a long way since Rebecca's time. Still, the combination is nice: quaint and homey, but all about comfort.

"Starving," Logan says, striding in from the bathroom in loose breeches that are *very* reminiscent of our setting. He lifts an eyebrow. "I made breakfast; you want to make dinner?"

I laugh and say, "Sure," but realize I have no idea what he likes. I consider making him a cheeseburger and fries but stop myself just in time. They're not *Logan's* favorites. I clear my throat and push my memories of sharing french fries with Benson aside. *Way* aside. "So . . . what are you in the mood for?" I ask, seriously wondering what this person I've *spent the night with* likes to munch on.

Our relationship is so weird—we know so little about each other and yet have spent lifetimes together. We feel so deeply for each other but have been a couple so short a time that we still haven't made it past the slightly awkward stage. Or the *I-want-to-grab-your-face-and-kiss-you-every-moment-of-the-day* stage, I think ruefully as I watch him stretch his long arms before yanking on a loose T-shirt.

I've seen the other Earthbounds around here, and most of them are not nearly as amazingly hot as Logan. I count my blessings that even if fate or luck—or whatever—had to deal me such a shitty hand in this life, at least the guy I get to be with forever is seriously smoking. Makes one believe in karma.

"When you were Rebecca you used to make me these awesome venison sandwiches, remember?" he asks.

I should. I should remember. And if I sit here long enough and sift through memories, I probably will.

But I need to get some food into him a little sooner than that.

"What else was on it?" I ask, in what's probably a really obviously faux-casual tone as I wrack my brain trying to recall if I've *ever* eaten venison. It feels even sillier to not be able to remember when I'm sitting in a replica of my old life. But I'm not coming up with anything.

"You don't know?" he asks, his eyes darting over to me with a flash of worry.

"Not . . . really," I say slowly. "It's—well, my therapist, who's dead now, thought it was because of the—the brain thing," I say in a mumble, realizing just how full of crazy *that* sentence was.

His jaw muscles flex a few times, not like he's mad, but like he's thinking. Then he smiles, and all the tension melts off his face. "I got it," he says, and before I know it he's holding two pieces of coarse brown bread with a huge hunk of meat in between them covered in a sauce I don't recognize. There's not a slice of tomato or lettuce in sight. He takes a bite and groans in pleasure. "Damn, I forgot how good these are," he says. "Do you want one?"

My head is already shaking from side to side. "No thank you," I say, staring at what can only be described as a man-sandwich. "I'll go with a wrap. You know, the kind with something healthy on it. They're called ve-ge-ta-bles," I say slowly.

Logan just makes a grunting sound and digs back into his sandwich. We both eat for several minutes and I think I've escaped his questions until he swallows the last bite of his meal and asks—with the same casualness I tried to *fake*—"So . . . you don't remember the sandwiches, and sometimes I feel like you don't remember . . . other things."

I had hoped to push this conversation off for a while—until we knew each other better. I should have known I couldn't hide something like this from the man who has known me since the beginning of time. "I don't remember much of anything, really."

A handful of words, but they took every ounce of my remaining courage to say.

"What do you mean? You said you don't remember the lives when we weren't together, but you obviously remember being Rebecca. You made all of this," he adds, gesturing at the room.

141

"I do! And you as Quinn, of course. But it's like remembering childhood friends. There's no clarity there. I—I see you do things, and a memory of you doing the same thing in the past will spring into my mind, but I don't think I remember as clearly as you do." I pick at the stitching on the quilt to avoid looking directly at him.

His eyebrows lower as he considers this. "What about beyond that? Do you remember being Jenna Farthing?"

I shake my head. "No." If anything, that's a completely new name.

"At all?" Logan asks, and now he looks genuinely worried.

"Nothing," I whisper. "I had vague memories of being Embeth, and Kahonda, and Shihon right after my awakening. I wrote them down in my journal." Which the Reduciates now have. "But Audra suggested that those . . ." Man, it's so hard to even say. "That those might just be me remembering *Rebecca's* memories. Oh, and some wispy memories as Sonya, but you didn't know me then." I still haven't told him about my dreams of her. With their constantly evolving endings, I don't know what's true and what's just my crazy brain making stuff up—and so I can't trust them. I want to; I'm convinced there's truth in there. I just can't tell the difference.

Logan opens his mouth like he's going to say something, then closes it again, having changed his mind.

It feels ironic to sit here in this room that is a replica of the only home I remember sharing with him. For him it's one of many. Hundreds? Thousands? I have no idea.

I should. I think. "Logan, do you remember *all* of your lives?"

He pauses, nods, and then tilts his head to the side. "Yes and no. I remember a few thousand years pretty clearly, but beyond that, it's like you said—a childhood memory."

Despite everything I've learned about being an Earthbound, the idea of remembering *thousands* of years is hard to even consider. It simply doesn't mesh with the experiences I've been having with my own memories.

"I have a few very, very shady memories of back when we were Earthmakers, before humans—but I don't know anyone who really remembers *that* very clearly. Despite the fact that we're still being punished for what we did," he adds sardonically.

"The beginning of the world," I say, and the bitter cast in my tone makes Logan give me a worried glance. I lean back on the feather pillows feeling suddenly weak. "You remember the beginning of the world," I explain. "And I can't even clearly recall the last life we shared."

"Hey," Logan says quietly, reaching for my hand and wrapping his fingers around my cold skin. "It's not like this changes anything." He squeezes my hand and waits for me to look up at him. "You're still *you* even if you don't remember everything." He lifts my hand to his mouth and brushes his lips across my knuckles in an exceptionally old-fashioned but gentlemanly gesture, and a flash of memory erupts in my head of him doing the same things as Quinn. Not just once—a hundred times.

Hope wells within me, and I blurt, "I remember more things all the time. Just now, I had a new memory."

"Good," he says. "But I really do want you to know that it doesn't matter."

Warmth spreads through me, and I finish my wrap even though I don't feel hungry anymore. I feel *full*.

A knock on the door startles me, and I give Logan a wary glance. "Do you think it's Alanna?" I whisper. "Or maybe someone telling me I should start work on the vaccine tonight after all?" Part of me hopes it is. I'm anxious to do *something*.

"That would be just *perfect*," he says with a groan. "I'll get it." He opens the door enough to peek out, but not enough for whoever is out there to see into the room. To see *me*. He's protecting me again, and I smile at the thought.

But then he swings the door wide, and a man and woman I don't recognize step just inside the doorway. "Tavia Michaels?" the woman asks. She sounds nervous.

I scoot to the edge of the bed but don't say anything.

"I—we need your help. Could you possibly come with us?"

"Where?" I don't like this.

"To . . . our holding cells, I guess you could call them," she says, sharing a telling glance with the man I assume is her partner.

"Not to be locked up," the man hurriedly adds; my doubt and fear must be pretty obvious on my face. "We need your assistance with one of the people we're holding. When the two of you were brought in yesterday, another person was brought in as well. A prisoner."

Prisoner? I glance at Logan, but he doesn't seem to understand any more than I do.

"I don't remember seeing anyone else," I say.

Her face pales. "He was brought in after you. In a different chopper. From what I understand, they raided the Reduciata base you two were held in after they got you away."

We stand in an awkward square of silence until the man with her gestures to the open doorway. "We can fill you in as we walk."

Logan and I start to exit, but the man lays his hand on Logan's chest. "We only need Miss Michaels."

Logan raises an eyebrow. "Are you two partners?"

They share a glance, then nod.

Logan looks toward the man, then gestures with his chin to the woman. "Would you let *her* go anywhere without you in a place like this?"

The man bristles but lets Logan pass.

"Is this person a threat?" I ask, fear starting to bubble up in my stomach.

But the woman is shaking her head. "He's human, so very containable. But he's fighting us so hard that we're having to keep him almost constantly tranquilized."

"Which wouldn't be a problem," the man beside her pipes in, "except that when he *is* conscious, he won't eat. He won't drink. It's been twenty-four hours, and he hasn't slept. We're worried about his health."

"Okay . . ." I say, even more confused. What does this have to do with me?

"There's only one thing he keeps asking for."

The hallway is silent as I look between them.

"You," the first woman says again. "Generally we wouldn't give a prisoner anything he wanted until he agreed to cooperate,

145

but with all the tranquilizer serum we've had to inject him with and his refusal to eat or drink, we're . . . we're afraid he'll hurt himself."

"Usually we would go to Daniel with this, but as you can imagine, he's so busy with the fallout from this morning's disaster that he's completely unavailable for anything else. That's why we came right to you."

"Why would he want me?" I ask, squeezing Logan's hand as a trickle of fear travels down my spine.

They look between each other, and I wait for them to reveal whatever it is they're not telling me. "We think it would be best if you see for yourself."

They lead us past the landing that looks over the extravagant atrium—still alive with people sitting in front of the blue glow of televisions—and then down a spartan hallway. Premonition hums within me, and my stomach churns. Every nerve crackles with alertness, but after the wringer I've already put my mind through, even that buzz feels feeble and sickening.

We stop at a thick set of double doors, waiting as the woman creates a key in her hand and unlocks three different locks. I raise my eyebrows at Logan, wondering why they would need such a thing.

Maybe I don't want to know.

But when the doors open I'm seized by panic.

It's not that it looks *exactly* the same as the Reduciata cells where Logan and I were held—I mean, the architecture is completely different and the walls are simply a nondescript cream instead of that stark, glaring white. But it has the same feel, and as I take tiny steps through the doorway I almost expect to see a huge Reduciata symbol, just like in our prison.

Instead, I see walls lined with three of those two-ways mirrors. Except that this time I'm on the other side. The side you can always see through.

"He's in this third cell," the woman says, and suddenly I wish Logan weren't here. That I was alone.

I deny the truth of my suspicions all the way down the hallway, and even when I come around the corner I tell myself a million reasons why it's not . . .

It won't be . . .

It *can't* be . . .

"Benson." The words are out of my mouth in a hushed whisper before I can stop them. I sway on my feet, and blackness starts to close in around my eyes. I have to reach my hand out to the wall to keep myself from crumpling.

"Tavia!" Logan's hands wrap around my shoulders, holding me steady.

Benson is sitting in the middle of the floor, his head resting in his hands. His shirt is gone, and from this angle I can see the Reduciata tattoo on his shoulder. It seems to grow as I stare at it, enveloping everything else about him.

"He says he won't talk to anyone but you," the woman says, her voice quiet, as though Benson were sleeping. As though he could hear us at all. But even as tired as he must be, and despite his slumped posture, I can see the tension in his shoulders, the tiny muscles clenching at his temple.

He's not asleep.

At least I can't see his face. That might break me.

As though sensing my presence, Benson shifts and starts to lift his head toward the glass.

No. I can't. I spin away from the two-way mirror.

"Not tonight," I mumble as the man and woman look at me funny. "I can't deal with him tonight," I clarify. I try to think clearly, but my entire brain has gone into shutdown mode. It just can't handle one more awful thing tonight.

The disaster in the South Pacific shattered my world, but Benson? He'll destroy what's left of it.

CHAPTER SEVENTEEN

The Curatoria lab is a welcome reprieve from the chaos of last night. But still, as much as I try to pay attention while Daniel takes me from one station to another, attempting to explain all the shiny, hulking pieces of equipment, my mind continues to return to everything that happened last night. Not just with Benson. Logan too.

As soon as we left the security wing, Logan began asking me who Benson was—who he was *to me*—but I kept refusing to answer his questions until finally he just stormed out of our room. I don't know where he went, but he was back by the time I woke up. He must have crept in after I went to sleep.

Which left *me* sneaking out this morning.

I'm going to have to talk to him—talk to both of them, actually—but at least for now, I have something else to do.

If I can focus.

"This one we're just about ready to release to the rest of

the world," Daniel says, stroking a white and silver machine whose function I can't remember. "I think they're ready for it." I see his hand suddenly clench, and he sighs. "Or they will be if there's anything left in a few months." He stares off into space for a few seconds, and then his head jerks up, he takes a deep breath, and his entire posture changes—like I've seen it do before within just the two days I've known him. It's uncanny, really. As though he changes moods like I change clothes.

It makes me question how real any of his personas are, but for now—after that terrible newscast yesterday—I force myself to shake off my suspicions. As much as I believed Sammi, she never did tell me what her mistrust was based on.

And Daniel admitted he'd made mistakes.

Either way, none of that matters now; I don't have a choice. I *have* to do this.

"Come in here before we suit up," Daniel says, beckoning me into a dim room. Inside, Daniel has set up what looks like a mini PowerPoint presentation.

"Do you know anything about viruses?" he asks, motioning me to take a seat in an office-style chair in front of a four-foot-square screen.

"Not a thing," I admit. "Not the sciency bits anyway. I know they make you sick. That's pretty much it."

"Okay, from the beginning then," Daniel says, clicking the mouse. A picture of a simple drawing of a square with some kind of legs . . . sort of . . . appears on the projection screen.

"Viruses are essentially made up of three parts," Daniel says. "The shell, the genetic material inside the shell, and an injection mechanism . . ." As he talks I can tell that he's struggling to simplify the concept, to make it understandable to me. But I barely understand the theory, much less the practical implications. After flipping through a couple of slides on the anatomy of a virus, he walks me through common treatments and tries to explain the mutations that made each ineffective against the Reduciata's bioengineered disaster. Pretty soon we're staring at a flowchart covered with words I can barely pronounce, much less define, like "replication inhibitors" and "spontaneous mutation."

"So what are we supposed to *do*?" I ask, because after all of that I still haven't the faintest clue.

"We need a new vaccine, but at this point we simply do not have time for conventional development. We have two electron microscopes that are many times stronger than anything any other lab in the world has—one for you, and one for me. I've already spent much of the last several months analyzing the RNA in the virus, and I think I have found the section responsible for replication, which is how the virus grows. I brought my most powerful Creators and Destroyers in to assist me, and we tried to use both powers to first destroy the original segment of the DNA and then replace it with a newly created segment that would fight the virus."

"I take it that didn't work."

He shakes his head. "We couldn't do it fast enough. The instant the segment was destroyed, the strand of DNA broke apart completely. That was when I realized I needed to not simply *create* a new piece, but *transform* the existing piece. I needed you."

"So you know which part of the DNA has to be changed?"

Daniel looks weary. "No. I haven't found the right *part* of the DNA yet. I've found what I *think* is the right section—a section of about ten thousand pairs. We'll need to go pair by pair, transform the DNA, test it against the RNA, and then move on."

Now I understand his weariness. "How long do you think it will take?" I ask in a small voice.

"It depends on how lucky we get," Daniel replies, and he tries to smile, but it feels like a grotesque mockery. "I spent four months finding the segment of the RNA that we needed, but I got pretty fast in the end. Hopefully with us working together, and a bit of good fortune, it will take a week or two."

May as well be forever.

But we have to try. Because who knows what piece of the world will disappear next.

"I . . ." He stops, purses his lips, shakes his head, and then continues. "I'm not sure I should even tell you this, but I don't want to hide things from you more than is necessary."

More than is necessary? I'm pretty sure I don't like the sound of that.

"We had an attack yesterday. Not here at the headquarters," he clarifies quickly. "But at one of our sentry stations a few hundred miles away."

"Reduciates?"

He swallows. "Reduciates who were specifically asking questions about you."

I try to shrug away his words—the way they make my heart race in fear. "Isn't that somewhat expected? I mean, you did just break me out of a Reduciata prison. It seems like they *would* be trying to get me back, right?" I don't add that they might be after Benson too. I mean, *he's* the one who knows Reduciata secrets, not me.

"Of course I knew they would come after you. But they're already closer than we expected and—" He waves his hands dismissively. "I probably shouldn't be burdening you with this. Besides," he says with a bright smile, "it's simply a sign that they know it's only a matter of time before we have the vaccine and they don't. I just want—I *need* you to understand how focused you are going to have to be. We want to work quickly and efficiently. We have people to save. Not just the humans, but the entire Curatoria. The Reduciata have essentially declared open warfare on us."

As if I didn't have enough pressure. I look down at the notes in my lap, and they look even less like English than before. I have to take several slow breaths to push back the dismayed tears that want to form.

"Now, Tavia," he says, pulling me out of my haze, "in order for this to work I need to teach you about the structure of individual strands of DNA. Not that I'm an expert," he says quickly. "The lab guys all taught me. But you need to know *exactly* what you're working with for your transforming powers to work." He clicks, and a picture appears of a double helix with about a dozen lines pointing to tiny parts.

"Daniel?" I ask before he can launch into his new lecture.

"What, Tavia?" And his voice is edged with an impatience that I understand, but I have to ask this first.

"You keep saying *vaccine*. Won't this also be an antidote?"

His jaw tightens, and I know the answer. "I don't think there's anything that can stop this virus after someone has already contracted it. It's simply too strong and too fast."

I swallow hard and nod as Daniel returns to his computer and starts telling me about the different parts of DNA. I try to focus—I have to learn this! Because even if we succeed in creating the vaccine today, it will still be too late for the thousands of people who don't know they caught it *yesterday*.

The sound of a clock ticking seems to fill my head, blocking out all other thought.

And it sounds like the countdown on a bomb.

CHAPTER EIGHTEEN

My back hurts from hunching over the microscope for hours, but even though I've been in the lab all day, I'm not yet ready to head back to my room.

It's time for me to face him.

I skirt the edges of the main atrium as I try to remember how I got to the "holding cells." The people I pass whisper about the virus—one hundred and fifty thousand dead from the disease, five thousand new cases today, this on top of the two million killed in the South Pacific. The countdown clock that echoed in my head in the lab grows louder and louder with each passing step.

And yet, I can't help but notice that for all the Curatoriates' talk about the virus and its effects, they still had time to redecorate the atrium. Today it has a Baroque theme. I scarcely had time to register it when I snuck away from Logan this morning, but now I see that intricate buttresses and colonnades have replaced the splendor of ancient Rome. Tapestries and beautiful swaths of silk and brocade drape the walls; suits of armor stand guard at every corner. There are even musicians playing ancient-looking stringed instruments, and today's dinner buffet, which I don't have time to partake of, unfortunately—a self-created bagel on the run will have to do—features a whole pig with an apple in its mouth surrounded by fruits and meats. Dozens upon dozens of candles flicker and glow in elaborate sconces on the wall, and an enormous fireplace—complete with a roaring blaze—fills almost an entire alcove. Two Curatoriates—a Creator and a Destroyer—must have spent hours decorating.

I put my head down as I walk along the stretch of railing in sight of the alcove below, wishing that I had left my hair down so it could fall over my face. I don't want anyone to see me.

Not even Logan.

Maybe *especially* Logan.

I hug the wall as I dart around the final corner and run into Alanna. Like, literally, bodies crashing. *Just great.*

Not only is she annoying and frustrating on her own, she's also incredibly loud. Not so helpful when I'm trying to be stealthy.

"Careful!" Alanna chirrups, her hands on my shoulders to steady me. "Wouldn't want to damage you any worse than you already are." She squeezes my arms and smiles patronizingly at me like I'm a little kid. I resist the urge to fling her hands away but can't help reaching up to pat my tightly braided hair, just to make sure my scar is still covered. Protected.

She notices nothing when I try to sidestep her to get away, simply falls into step with me. "Did you work with Daniel today?" she asks, her voice breathy and excited. I'm struck by how immature she seems compared to Audra, who must be at least ten years younger than her.

"Maybe," I grumble, hating that she brings out such surliness in me. But what else am I supposed to say? I'm certainly not going to tell *her* about Daniel's and my project.

When did it become mine and Daniel's? When did it become mine at all? It's not about me; it's for the world. To prevent the horrendous tragedy of yesterday from happening again.

Assuming we *can* do it.

Assuming we're not too late.

"—wouldn't tell us where you were. He's a squirrely one, your *diligo*."

"What?" I say, coming back to the present. "You were with Logan today?" I ask lightly. *The hell was she doing with Logan?* is what I think, but I don't want to cause a scene, or worse, raise suspicions about what Logan's doing.

Alanna turns to face me squarely now. "Yep, Thomas and I hung out with him for hours. Helped show him around. He wouldn't tell us where you were." For about three seconds she looks serious and more her age. Then her face crinkles into a childish grin and in her sing-song voice she chants, "But we gueeee-eeeessed." She leans forward before I can turn to walk away and says, "I assumed you two had slept in because . . . well, because he kept you up late last night," she says, waggling her eyebrows. "But Thomas said he saw you with Daniel this morning. Early." She stands straight and puts her hand over her heart with an exaggerated sigh. "That man, he sees everything. I'd be lost without him. Hands off!" she adds with her squealy laugh, and I can't make myself stay any longer.

"Listen, I really need to go," I say, trying to get by her. "What I really need now is a . . . a shower," I lie.

"I'll bet you do," Alanna says. "Make sure he washes you *everywhere*." Then she calls out in a suggestive voice, "Cleanliness is next to godliness."

"Yeah, uh-huh. Great," I mumble, then I push away from the wall, almost running toward the hallway that will lead me to the cells.

Fleeing.

I don't even care that she can tell I'm not going to my room. I have to get away from this woman. She irritates me more than our brief interactions can logically justify. There's just something so awful about her.

She calls after me, but I block out her voice and turn a corner, then slap my back against the wall just outside the security rooms and wait. For several minutes I stand there, but Alanna doesn't follow. No one comes around the corner. Why would they? Most sane people would avoid what is essentially the Curatoria's prison.

It takes several deep breaths before I feel truly in control, but by the time I find the strength to push away from the wall, I've reined in my emotions.

I'm ready.

Or, at least, as ready as I'll ever be.

I knock on the door and see the face of the woman from

last night, dressed in the same plain, cream-colored clothes. She looks tired, and I wonder if she's slept. Wonder how demanding her job as a warden is.

"Miss Michaels, I'm so glad you came before I got off shift," she says with a smile that speaks of a more genuine kindness than almost anyone else has shown since I've arrived here. "I'm hopeful he'll cooperate more if he sees we're willing to work with him."

I nod sharply. I've never wanted to run away and hide so badly. I square my shoulders and straighten my spine as I round the final corner and see him through the glass.

He's on his feet, braced against the wall with his hands in his pockets—still without a shirt, *why, gods*?—looking more than a little pissed. I'm so focused on Benson I barely register that someone is talking to me. I turn and face a man I don't recognize from last night—I guess it makes sense that there would be several security people who rotate shifts—as he finishes his lecture. I nod, though I have no idea what I just agreed to.

"Don't worry," he says, patting my shoulder. "You'll be safe."

Oh. They're worried about my safety. My *physical* safety. I should tell them they don't need to be concerned. It's only my heart that's at risk.

"Are you ready?" I look over at the quiet woman. Her hands are on the door handle.

Ready? Never. "Of course."

The door opens; I walk through.

Benson shoots away from the wall, instantly on alert. But his hands drop to his sides when he sees me.

159

"Tavia." The word is so quiet that even in the tiny, echoing room, I barely hear it. "I almost didn't believe you would come. I mean, they said . . . It doesn't matter," he finishes in a mumble.

My eyes can't help but wander over his bare skin. He looks so incredibly sexy in his current getup of faded jeans and no shirt. "Put some clothes on," I finally say, harsher than I intended.

Benson's entire expression wilts, and I can't look at him as I hold up a hand, conjuring a white T-shirt.

Just his size. The soft, brushed cotton I know he prefers.

I turn to the side and wait, my ears honing in on the sound of fabric skimming his skin as he pulls the shirt over his head. Only when I'm sure he's covered do I pivot to face him.

"You wanted to see me?" I say, my voice quivering. I don't know what to say. How to talk to this person who I thought could look into my soul only two weeks ago but who's now a stranger.

"They think I'm a Reduciate," he says so quietly.

"Aren't you?"

"I never wanted to be."

"Doesn't change the fact that you belong to an organization that has *killed* practically everyone who has ever mattered to me. Or Logan," I add, even though I know it's a low blow to bring him up.

"Do you really think one tattoo defines who I am? Forever?"

I start to speak but clamp my mouth shut again. Do I? And if he were to get a feather and flame symbol on the other side, what would that make him? Does his mark mean so much to me?

I wave my hand, and a table and two chairs appear. It's already too late when I realize it's the table from the library in Portsmouth. *Our* table. Creating is just too easy for me. My ability practically reads my thoughts. My *secret* thoughts.

"Sit," I say, grabbing my chair and plopping down into it. "Talk."

But he hesitates, standing there with his arms folded over his chest, not in a rebellious way, but more like he's trying to keep himself warm. He towers over me, but somehow he's the small one.

"Are you sure you want to hear the truth?" he asks.

"I don't see why not," I reply with a casualness I don't feel. "I'm the one who's been suffering the consequences for a mark that supposedly doesn't define you. I may as well know why."

"But then you'll know how much I lied to you."

I keep my eyes neutral but consider his words carefully. *Do* I want to know? The last time I heard the truth about him was when Marie told me he was a Reduciate. That revelation destroyed my confidence and kept me awake for days. Even now, I don't dare believe I can ever fully trust anyone again, much less *him*.

Could anything he might say today be worse?

"As far as I'm concerned, every word you've *ever* spoken to me was a lie," I say, looking up at him. "I don't think you're going to shock me." But even though everything I've said is technically true, it rings false at the same time. I *want* him to shock me. I want to be convinced that I was right to trust him—that I was wrong to ever doubt him.

A hollow pang reverberates through my chest as if my insides are asking me, *and where would that leave Logan?* I don't let myself answer.

"Sit," I command again. He's still for a few more seconds, and I wonder if he'll refuse. Then his whole body sags in surrender, and he drops into the seat and lays his head down on his arms.

"I don't have all night," I say after he's motionless for almost a minute.

He lifts his head just enough to peer out at me with those bright blue eyes, and a tiny piece of the ice around my heart cracks.

Maybe it was a bad decision to come see him.

It's too late now.

"I . . . I'm not really sure where to start," he says, his voice unsteady.

"How about with how you got here?" I ask, gesturing to the room around us.

"Same way you did," he mutters.

"What are you talking about?"

"We were in the same prison. The Reduciata one. Three days ago. I . . . I saw you for just a second and I tried to—it doesn't matter. It didn't work."

I almost forgot. The voice that struck me into stillness. The one that called my name. Of course. Of course it was Benson. He's not lying. And somehow that makes everything worse.

"When the Curatoriates came in and rescued you, they, like, raided the place after you were gone." He shrugs. "I convinced them to take me with them."

"Why the hell would they want you?" I don't mean to sound so sharp, but it doesn't make any sense.

"After you made my bars disappear, I ran after them. I wanted to get out of there so badly I didn't care that I was technically going to the 'other side.' I told them I had—well I didn't *have*, but I knew where they were keeping the painting from the cave."

My entire body stills, and I know my face must be pale. I turn my head, trying not to let him see.

"See, I had this theory that you could use it for . . . I guess it doesn't matter," he mumbles. "You obviously found a way on your own."

"How do you know I found a way?" I snap, paranoid all over again.

"Your hair," Benson says simply. "It's been more than five minutes and it hasn't gone short again. It was never long enough to braid before. It's cute," he adds, more to his lap than me.

"Keeps my scar hidden a lot more effectively," I volunteer. For a moment—just a moment—it feels like before. Then our eyes meet and I remember that I'm furious at him. "Why didn't they just take the painting?" I ask. "Why bother with *you*?"

He looks guilty now. "I told them I could see the Earthscript and that the Reduciates were using me for that."

"The what?" I narrow my eyes.

"The triangles. The ones you kept seeing in Portsmouth. The ones that glimmer."

My mouth falls open, but then I remember how he hesitated when I asked him if he could see the triangle over the door of a house I took him to in Portsmouth. "Benson," I say, my heart pounding. "Why can you see the triangles?"

He leans back against his chair now and lets out a heavy sigh. "Because my father is an Earthbound."

CHAPTER NINETEEN

"What?"

He runs both hands through his hair. "That's how I got into this whole thing in the first place."

"How long have you known?"

"Technically, it started when I was eight. Not that anything seemed weird at the time. As far as I was concerned I had a great life. Mom, dad, annoying older brother, but I couldn't really do anything about that. And then one day my dad came home looking really, really weird, and he told my mom he had to go find the woman he loved, and he left."

"He just left?"

"Didn't take a single thing with him."

"He must have done something that triggered his memories," I say softly.

"That's what they figured too."

"Who's 'they'?"

"The Reduciata."

I furrow my brows. "I don't understand how we jumped to them."

"Well, I've since learned that Reduciates often prey on what you might call the 'victims' of Earthbounds. Families that get left behind. Lovers, children, people who don't matter anymore," he finishes in a bitter grumble, and I clench my jaw at those words. First the woman at the Reduciata prison, then Daniel, then Logan, now Benson. I don't *ever* want to hear about people ceasing to matter again. "The Reduciates search for them just like they search for Earthbounds."

"Why?"

Benson lifts haggard eyes to me. "Because they can feed their bitterness and turn them into *weapons*. They've been doing it for ages. When some people in fancy suits came to my mom and told her they knew where my dad was and that they could help her give him what he deserved, she jumped at the idea." Benson waves his hand vaguely. "At first it was promises of child support and stuff, but eventually they told her the truth."

"And she believed them?" I remember how hard it was for me to believe it myself, even when I had proof sitting in front of my face.

"Not at first, but she did believe *me*."

I'm silent, waiting for him to go on, not understanding any of this.

"After the Reduciates told her what my dad was she backpedaled big time. She was sure she'd almost fallen for a scam. But then they pulled out a bunch of cards and asked both me

166

and my brother what we saw. My brother didn't see anything. I saw a bunch of shapes in what looked like sparkling paint."

I can hardly think enough to get the words out. "But you're not . . . you're not . . ."

"I'm *not* an Earthbound," Benson says with fierce determination—like it would be so awful if he were. "You can't just *make* a new Earthbound. But the children of Earthbounds sometimes have latent—watered down, I guess—abilities. Most commonly, seeing the Earthscript."

"Earthscript," I echo. The name sounds right now that I say it.

"I suspect the fact that I could see something she couldn't is the reason my mom decided to listen. And that's when my life really ended. Even more so than when my dad left. My mom became obsessed with her role in the Reduciata. They kept telling her that surely he had gone to the Curatoriates, but they could never find him. For years she worked for the Reduciata—doing anything they wanted—in exchange for them continuing to look for my father."

"Doesn't she know what they do? What they have planned?"

Benson shrugs. "As much as anyone does." He leans forward, his forearms braced against the table now. "You don't understand how it is, Tave. They feed your hatred and anger until you're blind to everything else. It's how she was. How she *is*," he amends. "So tunnel-visioned by her hate and desperation for revenge that nothing is more important than that. If she'd been allowed to just take time to heal and mourn and all of the things that normal people do, I think she would have been fine." He shakes his head. "But the Reduciata got a hold of her and they've . . . they've twisted her until she's almost unrecognizable."

"What about your brother?"

Benson cringes like I've slapped him. "They—they made a soldier out of him and . . . I don't even want to know what he's doing now. They probably tell him he's looking for Dad. I imagine after this long he'd actually kill him if he saw him."

My throat is tight, and I'm having trouble swallowing. "And what about you?" I finally choke out.

Benson's gaze is fixed on the desk. "I guess I was always a bit of a rebel. I didn't like what I kept hearing from these people. And they always wanted to use me for my ability to see the Earthscript. I started to lie and tell them I didn't see it after all." He gives me a pained smile. "I was little; I thought it was a good idea. I never considered that it would be painfully obvious I was lying. But things were at least bearable until we actually moved into a Reduciata compound. Before that I'd go to the library every day after school and stay until dinnertime. Hiding, basically. But once we moved I couldn't go *anywhere* without the Reduciata and everything it stands for being thrown in my face."

"But you still chose to become a member, eventually," I say, reminding myself of the important part. "You have the tattoo."

He chuckles dryly. "You're so fixated on that mark." He's silent for a long time, and I don't push him.

Though I want to.

"When I was twelve, my brother was fifteen and had just

been sent on his first 'real' mission—I didn't *want* to know anything about it. He decided it was time that his wimpy little brother became a true Reduciate. He went to the tattoo artist and told him that I'd said my vows, but that I was afraid of needles. He and couple of his buddies held me down, and I got my mark. End of story."

"He tattooed a twelve-year-old boy while he was being held down?"

"The world of the Reduciates is nothing like the world you know."

"Okay, fine . . ." My voice trails off. "But no one was holding a gun to your head when you met me."

Sob story aside, that's the crux of the issue. I can forgive him for getting involved in an organization he's been tangled up in since he was a kid. But everything he did in Portsmouth, he did of his own free will.

"They might as well have."

I scowl at him and wait.

"When I was seventeen they let me get my GED, and a few weeks later I was shocked but pleased to get into New Hampshire, despite a late application. Not that it mattered; I didn't think the higher-ups would let me go. I should have realized when they *did* that they had something in store." He leans his forehead on his clasped fists. "Wouldn't be surprised if they got me accepted to begin with."

"When was this?" I ask warily.

"A month after your plane crash," he says bluntly.

A pit forms in my stomach. I remember Benson asking

me—just a few weeks ago—how far I thought this whole con-spiracy idea went.

I don't think even *he* knew at the time.

"So they gave me a taste of real life, of freedom. Of ev-erything I ever wanted, really. And three months later they brought me in. To Marie. *Marianna* they all call her there." He lifts his head, his eyes lifeless. "As soon as the message arrived I knew I'd stepped into a trap. So I went in to see Marianna, and she told me about you."

"Told you *what* about me?" I shoot back, more a knee-jerk reaction than anything.

"Just the basics. That you were important; that they need-ed an inside agent to facilitate your memory-retrieval process. The plane crash," he adds in a mumble.

"You knew. *Everything*."

He nods, his eyelids squeezed shut.

"Why you? Surely they had dozens of people who could have done it."

"I was young. I was 'fresh,'" he says with quotey fingers, "as Marianna put it. I wasn't a Reduciate—not truly—and she thought I would be more convincing."

"She was right," I mutter half under my breath.

I don't know if he heard or not, but he doesn't respond. "And, of course, I can see the Earthscript. They wanted some-one who could really know *exactly* what was going on with you. And so they decided I was the man for the job."

"And you said yes."

"I said no," he whispers.

I sit, stiff, staring at him.

"And then they reminded me that my brother and mom were both under their control and that they could make their lives inconvenient. Or simply short."

I turn to the side so I don't have to look at him, and wish I had a curtain of hair to hide my face. Would I have turned a stranger over to an evil establishment to save my parents? I push aside the little voice on my shoulder that says yes.

"So I made a deal with them. I told them I would do this for them—help some brain damaged, crippled girl get her memories back—and in exchange they would let me go. Forever. And I would keep their secrets."

My mind latches onto the words *brain damaged* and *crippled* and I'm shocked by how much it hurts to hear them come out of his mouth.

"Problem is it wasn't just someone—it was *you*."

His voice sears like boiling water that feels warm for one instant before the agony sets in. "Benson—"

"I know, I know, none of that matters. . . ."

"But you kept going. Even after you met me."

"I had to. You saw how Marianna was—now you understand why she hovered so much while we were studying at the library." He fidgets in his chair and then adds, "I was watched every second by someone. If it wasn't Marianna, it was . . . Johnston. You called him Sunglasses Guy."

I want to throw up. More even than I have in the last half hour.

"I had to think of my mom and brother. Of my freedom. And then when . . . when you became more important than all of those things put together, it was too late. I was already

171

screwed. I tried . . . I tried to get us away but—" His words cut off and he shivers. "You don't understand how powerful they are. How fully they were integrated into every part of my existence. *Your* existence," he adds in a whisper. "I tried."

"Why do they want me?" I say, and even though he's lied to me a thousand times, I feel guilty asking him a question I already know the answer to, guilty testing him. But I can't afford to believe every word that falls from his lips. That's what I did before, and look where it got me.

Does he know the secret that I'm a Transformist? Because I sure as hell know the Reduciata does.

"That's why I kept following you," Benson says, his face taking on a sense of purpose that makes him look more like himself. More like my Benson. "They didn't tell me originally, but based on the little bit I was able to hear while they had me in custody, Jay—or, you know, Mark—he was right, it *is* about the virus." He pauses. "Tave, you're immune."

I glare hard at him, his words taking me completely off-guard. This doesn't have anything to do with transforming. Doesn't have anything to do with *anything*. "What?"

"You're *immune*. That's what Marianna said." He sounds excited now, and his features are so animated that I can hardly draw breath at the sight. "So I'm figuring they wanted me to help you provoke your memory process so that you could remember why you're immune so they can replicate it. She said they needed to find you and pick you up and start testing you." He suddenly sobers then continues, "That's why I begged the Curatoriates to take me with them, even if it was as a prisoner.

Why I told them about the painting and the Earthscript. I had to get to you. So I could find a way to tell you. We—we have to stop this before it kills everyone."

I rise to my feet, pushing the chair back with a loud squeal. "I am *not* immune. I guess I just have to decide if *you're* lying to me or if they were lying to *you*."

"Tavia, wait, please! Don't go."

I'm not sure what makes me stop. The pleading in his voice? The fact that my heart aches at the thought of leaving him again? Of walking away for good?

But I can't make myself do it.

"Tavia, I know I've done so many things wrong. But I swear to you, I will never, *ever* lie to you again. Never." His face is so open, his eyes begging me to believe him.

But I'm not sure I can.

I'm not sure I can believe any of it.

"I know that I've destroyed any chance of being *with* you again," Benson says softly. "But I'll spend the rest of my life trying to make up for what I did—earning your forgiveness—if that's what it takes. And even if what I overheard *is* a lie, it's got to be somehow useful to know what Marianna is *saying* about you. I don't know how to convince you I'm sincere, but whatever it takes, tell me, I'll do it."

I pause at the door. "I fell in love with a history nerd who liked bad puns and pastel clothes and hated math. Does that person even exist?"

Benson looks down at the desk and is silent for a long time. "From the day my dad left I never got the chance to be the person I wanted to be," he says, his voice hollow. "I planned to major in philosophy, not history; I do have a fondness for really bad puns; and I never want to wear Reduciate black again. Maybe *that* Benson wasn't quite what you would call the *real* Benson, but it's the person I always *wished* I could be."

After that I can't take it anymore. My heart is tearing itself to pieces, and if I don't get out of this room, I'm going to throw up or cry . . . or possibly both. I pull on the doorknob, desperate to escape, but the door is locked.

Of course it's locked.

I'm sure if I wait fifteen seconds someone will unlock it, but I'm too frantic. I transform the space around the door handle into a puff of air and shove my way out, staggering into the hallway.

"Sorry about that," I mutter to the people surrounding the door, but I don't stop to answer questions.

CHAPTER TWENTY

I slam the door to my room behind me, realizing vaguely as I turn the new bolt—one that I just made using my powers—that now Logan can't get in. With my back wedged against the heavy door I hold my breath and look around, finally releasing it when I see that I'm alone. No Alanna pounding the door behind me, no Logan lounging in the room in front of me. A few moments to myself, that's all I need.

Just a few moments.

I go to the bathroom and turn on the lights, staring at myself in the mirror. How can I look so familiar and yet feel like a stranger? I thought my life turned completely upside down when I found out I was an Earthbound two weeks ago. But now?

What am I, truly?

I'm an Earthbound; my powers make that clear. But even so, I have *unique* powers. Is it *possible* I'm also immune to this raging virus? Despite everything else? Isn't that too big a coincidence?

I am the most powerful Earthbound in the world. I am the *only* Transformist in the world. I'm also the only person who's immune? It seems like too much.

Unless . . .

Unless they're all tied together somehow. If one leads to the other, though I don't see how. Is that what my secret is about? But how could it be—I wasn't any of those things when I was Rebecca.

Was I?

I pause with the cold water running over my hands. What if the secret is bad? What if the reason I didn't tell Quinn wasn't for his safety, but because I was afraid? I hadn't considered that. Maybe it's a terrible secret.

I wish I could just remember!

I groan and let my hot forehead fall against the cool mirror. If only I had my backpack. By the time I woke up in the Reduciata cells, they'd already taken it from me. Surely they threw Sonya's braid away, dismissing it as nothing. I wish, wish, *wish* I had the braid now that Logan and I have resurged and I know that I can safely use it without wasting my final death.

That braid was the only key to her life in this entire world—the only method I could have used to figure out my dreams of her.

I wish now that I had used it, even though rationally I know I couldn't have taken the risk without having first made sure Logan and I wouldn't die forever.

And now it's gone. Despite my brief dreams—which may or may not reflect reality—whatever Sonya knew is dead with her.

I splash water onto my face as I think about what Audra told me. About how limited my brain is for an Earthbound—even though I seem pretty normal for a human.

But my memories? They're so inaccessible I may as well not have them.

Without my memories does it matter that I had past lives? Does it matter that there's an immortal soul somewhere inside my body? Maybe that soul will do nothing but lie dormant through this life as I stumble through it being *Tavia the Human* . . . plus superpowers. How much better is that than being, say, Audra the fully awakened Earthbound whose powers are still temporary?

I freeze, my hand on the faucet. I don't want to forget myself.

The last year of my life has been filled with so much joy and pain. There were days I wasn't sure I could survive. There were times my brain literally ached with the weight of the facts and feelings I threw at it.

But I wouldn't take them back.

Not even . . .

I look up and see my own haunted eyes and whisper, "Benson."

Not even him.

Yes, my heart rips in two all over again every time I think of that final night in Portsmouth—of that mark on his shoulder. But would I trade the pain of that moment for the memory of his heartbeat when I lay against his chest in the cheap hotel in Maine? I watch myself shake my head in the mirror.

I don't want to lose memories of love. *Any* kind of love.

But apparently I don't get a choice, because my brain can't put stuff in long-term storage. All my memories from this life. Of everyone.

Gritting my teeth, I slowly undo the tight braid on the right side of my head. I'm not used to my hair being bound so tightly, and it's making my scalp ache. But I'm safe here. I startle when someone fumbles at the doorknob, and for a second I'm afraid Alanna has decided to come by for a visit.

Then I remember I've locked Logan out.

"Sorry," I murmur when I open the door. "I changed the lock."

"It's okay," Logan says, smiling nervously. "As long as I can get to you, you can do whatever you want to the door."

"I was afraid you might be Alanna," I say, closing the door behind him. I avoid his eyes. I haven't actually talked to him since I wouldn't explain myself last night. Now I feel even *less* ready, but I know I have to tell him something.

Logan lets out a loud noise of disgust and kicks off his shoes. "Everywhere I went, they were *there*! Alanna and Thomas. I couldn't shake them. What's their problem?"

"Thomas seems nice enough," I say, pulling at my own shoelaces. "And *quiet*. I'm not sure how he stands her."

"Because she lets him grope her all freaking day long," Logan replies, sinking into a chair.

"What?" I ask, head shooting up.

"It was *awful*," Logan says, pulling me down onto his lap

once we're both barefoot. "They were seriously making out every time we stopped walking." I fold my knees against my chest, and he wraps his arms around me—all of me—his chin resting on my head so his voice reverberates in my ears. "I mean, I certainly wouldn't mind having my hands on *you* every minute of the day," he says with a hint of laughter in his voice, "but I have a degree of self-control. And some inkling of what's socially acceptable," he adds, sounding pissed now. We definitely agree on this topic.

"You should have seen the way everyone here avoids them," Logan says, rubbing his fingers in random circles down my spine, like he has to work out his frustrations. "They physically make way whenever the two of them come around. It's practically a shield the way they all scatter." A dark chuckle. "If I thought they were even *remotely* trustworthy, we could use that to our advantage." He shakes his head and leans back against the chair, his arms falling onto the armrests.

"Were you able to find anything out?" I ask, my eyes closing a bit sleepily as I lean against him. I didn't realize until now just how much working with Daniel today wore me out.

"The basic geography of this place. I'll draw you a map later. It's actually pretty cool—it's an underground pyramid, as far as I can tell. Like someone created it and then buried it in the sand." His head cocks to the side. "Actually, that's probably exactly what they did. But I couldn't really scope out anything with those two hanging around. I don't know what to do about them."

"Be mean," I suggest, only half-kidding. "Shout at them to get the hell out of your face?"

"No joke."

We sit in silence for several minutes, me listening to Logan's heartbeat, Logan thinking thoughts I can't predict as he rubs at my knotted spine.

"So, are you ready to tell me who that guy in the cell was?" he whispers. "You seemed pretty shaken up about him."

My whole body tenses, but I don't pull away. "His name is Benson," I say cautiously.

"How do you know him? From this life, or another one?"

"Oh, this one," I say quickly. "He's human. He's from Portsmouth. From before."

"Was . . . he your boyfriend?"

"Not exactly." I push up from Logan's chest and look down at him, trying to keep my face unreadable.

"He has a Reduciate mark." Logan's voice is steady, but there's a tense undercurrent.

"He does," I answer tentatively.

"So I assume you're going to have nothing to do with him."

"Well, I think I should . . ."

"Tavia!" My name explodes from his mouth. "You know as well as I do that the Reduciates are dangerous. They killed my family, captured us, and trapped us in a cell. And that's just in *this* life. You can't trust them."

"We thought we couldn't trust the Curatoria and now—"

"And now we have no other choice. Don't forget that the only reason we decided to put even an ounce of faith in the Curatoriates is because they have the tools you need to help you figure out the virus and whatever else is going on with you."

I rise from his lap and fold my arms across my chest at the phrase *whatever else is going on with you*. The hell does that mean? My brain injury? "I *do* realize that and—"

"I hope so. And I hope you *remember*," he says with an emphasis I definitely don't like, "that it's because of the Reduciata that the virus exists in the first place. If this guy is a member, then you should stay away from him." Logan looks up at me and only now seems to sense the change in my mood. The anger brimming at the surface. "For your own safety," he adds, quieter now, but not backing down.

"He changed his mind," I mumble, realizing that I believe at least that much of Benson's story. "He's the one who told Daniel about the painting that helped us resurge."

Logan hesitates now. "So he's on *our* side?"

"Absolutely." I don't say that what's more accurate is that Benson is on *my* side.

But Logan's not convinced. "Then why is he a prisoner?"

"It's complicated."

"That's all I get?"

I'm silent. Answer enough.

Logan sighs loudly and runs his fingers through his hair. "Okay," he says softly. "I'll back off. But let me just say this. Be careful." Before I can interrupt, he adds, "I *trust* you. But if you go back to see him—talk to him, whatever—I hope that maybe you'll bring me along." He says it lightly, almost casually, but I can feel how strained his voice is. How worried he is.

At least he says he trusts me. After a long moment, I nod and give him a weak smile.

He studies me for a long time like he wishes he could read my thoughts. I'm just starting to squirm when his face relaxes. "Your hair is cute."

I stare in horror—his words are so similar to Benson's, and right after arguing about him? Could he have . . . I stop mid-thought, remembering that I let down only one side of my Dutch braids and that I probably look pretty funny. I self-consciously tuck the loose waves behind my ear, shuddering as I inadvertently brush against the scar.

Logan reaches his fingers up and lightly touches the crooked line across my scalp. "Why don't you just get rid of it?"

"What are you talking about?"

"If you can transform things, it seems like you could just transform your scar into regular skin, right?"

I feel simultaneously excited and repulsed by the idea. "Feels like . . . cosmetic surgery."

He shrugs. "I guess it is. But it's hardly a bad boob job. I mean, it obviously bothers you. At least, it bothers you when other people see it, or touch it."

I shiver at the memory of Alanna's fingers on my scalp.

"Think of all the people you would never have to explain it to. Ever. It might help you to . . . move on, I guess." He pauses, then adds, "There's just no reason to keep it if it makes you unhappy."

He's not wrong. But it feels like closing a door on a part of my life. Not a *good* part, but am I ready for that?

"Come here," Logan says, pulling me toward him as he rises from the chair. "I'll help." We stand in front of the mirror, and Logan sweeps my hair carefully to the side and holds it back. It's strange to let my scar be so exposed in front of anyone else. Even Logan.

"Do you hate it?" I whisper.

"How could I hate any part of you?" He bites his bottom lip, then meets my eyes in the mirror. "It's just that I think it reminds you of everything that went wrong in your past. Maybe without it you could turn more fully to your future. *Our* future." He leans forward, and I can see him peering closely at my skin. "But the scar itself." He shrugs. "I couldn't care less."

That makes up my mind. My brain may be broken. I may be more human than goddess. But no one *else* has to know. I draw in a deep breath and squeeze my eyes shut, picturing a new kind of skin. Flat, pale, filled with tiny hair follicles. I open my eyes and feel for the scar. "It's gone," I say to Logan.

"Like it was never there," he replies, giving me a kiss on the side of my neck that makes the skin there tingle. Then his lips move lower, pushing my shirt away to trail along my shoulder.

I nod my head in silent agreement. But an hour later my fingers still search for my nonexistent scar.

"I forgot to ask you how things went with Daniel today," Logan mumbles, already nearing sleep. We both worked today—me on science, him on spying—we're both tired. We're both trying to deal with lives that have changed so much, so fast. I lay tucked against his shoulder in the darkness, my hair flowing around my shoulders in waves from the braids I may never wear again.

"Slow," I say. "And difficult. Science was never my forte, and I'm essentially having to catch up via CliffsNotes."

"I know you're going to get it," Logan says, and I'm surprised by the intensity in his voice. "You always manage to do anything you set out to do. Even when I would tell you it was impossible—you'd find a way. I know you can do it again."

Everything inside me melts as I realize I can borrow some of his confidence to make up for my own. I'd been so focused on what *I* had to do that I forgot Logan is as wrapped up in this as me. And I haven't been making it easy for him. Especially with piling the Benson stuff on top of everything else.

I think of our argument about Benson and feel a little silly. I'm causing Logan so much stress, but in the end, he still trusts me. Still loves me. He may not be with me every moment of the day, but wherever I am I can carry his love and confidence with me. I wrap my arms around his chest and squeeze as hard as I can in a silent thank you for his never-ending belief in me.

It makes me want to be with him, to be part of him. To show him how much he means to me. In moments I want him so badly I can hardly hold back enough to not hurt him as I claim his mouth with mine. Aching, needing, taking his strength as my own.

I need him.

Need my partner.

With our flushed skin pressed together along the length of our bodies I abandon myself and wonder how I ever could have forgotten him.

This other half of me.

"I love you," I whisper, then smile when the words ring with truth.

CHAPTER TWENTY-ONE

"There you are," Daniel says after I spend ten minutes donning a hazmat suit, being doused with disinfectant, and traveling through two air-locked chambers.

"I'm sorry," I say, sliding onto the stool I made very good friends with yesterday. I neglect to tell him the reason for my tardiness: too much time spent dawdling with Logan. Okay, kissing Logan. I've realized that I can't face the virus without him.

"Don't be."

I dismiss his words as polite niceties until he lays a gloved hand on my arm and says, "Really, Tavia. I know you're taking the need for a vaccine as seriously as I am, and if you feel that you need an extra hour or two of sleep, I'd rather wait than miss something because you weren't alert enough. I trust you to be the judge of your own state," he says, then turns serenely back to his microscope.

"I had to get breakfast," I blurt, needing some kind of excuse that doesn't have anything to do with sleeping. I've committed myself to curing the virus, but I won't let Daniel tarnish the minutes I spent drawing strength from Logan's arms. "Daniel?" I ask, not only to change the subject but because it's been bothering me. "Why do they keep bothering to redecorate the atrium every day?"

In the process of grabbing some breakfast—which was the truth, or at least partially—I took a few moments to check out the new decor as I ate a warm sesame bun coated in sugar. The theme today was ancient China, and beautiful golds and reds filled the towering walls in the form of paper lanterns and dragons and butterflies. Painstakingly painted scrolls at least eight feet long hung from one wall, and enormous vases graced nearly every corner. A huge dragon's head arched majestically over the biggest alcove.

Instead of being filled with amazement and appreciation, it all made me angry.

"It doesn't matter what kind of fantastic world the decor of the main atrium mirrors," I say hotly. "We still exist in the *real* world. The world where people are dying by the thousands. Why are we wasting our time and resources on *interior decorating*?"

Daniel smiles in a way that manages to be both kind and patronizing at the same time. "What do you suggest they do, Tavia? Go mop sweaty brows of doomed patients and risk catching the virus themselves? We're all waiting for you before we can act."

I turn my face away, hating that I should have realized that.

"And in the meantime, what does it hurt to instill a sense of normalcy and keep everyone busy? Do you understand?"

"Yes," I mumble.

We work silently for a long time before Daniel says, "I heard you went to go see your old friend last night."

My head shoots up. "Are you watching me?" Again I wonder if I really am free here. Even if they are letting me roam about of my own volition, is it truly freedom if they also monitor my every move?

"I watch everyone, Tavia."

"Not me," I say without really thinking.

"Everyone," Daniel says, and his voice is hard for several seconds before his eyebrows arch and he smiles. "Actually, if it makes you feel better, even though I *can* watch anyone, it was *him* I was keeping an eye on last night. Your Portsmouth friend."

My heart pounds at his words. I've never mentioned Benson to Daniel and hoped I wouldn't have to. I don't know that I really thought I could keep him a secret—he's *Daniel's* prisoner, after all—but I did hope I could at least hide our past relationship. "You know about us?"

Daniel nods. "Since we raided the prisons you were being held in. I was glad they brought him back once I realized just who he was."

"Who is it that you think he is?" I ask, not sure why I'm suddenly on the defensive.

Daniel hesitates, studies me. "I don't know everything," he

187

says, as though not sure what he should tell me. "I do know he was your friend, that he helped you find out who you are. But I also know that he's a Reduciate."

"Was."

Daniel just tilts his head. "Maybe. But I'm not willing to risk the headquarters on his word."

"He gave you the painting."

"Not exactly. The painting was hardly in his possession, but yes, he did bring it to our awareness."

I'm silent for a long time. There's something bothering me about Daniel's story, but I can't put my finger on what it is. "You didn't tell me," I finally settle on. "Even when I specifically asked where the painting came from."

"I didn't think it was necessary. You were with Logan. That's what you wanted."

"What else are you hiding from me?" I don't bother to hide the accusation in my tone.

He stands, and the stool scoots back and almost falls. "Tavia, I put my entire organization in danger to get you here. I think that what secrets I know and don't know should be far down your priority list."

"What do you mean?"

He slumps onto his stool, and all the steam seems to rush out of him. "We've had another outpost attack, closer this time. I'm afraid I may have compromised our location by bringing you directly from the Reduciata compound to here. I was in too big a hurry." He sighs and stares at something just over my shoulder. "I should have taken you to several decoy locations to throw them off. But I needed you and quickly."

Guilt swirls in my stomach, but I remind myself that I did not make that choice for him. Even if it's linked to me, it's not my fault.

I rephrase my question. "Is there anything else you know about me that *I* ought to know?"

He smiles wearily now. "I have forgotten and remembered so many secrets in my lifetimes, I could tell them until we were both old and gray and still there would be more. And I suppose it's possible that some of them have to do with you." He smiles, but there's a heaviness in his eyes that speaks of years of exhausting leadership. I think of the weighty responsibility *I* feel to prevent another disaster like the one in the South Pacific and realize that Daniel feels the same way.

But for the entire *world*.

For lifetime after lifetime after lifetime.

And he doesn't have a partner to help him bear it.

Of course he knows secrets—knows things I don't know, will never know. He won't tell me everything he knows any more than I'll tell him everything *I* know. Our secrets don't matter, nor do our pasts.

"It wouldn't hurt to talk to him, you know. About what we're doing here," Daniel says after about an hour of near-silent work scrutinizing strands of RNA on the electron microscope.

I stare at Daniel, completely uncomprehending. "Of course I tell him what we're doing. I tell him everything."

"Not Logan. Benson."

"Benson?"

"The Reduciate boy."

I give an annoyed sigh and turn back to my screen.

189

"Seriously, Tavia. I can't tell whether he has truly changed his loyalties or not, but while he is in our cells, he's harmless. He won't talk to me, he won't talk to my interrogators, but maybe—if he knows anything at all, *and he might not*—he'll talk to you."

I start to retort that of course he doesn't know anything, but his final words to me echo through my mind. *You're immune.*

For the first time I wonder just what kind of technology they have in that cell. Does Daniel already know what Benson told me? Is this some kind of a test? Or does he really think I can get Reduciate secrets out of Benson?

And can I?

"Maybe I will," I say softly.

"Might help you sort out everything with him too," Daniel suggests.

I nod, and in unspoken agreement we both turn to the same box of samples we were working on yesterday.

"Oh," Daniel adds, "and probably best not to mention it to Logan."

CHAPTER TWENTY-TWO

At least he's got a shirt on this time.

The security team, in their matching off-white out-fits, looks at me funny, but they let me into Benson's cell. They seem hesitant, but then I invoke Daniel's name. It's kind of magic around here. The two people who came to my room probably would have let me in without question, but I don't see them here tonight.

I take just a few seconds to watch Benson unawares as they unlock the heavy door. Watching him through the glass gives me that same guilty feeling as eavesdropping, but I can't help it. This is *him*. No masks or disguises, no lies or half truths. Not trying to impress me or give me careful smiles. Just Benson, bored to tears, in a Curatoria prison.

He turns as though he can feel my eyes on him, and I look away—even though he can't see me. *Our* table is still there.

Not that it matters, exactly. But it makes everything feel like the past. When things were still good.

I wonder why they let him keep it. He could use it for . . . I don't know, something. But then, he's human. I believe the words the woman used when she came to my room were "very containable."

And what chance does a human have against a team of Earthbound security guards, really?

The woman finally gets the door unlocked, and I walk in. I want to look confident, assured.

Unaffected.

But acting isn't one of my better skills. All I can hope is that I don't look as terrified as I feel.

I've been *sent*.

And I came alone.

Truth is, I don't really know what I'm doing here. I'm not Daniel's errand girl to be ordered out to fetch information. And after last night . . . well, let's just say that even as the door opens I almost pivot and run back to Logan.

Maybe I should. He was wonderful last night. And he did ask nicely for me to bring him along next time. Once he got done blowing off steam.

But Daniel said . . .

I shake the doubts from my head. I'm here now—there's really no backing out.

I stand silently as I hear the bolt click behind me. Locking me in. The lock is for Benson's sake, not mine, but that doesn't help mitigate the sense that I'm also a prisoner.

We stand silent, avoiding each other's eyes for at least two minutes. The longest two minutes I've ever known. Finally, I raise my chin. "Let's be clear: I believe your story, but that doesn't mean I trust you."

"Hello, Tave. It's nice to see you too," Benson grumbles, walking forward and slouching into a chair.

I run my fingers through my hair nervously.

"Wait." Benson stands back up, and I put my hands out in front of me as he gets closer.

He stops at my gesture. "What happened to your scar?"

I should have known he would notice. "I got rid of it."

"Why?"

I shrug. "There was no reason to keep it. It made me unhappy," I add, parroting Logan's words.

"Did *he* tell you you should?"

"Does it matter?"

"So you got rid of it because *he* disliked it?"

"No!" I protest, almost at a yell. "He didn't care."

"It's part of who you are, Tavia. He wants you like you once were—whole and perfect—not the *real* person you are now."

I point a finger at him, and I'm so angry it shakes. In my mind I see an image of Logan from last night, as he told me he trusts me, that he could never hate any part of me. That he believes in me. *Why am I here?* "You have no idea what he's like," I almost spit at Benson. He backs up several steps, looking defeated.

"You're right," he says. "I don't. I'm just saying how it looks."

"Well, you're wrong."

"Great, I'm wrong," he says, falling back into his chair.

I sit too, but I crouch on the very edge of the seat, my hands clenched together and squeezed between my thighs. "Are they treating you okay?" I ask, remembering the Reduciates' attempt to starve and freeze me. No matter what he's done, I still want Benson treated humanely.

"I'm in prison: I get one ten-minute shower a day, three meals, all the bottled water I care to order, and at night they give me a mattress. But you know what?" He looks up, and when our eyes meet, the blue seems to burn into me.

"What?" I whisper.

"I'd take way worse to stay away from the Reduciata." He does this shrug thing with only one shoulder. "And be closer to you." His voice cracks on the last word.

"Benson, I—" I put my elbows on the table and drop my forehead against my hands. "I can't . . . you can't . . ."

"I know. I *know*." He squeezes his eyes shut. "And I tell myself that a hundred times a day. But then I see you and I—" He reaches out and grasps my hands before I can pull away. "Tave, you have to understand. I was a pawn as much as you were. And even with everything, I *chose you*. Over everything, everyone. I know that maybe it will take time, but—" He gulps, and I can only stare in horror. "Can't you see that as soon as I *could* make the right choice, I did?"

"Benson, please. I—" I'm gripping his hands so tight my fingers are white and they ache, but somehow, he's still clinging harder.

"I thought it would be enough just to help you—hell, to see you alive! That I could honestly just be happy for you. But I can't. I have to at least try. I'm not sure I can last in this place without going crazy if I don't know there's some kind of chance. A trickle of hope. Something. Please."

It's a good thing there's a table between us, because that's all that's keeping me from going to him, and I know I can't. It wouldn't be fair. "Ben, I'm with Logan. You know that."

"I know. I *know*! And who would understand that better than me?" His hands are still latched onto mine, but he leans forward now, laying his head on his arms, and I want to run my fingers through his waves. "But I didn't know it would be so hard. When you were in here yesterday, I thought . . . I thought maybe . . ."

I start tugging at my hands now, trying to take them back, but I don't think he notices.

"Tell me you love him."

I stop pulling. "What?"

"Logan. Tell me you love him. That he's everything you could ever want. That he will make you happy every day for the rest of your life, and you're certain."

"Certain of what?" My voice is shaking.

"That you'll never want me again."

My whole body stills. My throat closes in on itself, and I wonder if this is what anaphylactic shock feels like. I told Logan I loved him last night—why can't I tell Benson? *I love Logan. Say it!*

"Set me free," Benson mumbles into his arms, not noticing my battle.

I try to speak. To say the words. But somehow it's easier to lie to myself than to Benson.

"This halfway thing—I can't stand it. I need you to—" He

looks up right at me and his voice cuts off and I wonder what he sees. "You don't. You . . . you're not sure."

I close my eyes, turn away. "Of course I'm sure. I have to go." I walk over and knock on the door for them to let me out, but Benson is right behind me.

"Give me a chance then, Tave. I will show you. I will make sure you never doubt me again, I—"

"Shut up!" I scream, clapping my hands over my ears. "There's not a chance, Benson. I can't. I can't. I—"

"You need to step away, Mr. Ryder." The tallest security guy is there, and Benson drops his hands and backs up until he hits the wall on the opposite side of the cell.

I slip through the door in front of the guy and nearly run into Logan.

"Logan." I know the guilt must be shining in my eyes. Practically sloughing off me in waves. "How—how long have you been here?"

"Long enough." His jaw is tight, but his eyes never leave mine. "Alanna told me she saw you heading down this way. I just came to walk you back. In case you were upset. I was worried."

"You didn't trust me."

"It's not about trust. I was *worried*."

I duck my head and walk past him out of the security wing. I know he'll follow, but I don't want to have any more of this conversation in front of the security team. And I really don't want to have it where I can see Benson out of the corner of my eye.

"I told him I was with *you*," I say as soon as we've cleared the heavy doors. "You heard me!"

"I heard a lot of things," he says, jamming his hands into his pockets. "I asked you to please not visit him without me. I thought we agreed on that, but maybe I was wrong." He turns his back but faces me again two seconds later. "Tavia, you told me he was *no one*."

"He wasn't my boyfriend. Not actually." But he's right. I lied.

"He's just in love with you."

I have nothing to say to that.

"Are you in love with him?"

I swallow hard. "I was."

"Are you still?"

I want to say no. Try to force my mouth to form the word. But all that comes out is "I don't know."

The sound of his gasp makes me jerk my head up—really look at him. Logan's hands are buried in his hair, and he seems like he's trying to physically hold himself together. "You don't know." He lets out a wry chuckle that sounds like broken glass. "After everything, you don't know if you might be in love with someone else. How can you even—he's a human, Tavia!"

"So?" My indignation finds its voice. "That doesn't make him less."

"Yes, yes it *does*! He is *so* much less than this. Than *us*! Than our eternity together. How can you not see that?"

"How about your parents?" I jab back, finally finding the courage to just say it. "Are they *less* too?" I don't get it; I know he *can* feel deeply. The depth of the emotions he feels for me is so cavernous it's almost frightening. But apparently none of that applies to the people who *raised him*.

"Yes!" he bursts out, as though it weren't a shameful confession. "Everything human is less than what we have. You used to understand that. Nothing and no one in the world is more important than what we have together. And you *don't know*?" He spits the last two words in disgust. He takes a deep breath and seems to take control of himself as he straightens. "You lied to me. You're hiding things. The last time we were together—when we were Quinn and Rebecca—we shared everything. The only secret we had between us was your big secret. The one we *both agreed* was too dangerous for me to know."

An entirely new kind of guilt fills my belly as I remember wondering if I wasn't protecting him, but myself. And I feel more guilty when I don't speak up. Even now.

"The one *you* don't even know now," Logan continues, not noticing anything. "And now you're sneaking around? Lying about your past? What happened to you?"

I feel tears build up in my eyes, and I'm not sure how much is from sadness and how much from anger and hurt.

And shame.

I did lie to him. I knew I was doing it and I did it anyway. He deserved the truth.

He's waiting for an answer. But I don't have one. I retreat instead.

I turn and run down the hall, not looking back.

I run from Logan.

I suppose I run from Benson too.

After leaving the security hall I'm not sure where to go. All I know is I can't face him. Can't go back to the room we've shared for three days. And three nights.

Can't go back to that replica of our perfect life as Rebecca and Quinn.

When I reach the stairs that lead down to the gold and red splendor of the main atrium, I pause before descending. For nearly ten at night the atrium is still very much alive. The huge television has extra couches in front of it, and there must be at least fifty people staring at the newest report from the Pacific. The reporter's words reach me as I draw nearer.

"Responders on the scene of this disaster now believe the death count will exceed two million and possibly be as high as two point five. This on top of the now over a quarter of a million deaths from the still untreatable Kentucky Virus. A number that also continues to grow each day. It's a scary time in history, Bob."

As I walk numbly by, it's hard not to become trapped in the hypnotic tragedy. I think of Logan's reaction to his family's deaths—even Benson's story of his father—and I can't help but wonder if these other Earthbounds truly feel the loss of human life or if their tears of sorrow and empathy are a learned reaction—what they know they're supposed to do but not reflective of what they actually feel.

Regardless, I don't belong here.

Once I'm in a deserted hallway where I can't hear the sounds from the atrium anymore, I glare at a blank wall and picture a small—almost tiny—room behind a very simple door.

I close my eyes, make a wish, and with the last vestiges of energy left inside my body, I push open the plain white door of my creation.

I walk into a replica of my bedroom from my parents' house in Michigan. A plate of my mother's homemade ravioli in cream sauce waits for me on the tiny desk I used to do my homework on. It smells just like I remember it, all garlicky and delicious. I breathe it in, savoring the memories of Thanksgiving and Christmas and casual weeknight dinners at home.

And then I close the door to the world of the Earthbound.

CHAPTER TWENTY-THREE

"He's dead."

"When?"

"Just a few weeks ago. They made it look like an accident—like he drank himself to death, really. But they helped. I'm sure of it."

"How are we going to tell her?"

I stand with my back against the wall, eavesdropping, tears running down my face. My partner, my diligo, gone. For this life, anyway. But it feels like forever. And just when I need him so badly. When I came here—to these Curatoriates I don't trust—it was because I knew the Reduciates were closing in on me, not him.

But apparently I was wrong.

What now? I have more reasons than ever to stay out of the Reduciates' hands. I fiddle with my necklace, turning it from silver to gold—back and forth. Little bits of practice that don't terrify me too much. I think back on my last few moments as Greta. In that life, I knew why I was being killed.

But the way they killed me. They were certain it would be forever. But here I am. Changed. Is that what made this happen? It's the only reasonable explanation I can come up with.

Do the Reduciates have any idea? I know they'll hunt me forever to keep me quiet, but do they know about my powers too? My strength? They wouldn't kill me if they did—I'd become their lab rat. I can't let that happen.

The girl continues to talk with her dad, discussing my future, how to keep me safe. But they don't know how. They only think they do. I've always known this place was temporary at best. I of all people knew better than to think I could stay with Curatoriates.

But what now? It's been almost two hundred years, and I'm no closer to fixing the problem than I was as Rebecca. Or Greta.

First things first, I have to leave. I'm pretty sure I haven't left any trace. Any proof.

But that Samantha—the old man's daughter—she was looking at me funny yesterday.

She's too smart for her own good. I can't risk her figuring anything out.

It's time to run.

Again.

I jerk straight up in bed, my whole body damp with sweat, heart racing. I'm not sure why; this dream was way less terrifying than the ones I had in Phoenix. But so many names!

I feel the clarity of the dream melting away already, so I create a notebook and pencil in my hands and begin scribbling everything I can remember.

Greta, new powers, transforming the necklace, the secret, a *change*.

When three pages are covered with what I saw, I finally take a breath and force my shoulders to unclench. After flinging the covers back, I get to my feet and start pacing—a nervous habit I'd been forced to give up when my leg was always sore. It feels strange to be glad I can do it again.

Thoughts swirl wildly through my head. Greta. Another name from another life. But she seems to be a key. Whatever happened in Greta's life is what Sonya thinks led to being able to Transform.

Plus the secret.

My feet jerk to a stop. I was right. Transforming *isn't* the secret. Not the one Rebecca had. There's something else. Could Benson be right and I *am* immune? But how far back could the virus have possibly existed?

I remember the brief vision I had in Portsmouth of being a tiny, cold child who was shot by Marianna. They were talking about an antidote.

Is it possible? Is my immunity the great secret? That particular short life came right before Rebecca's—time-wise, it could work that way.

But how would Rebecca have known?

And even if it's true—if Benson's right—wouldn't Daniel be studying *me* instead of having me develop a new vaccine?

Assuming they could hold me, a voice says in my mind.

That's right. How could they hold an incredibly powerful Transformist against her will?

Maybe in the grand scheme of things, this way is simpler. And I guess it stands to reason that altering an existing vaccine could be easier than creating a new one—even from someone who's immune. Taking my blood, studying me, would be a risk. Just fixing a not-quite-perfect vaccine, more of a sure thing.

Plus they get to spy on me while I work for them.

There's something else I'm missing, and a headache starts in my temples as I try to sort all of the information I have.

Daniel. He's not a Reduciate. It was the Reduciata I was always running from.

If the true secret is that I'm immune, maybe Daniel doesn't know.

And everything—*everything*—is leaning on this dream being a true memory, not just a stress dream. And I have absolutely no way to verify *that*. I growl and kick a cedar chest at the foot of my bed.

In the end, nothing has changed. Walls and bars don't trap me the way they do Benson; I have a prison of my own conscience. Even now, having figured all of this out, I know I can't leave.

If I do, the entire world dies.

I sink down onto my bed. The one that *looks* like my old home. But it's all pretend. I'm homeless in this veritable world beneath the desert sands. Homeless and alone and possibly a prisoner.

In the stress of the moment last night, this is what I made. A copy of my old bedroom. Of my old life. It's not that I'm trying to turn back time, exactly. Or even that I would go back and opt out if I could. It's that I needed a chance to just be Tavia again. Is that so wrong?

My stomach rumbles, and I create a breakfast of my mom's buckwheat pancakes, paired with my dad's fresh-squeezed orange juice. Then I linger. No, I'm putting off the inevitable. Because I'm not sure I'll ever be able to come back here once I leave. It's nice to feel like I'm sixteen again. Just for a few minutes. To be a person who hasn't been betrayed yet. Who didn't lie to her lover. Who doesn't have the fate of the world resting on her shoulders. Who isn't protecting secrets even she doesn't know. Tears fight their way up my throat, but I shove them away. I won't cry. Not today.

I spent my tears last night. Today I am strong. I *will be* strong.

I peek out the door, and when the hallway is clear I step out, transform my door into a plain wall, and then try to figure out exactly where I am. Luckily it doesn't take too long, and I'm pleased to discover I can get from my room to the lab without having to cross the atrium.

Because the truth is, I don't want to see *anyone* this morning.

When I reach the lab I suit up silently and sit in front of the microscope for about fifteen minutes before Daniel joins me.

"I'm sorry," he says. "They didn't tell me you'd arrived."

"It's my fault." I can hear the misery in my voice. "I didn't really check in."

Daniel looks at me for a long time, and even through the mask over his face his eyes look . . . they look *fatherly*. I'm not sure I want him to look at me that way. "You don't seem very well."

I turn away and scoot my stool closer to the microscope. "I'm ready to work, that's the most important part."

But Daniel stops me with a hand on my shoulder. "Did you find out something distressing from Benson?"

"No," I say, though my entire body stiffens when Daniel says Benson's name. I hate that he's twined up in all of this. "I didn't find out anything, really." *Except that I don't want to give him up*.

"Are you upset over the things Audra told you?" Daniel asks.

"How do you know about that?" I ask, my tone blatantly accusing.

"I know most things that happen here, Tavia," he says with no inflection. "I'm afraid you'll have to become accustomed to that."

My gaze drops from his, because I'm not sure if I should be angry at *him*. His house, his rules. Including intrusive spying. "I know," I mumble, avoiding the argument.

"The deaths in the Pacific Islands?"

I shake my head. "I can't even bring myself to think about what happened there for very long. It's too much."

Daniel looks like he's trying to come up with something else, and I have a feeling if I don't fess up he'll start naming other things I *should* be upset about. I don't think I can handle that right now. "I—I had a fight with Logan last night." I try to meet his eyes the entire time, but my courage fails me and I say the last few words to his feet. It's not completely a lie. But the drama with Logan doesn't feel nearly as draining this morning as the fact that I had a dream that may or may not be full of answers. And I have to decide what's true.

"Ah, lovers' spat. Those are never pleasant."

Spat? Not exactly. I run my fingertips along the box of slides, wishing again that I somehow had the braid from Sonya's life. To confirm or deny all of my dreams. Not knowing is maddening.

"He was looking for me last night, and someone saw me and told him where I had gone," I say, making myself talk about my romantic saga instead of what I'm really thinking. "He walked in at a bad moment."

"Oh," Daniel says softly and sits down on the stool beside me. "Oh, dear. Maybe I shouldn't have encouraged you to go—"

"It's not your fault," I say miserably, cutting him off. And it isn't. My meeting with Benson *should* have been completely innocent. I mean, I *knew* people were watching us. I just didn't think Logan was one of them.

The lights above us flicker, and a knot of fear catches in my throat. But five seconds later everything seems fine.

"What was that?" I ask.

"Almost certainly a sandstorm. We've had some really awful ones the last few weeks."

I think of the other crazy weather phenomena I've seen. "Do you think it's one of the effects of the virus?"

"It's certainly possible. But don't worry. As you discovered the first night you came to us, we have excellent generators. For the essential electric needs, that is."

True. But the overhead lights in our candlelit bedroom evidently didn't make the list. Not that I'm complaining.

"Tavia." Daniel hesitates and then moves his stool an inch or two closer. "Do you still have feelings for this human boy? I know it's not my business, but now I feel guilty for having sent you to him. I never thought that he . . . well, it doesn't matter. But, do you?"

The crying lump is clogging my throat again, and all I can do is nod miserably.

"Even . . . even now? After remembering Logan?"

"That's what *he* asked. I don't understand why everyone thinks that remembering former lives makes this life not matter!" Daniel draws back a little at my vehemence, but I keep talking. Almost shouting. "Logan is the same way. He said that Benson is *less* just because he's human. And he doesn't seem to care at all that his entire family died a week ago—were *killed* a week ago. When my parents died—" Even now, saying the words out loud makes my chest ache with emptiness. "When they died I felt like a piece had been ripped from my heart. Like part of me was dead because they were. And when I remembered everything, that didn't change."

"But you didn't remember everything, did you?" Daniel asks.

My mouth snaps shut. "I guess not," I say softly.

"It's hard to explain the complete change in perspective if you haven't experienced it. It's like . . . like living your whole life as an ant. Then one day, you turn into a giant. And there are other giants. In fact, an entire world you never knew existed. How important do all of those little tiny ants seem to you now?"

"But ants do still matter . . ." I reply. The words seem hollow even to me. I don't like the sense Daniel is making.

"We don't physically change, but all of the sudden, this tiny speck of time that is a single lifetime is so small. And the people in it, well, they're practically infinitesimal. Except for one person."

I look up at him, remembering that he hasn't found his partner yet. There's a sheen of tears in his eyes, and his voice quavers a little, though he gains control quickly.

"So now you have Logan. And he has remembered. And in the enormous span of time that is his many lives, there is *you*. You are, for lack of a better comparison, his sun. And here you are, telling him that you still have feelings for this *ant*. This tiny, insignificant ant."

"He's not insignificant," I instantly retort.

"But he *should be*," Daniel says with a calmness that shakes me to my very soul. "And to Logan, he is."

I remember the impression I had the other night that Logan loves me more than I love him, and my hands begin to tremble.

"It's not simply the thought of losing you to someone else—though certainly that would be hard enough for anyone, human or otherwise. But losing you to *him*? Can you see why it's so unnatural that Logan can scarcely even comprehend it?"

I do. I feel awful reducing Benson to such terms, but I understand. Or at least as much as I can without having the full memory that Logan does.

"I'm not telling you what to do. I'm not even telling you that there is a 'right' choice. But—" His face crumples into an unreadable expression, and he shakes his head. "That's not true. I'm rooting for Logan. The two of you are meant to be together. If I found my . . . my partner only to discover that

209

she wanted to stay with someone else I . . . I would lose my entire purpose. Any reason for living." He turns to me. "The human boy will get over his heartbreak. But Logan? You reject him and you may as well thrust a knife in his heart. It's simply a fact." He looks at me with such pain in his eyes it's hard to meet his gaze.

"Now," he says, and I can hear the strain in his voice, the forced cheerfulness. "Let's get to work."

CHAPTER TWENTY-FOUR

Five hours later I want to slump over my microscope and wail. After two and a half days of painstaking analysis, we've still gotten the exact same result from every DNA sequence I've transformed.

Which is *nothing*.

No reaction whatsoever.

After a while I'm not productive anymore; I start botching the transformations. And then Daniel gets cranky.

Like now.

I can't tell if he's angry with *me* for not being good enough, or if he's frustrated at himself for pushing me too hard.

"Take a break," he says at twelve forty-five, in a tone that brooks no argument.

I brook anyway. "But I have fifteen more minutes."

"To what?" he snaps. "Do the same section over and over?"

We're both stressed—we're both desperate. It was only a matter of time before one of us lost our temper. But every minute of break I take makes me feel guilty. What if the *very next* matched pair in the viral RNA is the right one? Or the one after that?

But that's a train of thought with a bridge out ahead, and if I followed it I'd make myself work all through the night. And the next day.

So instead of arguing, I nod and slide off my stool onto legs that feel like jelly.

I decide to spend my hour-long break back in the room I created last night. I like it—love the illusion of being back in Michigan, where life was simple and wonderful. I glance behind me right before I turn down the final hallway and meet an unfamiliar pair of eyes.

That immediately looks away.

I don't know that I would have noticed him staring if it weren't for his blond eyelashes. Light blue eyes surrounded by thick, blond eyelashes. I glance up and see the lashes are paired with dark strawberry-blond hair that's almost perfectly rust-colored. The rest of him is pretty nondescript—average height and build—but his hair is rather distinctive.

I give him my back and wonder just how innocent that little encounter was. Is he watching me? He did look away like he was guilty. Or, at the very least, didn't want to be seen looking. I had intended to head to my new room, but now I'm not sure I should even turn down that hallway.

I remember a joke kids used to say at school in Michigan:

Is it still paranoia if they really are all out to get you? It suddenly doesn't seem very funny anymore.

Before I can dwell on this new development for very long, something reaches out and grabs me, pulling me through a doorway that wasn't there a second ago. I start to scream, but a hand claps over my mouth and Alanna's face blocks out my vision.

"Don't do anything stupid or everything Sammi and Mark worked for will be wasted."

I'm so shocked I can't move, much less speak.

Or scream.

"Are you calm?" Alanna asks, sounding absolutely nothing like the person I've been avoiding for the last three days.

I nod, my eyes still so wide I must look like I'm in shock.

Maybe I am.

There's a distinct possibility I'm hallucinating.

A light brightens, and I see Thomas and Logan standing behind Alanna, the two males mirrors of one another, arms crossed over their chests. But the moment Logan's eyes meet mine, his arms fall and the defiance in his stance disappears entirely.

Logan? The innate wrongness of this whole situation is multiplied by the fact that he's here. Unrestrained. Like he *wants* to be with *them*.

"What the hell is going on, I swear you have *ten seconds* before I am gone and don't even think you can stop me," I say in one long string without pauses.

Alanna steps forward. "Short version: We've been working with Mark and Sammi for about two years now trying to find out what Daniel is up to, and I think we can trust you to help continue our efforts."

I gape at her, but even her *appearance* seems altered without the vapid look I'm used to. Standing before me is a woman with a confident stature and intelligent eyes. If it weren't for her rather gaudy clothes I wouldn't believe it was her at all.

I'm struck still, unable to think or speak or move. I don't know how long I stay there, stupefied, before I cough out, "Well, that is one hell of a disguise."

She rolls her eyes. "I know, aren't I an absolute bitch?" She takes a loud breath. "I know this is sudden. Honestly, we wanted to wait longer, but with everything that's happened and Logan being a rather conspicuous spy," she says, shooting an annoyed look at Logan, "not to mention our sources saying you're not making much progress in the lab, well, we had to take the chance."

My mouth is open at the fact that not only does she know how pathetically things have been going in the lab but that she's basically just thrown it in my face. I'm so angry I can barely think straight.

But I'm cautiously curious too.

"Here," Alanna says, making a gesture at Thomas. "Sit."

A table and chairs appear. "I thought you were Destroyers," I ask suspiciously, my eyes darting about the space that can hardly be called a room. There are walls, and they're straight, but it's an empty, bare space that is more an organized absence of where a wall *used* to be than a proper room. A tiny voice in my head whispers that I could do better—that I *did* do better last night—and I wonder if this is what Daniel means when he tells me I'm "stronger."

Alanna sucks in a fast breath, then says, "*I'm* a Destroyer, but Thomas is a Creator. We've spread the misconception that we're both Destroyers, so he can never use his powers in front of anyone. Ever. But we've decided to trust you." She takes a seat on one of the chairs, and her face is so calm and serious she actually looks like a different person. "Mixed pairs are very, very rare. In fact, as far as we know, there are only two sets of us. Maybe that's where the story really begins, actually."

We gather nervously around the table. Thomas and Alanna immediately sit together, leaving Logan and I to also sit side by side. I tentatively meet his eyes, and a momentary truce passes between us. We're both too curious to find out what's going on with these two to let our drama stand in the way.

For now.

"Most people associated with Earthbounds assume, like you, that all *diligos* are matched pairs, and most of the time they're right," Alanna says. "So Thomas and I are, well, you think it's tough being objectified as a woman, wait until you're objectified as a god," she says dryly. "We're the perfect combination."

I cringe inwardly, realizing that—technically—I'm the perfect combination all by myself.

But I'm not ready to tell them that. Not yet.

"And so everyone wants us," Alanna says in that sensible voice that I'm still not used to. "Every time we've managed to find each other we've done our best to stay off both the Reduciata and Curatoria radars."

I look between them, confused. "Then why are you here? This is pretty damn close to the Curatoria's radar."

Alanna looks to Thomas.

"I'm a scientist," Thomas says after clearing his throat, as though he hasn't spoken in a long time. Remembering how quiet he always is, I wonder just how long it's actually been. "And about forty years ago—in a past life, and without any memory of my Earthbound identity—I was a doctor, and I had a patient come to me. She had a sickness I couldn't identify, but it was obviously killing her and killing her quickly. I took samples of her blood, and none of it made sense to me. The illness simply wasn't acting the way it was supposed to."

"Do you think it's a version of the virus we have today?" I ask.

"I do." He hesitates and looks uncomfortable in a way that I recognize as extreme shyness. I wonder if that shyness comes naturally or from lifetimes of isolation. Regardless, he continues, "While I was examining her, she left the man who had brought her in back in the waiting room, as was the custom back them. As soon as we were out of his sight she started raving to me about the witchcraft and magic she was being exposed to. I dismissed her ramblings as craziness, whether natural or brought about by her disease. But now—in a different life and with my memories restored—I believe her."

"Do you think she was a prisoner of the Reduciata?" Logan asks, leaning forward now.

"No, no, I don't," Thomas says, his voice firm, determined, even in its quietness. "Because the man who brought her in was Daniel."

A silence settles among the four of us as we all continue to try to figure out how much we can trust each other. Even in the face of this bombshell.

"Tell her the rest," Alanna prompts, her hand on his shoulder.

"That night, I was run down by a car and killed. I don't think it was a coincidence."

Tingles run up and down my arms as I try to take this all in. "What does it mean?" I finally say, unable to loosen the knot of mystery in her story, even though I can sense its significance.

"It means many things," Alanna says, and Thomas looks relieved that she's taken over. "For starters, it means that Daniel knew about the virus forty-three years ago."

"But . . . it wasn't even around," I say, before remembering having that very thought this morning after my newest dream. "Unless—" But what can I say?

"Unless he was helping to develop it all along," Logan says, unknowingly coming to my rescue.

"Or trying to cure victims whom the Reduciata tested it on," I counter, not sure why I'm defending Daniel. Except maybe that he looked so sad this morning.

"And then killing off witnesses?" Alanna asks with a sharpness that makes me think of her disguised self for a second.

"You don't know that for certain," I whisper, thinking of the pain in his eyes when he talked about his lost partner.

But if Thomas really is telling the truth . . .

"It makes sense, Tavia," Alanna says. "I don't understand why you're arguing so hard against it."

"Because I would like one damn person in this entire world

to be who they told me they were," I snap, mortified to realize that not only am I yelling, I've risen to my feet.

"Then you're in the wrong world," Thomas says, and his voice is so quiet I barely hear it, yet the truth of it pierces me to my very soul. "Every Earthbound I've ever met is wearing a disguise of one kind or another."

I force my knees to bend—to put me back into my seat. This isn't about me, about Logan or Benson. It's not about Sammi and Mark or Alanna or Thomas.

This is about *Daniel* and the salvation of the entire world.

"Why hasn't he recognized you?" I ask.

Thomas grimaces and Alanna giggles, sounding more like the version of herself I've come to loathe over the past few days. I don't understand the reason for the sudden reversion until she slides a faded Polaroid over to me. It's Thomas, I guess, but he totally has shoulder-length shaggy hair and a big moustache. And let's not even get started on the skin-tight polo.

My eyes flit from the photo to him and back again a few times before Logan takes it from me to have a look. A laugh builds up in my throat, but it's accompanied by a strange pain. "I see," I say dryly, looking at the handsome, clean-cut man across the table from me. Sammi once told me that if the Earthbound didn't look the same from life to life, the brotherhoods would never be able to find us. But "the same" is such a relative term.

I don't look quite the same, Thomas doesn't look the same, even Quinn and Logan don't look the same, exactly. I'm starting to think that some of the claims both the Reduciata and Curatoria make about their files and records must be partly lies. Or, at the very least, stretching the truth. A pair of Earthbounds that both groups have been looking for for centuries has been living right in the Curatoria headquarters and no one has realized?

It makes me feel oddly hopeful that maybe I can make it through this alive.

"So when you got your memories back you remembered this?" I prompt.

Thomas nods. "By that time I was living a different life, of course, but I remembered that last fateful day, and I knew I had to find Alanna and we had to do something. We've never trusted either organization," Thomas says, "but the Curatoria always seemed like the lesser of the two evils, so to speak."

I raise one eyebrow—it's essentially word-for-word what Logan and I decided.

"So we came back and gave some sort of sob story about how we hadn't connected in ages and hadn't come in contact with the Curatoria in a thousand years. They had no record of us, but they gave us our vows and we"—he glances at Alanna—"we acted very enthusiastic, so they let us in."

"If the Curatoria has one glaring fault, it's letting too many people in—no offense," Alanna adds, glancing at us. "So Thomas and I started poking around, and we thought we were being subtle, but Sammi, she's smart. She caught on." Alanna laughs sadly. "She cornered me one day and straight-out threatened me. Bold little mortal thing. She was old family Curatoria—loyal to the bone, that one. But when I explained to her what Thomas had seen, the little bit we'd managed to uncover, she decided that she needed to look into it for the good of the Curatoria as a whole." Alanna swallows hard. "She was always so loyal to the *ideals* of the Curatoria. To the organization. In the end she didn't want Daniel to ruin it, and that's why we started working as a team."

"And when they were asked to come and pretend to be my aunt and uncle?"

"We were certain that either we'd been caught or it was the luckiest break we'd ever gotten. I'm still not entirely sure which. After . . . after they died we weren't sure if we should stay. We decided we'd give it one month and then we'd go out and try to find you ourselves. Not that we had any idea how we were going to do that. Luckily, you found us instead."

"Why didn't you just tell me who you were?" I ask. I don't bother adding that technically it was Daniel who found me.

"Because you were Daniel's prisoner."

Prisoner. Is that what everyone here thinks of me as? But didn't I come to that very conclusion this morning? A prisoner, one way or another.

"I had no idea where your loyalties lay. We decided we had to keep acting just like we do with everyone else until the time was right." Her hand slides across the table and touches my arm lightly. "I'm sorry I was so awful that first day. I had to get into that room and destroy any evidence Sammi and Mark might have left. I should have done it before but . . ." She shrugs. "I wanted to believe they were coming back. When suddenly you had already moved in, I knew I had to act fast. I had one chance to get rid of their stuff and throw you off at the same time, and I'm afraid I made the most of it."

I have a weird urge to cry at her apology. Because the consequences have already happened. I had never felt so blatantly affronted, and, in the end, it was Alanna's actions that convinced me to get rid of my scar.

But now's not the time to tell her that.

"And after that?" I said, my voice still cold.

"I tested you. Provoked you. Wanted to see what you would do and how you would react. I wasn't ready to put my life in your hands." She doesn't drop her eyes from mine the entire time. "To be honest, I'm still not one hundred percent sure. But we don't have the luxury of time anymore."

Funny that. "Me either," I say, rising to my feet. "Daniel will notice if I'm late back from my lunch break." I halt when everyone just looks at me in shock and maybe a bit of horror. To be honest, it makes me a little angry. "What do you expect me to do? I can't stop. I'm . . . I'm the only hope anyone has of beating the virus."

"We don't want you to stop," Thomas says, clearing the expression on his face. "I just didn't think we'd have to wrap everything up so quickly. Maybe . . . maybe we can talk later? And—and if you wanted to tell me about the work you're doing, I might be able to help."

I nod, but even though everything's shouting at me that they're telling the truth, that doesn't mean that they're *entirely* in the right either. What proof do they have, really? If Daniel were trying to poison the world, why would he bother to develop a vaccine when he could just focus on finding his partner and then hole himself away until the world was dead? This meeting with Thomas and Alanna hasn't made things clearer; if anything, it's made them more murky.

I wish I could talk to Logan. Or Benson. *Really* talk. But I can't help but feel like that ship has sailed. Maybe they both have.

"I should go," I murmur, feeling like I'm somehow quitting by leaving. But I don't know what to do, and being here isn't helping me think clearly.

"You two leave first," Alanna says to Logan, and I seize up with panic—I'm not ready to be alone with him. "We'll follow when the coast is clear." She grips my shoulders with both hands. "And I apologize for the awful things I'm certain to say when I next see you. I need to 'keep up appearances,'" she winks, "and my terrible personality gives us a degree of privacy you wouldn't believe. Between that and the rather unacceptable level of PDA we engage in, no one here can stand us. I've seen people literally run in the other direction when they see us."

I don't doubt it. I'd basically started doing that very thing. I just give a silent nod and then turn to the door without waiting for Logan to follow.

He trails behind me anyway.

"Tavia," he says, catching up as soon as the door closes behind us. "Just give me fifteen minutes. Ten. One. *Please*," he says, grasping at my hand now, "I'm begging you."

I look up, and my eyes are caught in his. I read the world in his eyes. A world of sorrow and regret, of love and loss, of ache and fulfillment.

Then you're in the wrong world. Thomas's words echo through my ears.

I'm not hiding anything, I argue to myself. *Not anymore*.

But I don't know that.

Even Logan can't truly answer that for me. It's been two hundred years since he knew me. I can't comprehend being a liar, a murderer, or anything like that. But having a brain injury has changed so much of me—even my personality. Maybe before that I *would* have seen this kind of capability within myself.

Maybe I've actually done something awful. Maybe *that's* why the Reduciata are looking for me. Maybe the real reason I couldn't tell my secret to Logan is that my secret is I'm part of this whole conspiracy.

I unconsciously grip Logan's shirt in my fists as I realize that maybe I really am immune.

And maybe it's because I *helped* develop the virus.

In my dream this morning Sonya worried about "fixing the problem." Is that because she—I—created it?

CHAPTER TWENTY-FIVE

I sway on my feet a little as I try to convince myself it's not possible.

But how the hell do I know that isn't *exactly* what happened? Exactly why Daniel wants my help. Maybe even why he sent me to the medical department: to try to get that progress back.

There are so many things I don't know about myself, and when I look up into the eternity of Logan's eyes my heart drops as I wonder if, despite my powers, with everything that has happened—everything everyone except me remembers and feels and *knows*—maybe I'm just an ant too.

"Can't we just go somewhere and talk?" Logan asks, and I look up at him like his voice is my anchor to the earth, keeping me from being swept away by everything I've discovered in the last hour.

Time. I have no time. I pull the phone I'm not allowed to

use from my pocket. "I've got about ten minutes before Daniel notices I'm not back," I say. "That's all I can give you."

"Where should we go?"

I have no idea. I feel like I've only seen about 10 percent of this cavernous place, and I'm too tired to make a room of my own.

"We can just sit here," Logan suggests, somehow sensing how overwhelmed I am.

I nod gratefully, and we slide our backs down the wall and sit next to each other on the floor, our thighs touching in some form of a stalemate.

"I should have told you."

His jaw tightens at my admission, but he just shakes his head. "I shouldn't have yelled."

"I did tell him I was with you."

"But you're not sure. I heard that part." He continues without giving me a chance to deny it. "And I just can't understand it. Is it because of . . . of the problems with your brain?"

Even though I've told him all the basics about how my brain injury affects me, affects my past memories, I didn't tell him what Audra told me about how I likely won't remember this life at all. And I find myself holding that one piece of information back even now. I can't confess to him just how messed up I am. But I do nod. I can't avoid the question entirely.

"Is it ever going to . . . heal completely? Give you back the things you don't know now?"

"No. I might be able to recover more if I can collect artifacts from other lives, but I don't think it's going to be much clearer than what I remember about being Rebecca." I don't meet his eyes. I can't bear to see the disappointment. "Does that change things between us?"

The silence lasts long enough that I have to look up to make sure he heard me. He's staring at me with a twisted expression of horror. "How can you even ask that? The only thing that ever—*ever*—stands between us is not knowing that the other one exists. If I found you nearly dead, in a coma on life support, I would sit by your bed and hold your hand until your last heartbeat. This is—this is nothing compared to that."

Warmth spreads from the top of my head down as he looks at me with glittering, almost worshipful eyes.

"In my last life I was a man named Darius," Logan says after a long pause. "I fell in love and got married young. Nineteen. Everyone told me I was an idiot, but I was head over heels in love, and it seemed like the most natural thing to do."

I wait for a surge of jealousy, but it doesn't come. I can't deny him a life—a love, even—before he knew about me. I would be a hypocrite at best.

"We got married soon after we found out she was pregnant. It was an accident, but we were happy. So happy."

"What happened?" I ask breathlessly.

"Car wreck. Multi-car pileup. No substances involved. Just one of those things. They were both killed. I thought . . . I thought I would literally die of a broken heart." He rubs his hands over each other like he's suddenly cold. "I started drinking heavily. Became an alcoholic. Died in my forties after an utterly wasted life."

Oh gods. The dream. Sammi's father said the Reduciates made it look like he drank himself to death. He doesn't know.

226

I'm completely unaware of my tears until I feel one tickle my chin. I turn away and try to subtly scrub my cheek. What am I supposed to do? Tell him? I have no idea what the *right* thing to do here is. So I stay silent.

"But I look back now—after remembering everything—and all I can think is, 'Well, that was a shame.' I don't feel the same grief for her that led me to fritter away my life. She—both of them, really—feels like a passing fancy. Just so *small*." And I shiver a little as he uses the same word Daniel did yesterday.

"Nothing else in the world, in any of my lives, matters a *fraction* as much as you do." He shrugs. "Obviously I don't *like* that it's not the same for you. But I'm not going to let that stop me from loving you."

"But you loved your family," I blurt, just needing to say it. To hear him say something about *them* after what he said last night.

"I did. And they were *wonderful* people. I don't want you to think I don't care. Or that they don't matter."

"Do they?" I whisper. Because I'm not convinced at all.

He's still for a long time before he nods. "They *matter*," he says hesitantly, "but not the way you do. If I ever lost *you* . . ." His voice trails off and he shudders. He turns to me, his eyes shimmering. "I vow, I swear on everything I hold dear in this world, on my very eternal life, that I will never, *ever* give up on you. No matter what happens. Never," he says, his voice almost vicious in its intensity.

All the feeling drains from my limbs.

Two boys, two vows, two loves.

Slowly, so slowly, I raise my eyelids, peer through my

lashes. I know when I look into the chasm of adoration in Logan's eyes that I have never been loved so deeply and completely by anyone in my life as this boy in front of me. Even the love my parents have for me seems pale compared to what I see in his eyes.

And it frightens me.

But how can you deny something this immense? I don't think any human can, and for the first time I understand a sliver of what the Earthbound around me keep saying—about the depth of love humans simply can't comprehend.

But I may as well be human because I *don't* understand it. Where does that leave me?

As though he can't help himself, Logan leans forward and brushes my lips with the softest kiss I've even known. So soft I wouldn't have believed it happened except that my lips are on fire from the merest touch of his mouth.

"Tavia," he whispers, "come home."

I choke on a sob and shake my head. "I don't have a home."

"*I'm* your home. Let me hold you tonight. Please."

"I don't know." The words are so quiet even I barely hear them.

"I'll wait," he murmurs, not moving forward to try to kiss me again, just sitting there, our mouths maybe two inches apart—just close enough to share the same breaths. He lifts his arm and hands me a perfect, freshly created blood-red rose. With no thorns. "I'll wait forever. Because what we have, it's worth it. It's worth anything." Abruptly he pushes to his feet, and the space in front of my face feels more than empty. And in a fierce voice he says, "And I'll fight to get it back."

CHAPTER TWENTY-SIX

Daniel looks up when I walk in fully suited. His annoyance is gone, but his expression still holds a question.

"I'm ready now," I say. At the very least, I'm fully awake after everything I've heard in the last hour.

I don't trust him. I'm not certain that I really ever did, even before hearing Thomas's story. I believed in Mark and Sammi. Maybe they were wrong, but I was inclined to believe they were *right*. Still am. Because of them I've never fully confided in Daniel, and even when I felt like we were developing some kind of camaraderie, I still wondered.

Now I do a hell of a lot more than just wonder. Could Daniel really be behind the *creation* of the virus?

Worse, could I have worked with him so long ago?

Did *we* make me immune?

First things first, there's got to be a way to figure out if it's true. If I *am* immune. I try to remember everything I ever learned in science and finally come up with what I hope is a decent plan. It's another hour and a half before Daniel leaves to use the restroom and I finally get my chance to put it into action.

As soon as he's stepped through the doorway into the first decontamination area, I create a pin and poke my fingertip. I close the hole in my glove as quickly as possible just in case Benson is wrong and I can get infected. A very tiny smear of blood sits on a slide, and I take a droplet with a micropipette before reaching for the disease samples. Even after three days I'm still squeamish about their origins, but I squelch the thought and mix the blood and virus on my slide.

I follow all of the procedures I've learned by rote, creating a stain, transforming the water into a fixative, and finally, with one more glance at the lab exit, I slide my sample into place.

The tiny droplets are still far too big, and I use my powers to strip away more and more layers of cells as I increase the magnification, until I'm left with a handful of single cells I can look at in detail.

I'm not sure just what it is I'm seeing, and I turn a knob to zoom to the level I'm accustomed to.

And my hands start to tremble.

There are the strands of viral DNA inside the nucleus of my blood cells. But instead of beginning the replication process, the double helix strands are coming apart. They're literally falling to pieces in front of my eyes. The nuclei in my blood cells aren't simply repressing the virus, they're *destroying* it!

It's true. I'm immune.

I'm immune, I'm a Transformist, and I'm the most powerful Earthbound in the world. That's got to be the secret. Or . . . three secrets. I'm just missing whatever connects them all together. And yet, something—a voice inside me that I'm petrified to listen to—tells me I still don't know everything.

What more could there possibly be? Everything is straining credulity as it is.

I hear the unmistakable sounds of Daniel returning, and I stare at the view before me, trying to memorize each part, knowing I have only seconds. The air lock releases with a hiss, and, with a twinge of regret, I transform the sample in front of me to the viral strand—so familiar now I can simply *create* it—and a strand of generic DNA that I'm certain won't align correctly with the split virus strand.

But it'll look legit enough to keep Daniel from suspecting anything.

Probably.

"That one didn't work," I say as soon as he comes to stand behind me. I transform the entire slide into a puff of air, the way I've been doing all day—less cleanup for the lab techs—before Daniel can get more than a glance at it.

He's silent for a brief moment, and guilt makes my heart race, but after another couple of seconds he sinks down onto the stool beside me and asks, "How are you holding up?"

"I'm doing okay," I say, hoping he doesn't hear how fast and shallow my breathing is. "It's just monotonous."

"Well, hopefully it will get exciting soon," he says. But I hear hopelessness in his voice. Just a touch. "We've had . . .

another attack. The closest of the three this time. I'm giving us twenty-four hours more—maybe I could stretch it to thirty-six if we're making progress—then we'll need to relocate."

"Where could be safer than here?" I ask, verging on panic.

"Usually nowhere," Daniel says with a sad smile. "But if they find us and there's any chance they could get in, destroy our progress, then someplace less protected but more secret would, I think, be safer. Temporarily."

Still, twenty-four hours. It feels oddly specific. One day. I can't help but wonder how much progress he thinks we could possibly make in those twenty-four hours, but the discovery I just made makes me want to work harder.

Except that we've been trying to find a DNA/RNA match-up for days and *nothing*. But after that one tiny experiment with my blood, I have something to work with! *If* I knew the science better.

Do I dare to tell Daniel about my blood? Surely it would help things move forward more quickly. Don't I owe the world that? Unless, as Thomas suspects, he has sinister intentions. If that's true, it seems more likely I owe it to the world to keep silent.

Then I remember what Thomas said this afternoon. That he was a doctor, a scientist.

That maybe *he* could help.

Maybe I can get Thomas into Benson's cell, and we can all share what we know.

Suddenly I'm incredibly impatient to get out of here and find Thomas.

"Daniel?" I say, my plan still forming in my head. "I'm

starving, and I know I can create food and all, but I thought maybe I'd go down to the cafeteria and clear my head for a little while and then come back up and work late tonight."

He looks at me for a long time, and I wonder if he can sense my lie. My half lie.

"I'm certainly not going to say no," Daniel says. "Truth is, you don't need my permission at all. I'm just concerned. I—*we* need you, and I don't want you to burn out."

"I won't," I promise, already pushing my stool back.

I get lucky and hear Alanna's faux shriek as I'm about halfway down the stairs to the main atrium, which is Renaissance-themed today, with the serving staff bustling around in either corsets or breeches. My first thought is how incredibly unfair that is for the women, until I see two clearly female staff members dressed up like the guys. Well, okay then. If the others *want* to wear corsets and not breathe, that's up to them.

Trying to be subtle I nudge up to Thomas and incline my head. He follows me to the buffet table, and I get a plateful of food as a prop while I whisper to him.

"Do you know where the holding cells are?"

"Are they down the plain white hallway south of our rooms?"

"Yes. Do you think you can meet me there in five or ten minutes?"

"Of course. Anything you need."

"There's a prisoner there I want you to talk to. About . . . well, I'll tell you there." I hear the squeal again, and this time it makes me grin. "Bring Alanna," I add. "Tell her we're going to need *a distraction*."

"Her specialty," Thomas says, peeling away from me.

I'm glad to be holding on to something to keep my hands from shaking as I walk toward the holding cells. When I pass the hallway that would take me to the room I technically still share with Logan, I can't bear to look. Later. All of that will have to come later.

I take a moment to catch my breath at the doors of the security wing—this is where everything went so wrong only twenty-four hours ago. But I don't have the time to indulge in my personal drama. I straighten my spine, raise my chin, and push through the doors. I don't really have to say anything to the security staff this time. They know I'm allowed to see Benson, and I imagine we all feel a little awkward after last night. The tall woman gives me a weak smile as I walk through the door, and somehow that makes me feel better. I like her.

Benson doesn't jerk up or even rise to his feet as I come in. He's slumped in his chair with his knees pulled up in a posture that could look defeated, but doesn't. It looks rebellious, like he's intentionally daring some teacher to walk by and tell him to put his feet on the floor.

"Have they fed you yet?" I ask without introduction.

"I got a sandwich an hour ago. You know, for a bunch of people who can make any kind of food they want, they certainly haven't manifested any degree of imagination with me."

He's clearly past the despairing stage and on to belligerence. He's miserable. I know it's my fault. But, well, it's *his* fault too.

Though I don't feel as angry as I did before. Like last night's blowup put us on even ground. Strangely, it feels like we're back at our library in Portsmouth and he's had a bad day.

To be honest, the comparison makes me want to cry, but I shove my feelings back for now and take a seat.

Benson hastily straightens up and knocks the table with his knee. Coffee slops over the edge of his mug and onto the table. "Sorry," he says, laying his napkin over the spill and soaking it completely. "I didn't think you were actually going to . . . to sit." He searches for something else to clean up the mess.

"Allow me," I say dryly. I've finally gotten to the point where I actually think to use my abilities. I flick one finger, and the sopped napkin and spilled coffee disappear entirely.

Replaced by a new, steaming cup.

Benson doesn't look as shocked as I expect, and I have to remind myself that he's spent half his life surrounded by Earthbounds.

And then lying to me about them.

Forget that for now. "Here," I say, setting the plate down between us. "There's plenty for two."

I guess I hadn't consciously realized that I had filled the plate not with my favorites, but Benson's. But when his eyes light up at the barbequed wings, the heap of raspberries, and a chunk of soft brie with crackers, I'm glad I did.

"I can't stay very long," I whisper, leaning in close.

"You don't have to explain," Benson says, popping two raspberries in his mouth. "I'll take your company for as long or short a time as you can give me." And he attempts a half grin, but things are still too unsettled between us, and it doesn't last very long.

"You were right," I say.

"About . . . what?" he asks. And he looks nervous.

"About my blood," I whisper after I swallow. "I'm—" I look around, then mouth the final word, shielding my mouth so that no one else can see. "Immune. I'm . . . I'm trusting you with this," I say, even as I think it rather odd that I'm trusting him with *anything*. But I don't tell him more. Hell, I haven't told *anyone* everything. But especially not him. Not after . . . just no. Only this one part that he helped with. That's not betraying anyone, is it?

"I'm glad," he whispers after a long pause. "So you definitely won't die."

"Not from the virus," I mutter.

"Good enough," he says softly.

I turn to look at him. I know I shouldn't, but I do. And see just what I expect.

Rawness.

Regardless of the lies his mouth may have said, Benson has never been able to lie with his eyes. I always knew when he was troubled, worried. I often knew when he was lying; I just always thought it was about something small.

Now his eyes are burning with hope.

And I put it there.

What have I done?

I can't look—not at something shining so brightly it's almost blinding. And not when a tiny part of me wishes I had the same ability to believe.

I hear the door click behind me and glance back to see Thomas's profile. Right on time. Now maybe I can get some answers. I face Benson again to explain our guest but swallow my words at the look of horror on his face.

I turn back to Thomas slowly, afraid of what I'm about to see. I should have kept looking at Benson. He nearly knocks me over as he flies by, and I let out a shriek as he plows into Thomas, knocking him flat on his back. Benson begins to pummel him with his fists as Thomas flails, trying to grab the fast-moving hands.

"Son of a bitch! I should have known. Lying bastard!"

All around me is a cacophony of chaos as the security personnel rush in and hands reach out and drag the two of them apart, Benson still shouting.

Alanna runs to Thomas—her entrance totally unnoticed in the scuffle—reaching him as he wipes a hand across his mouth, smearing the blood. He grabs Benson around the arm, and no one stops him. "It's okay," he says quietly. "I'll be fine. He'll be fine. It appears I need to have a little chat with my son."

CHAPTER TWENTY-SEVEN

Benson wrenches his arm away from Thomas. "Get your hands off me. I'm not your son. Not anymore."

"I don't give a damn what you think of me," Thomas hisses, grabbing him again, pulling him close in a sham embrace, and I barely hear the words Thomas rasps into his ear. "Shut the hell up or you are going to *ruin everything*." Something in Thomas's tone makes Benson still. Makes Alanna and me still too. A deadly edge that reminds me that I've only ever seen one side of this man.

The security people look at me, and I nod with as much decisiveness as I can muster. They appear wary, but ultimately retreat. As soon as the door closes, Thomas crosses his arms over his chest and says, "Would you like to tell me just what the hell you're doing here?"

"How about you tell me what the hell *you* are doing here?" Benson retorts.

Alanna snorts beside me. "Boys," she whispers.

They stand facing each other, and I see the resemblance now. I wouldn't have noticed the similarities between them without knowing to look, but they're both tall and have the same hair and eyes, and it makes me wonder if—subconsciously—that's why I liked Thomas more easily than Alanna, even *after* I knew her secret. Their profiles are similar as they stand, so tense, the blood smear on Thomas's face looking incredibly macabre. Benson is still lanky and thin, but in Thomas I can see the way he'll look when he's older and his shoulders fill out.

And I am *not* disappointed. I cough to cover my completely inappropriate grin.

The small room is filling with a tension so thick it seems to hold our bodies in suspension, when a click from the door releases the spell and we all turn with soft gasps.

It's Logan.

"Hell's sake," Alanna says. "Come in and close the door."

Logan steps fully into the room, and my heart slows.

Both of them. Together. Like worlds colliding, and the only possible result is that they crash and shatter.

I hear a clatter and a yelp and imagine my thoughts brought to life as I whirl back to where Benson has backed up and tripped over his chair. His face is white as he stares at Logan from where he lies sprawled on the floor. I'd forgotten that the last time Benson saw Logan's face it was in a two-hundred-year-old newspaper.

"What's going on?" Logan says quietly, taking in the expressions of dismay all around him. So much for keeping everything on the down low by meeting in a freaking prison.

"My *son* apparently decided to take one look at me and hit me in the face," Thomas says simply, as though that were all the explanation required.

"Then why is he staring at *me* like I'm a ghost?" Logan asks.

"Because you kind of are," I say. "The last time he saw you it was in a newspaper article about you as Quinn Avery."

Logan's eyes furrow. "You told him about Quinn Avery?" He's asking me, but he's glaring at Benson.

I swallow hard. I guess I didn't really explain everything last night. "Because he helped me find you." I hope I sound calm. Casual.

Logan just sighs in frustration . . . and maybe a touch of defeat.

"Oh no," Thomas says. "Please don't tell me you're the library friend from Portsmouth."

Benson wordlessly spreads his hands out to the side in a *here-I-am* gesture.

Thomas glances at Alanna. "This is why we should have insisted on photos. A simple description clearly doesn't cut it. If Mark and Sammi had sent us a photo I'd have realized it was Benson."

"This is *Benson*?" Alanna asks, wonder in her eyes. "Benson, I—"

"You are the last person I want to hear *anything* from," Benson says, cutting her off.

"Yeah, maybe you should leave, Alanna," I say, letting myself sound bossy and superior. "We have a *lot* to talk about. I'm sure Thomas told you why you were supposed to come, but I think you're no longer wanted in this room." *Please, please, please* let her understand. When I told Thomas I needed her to be a distraction I meant, like, making noise in here or something while we discussed biochemistry. Now I seriously need her to divert the security people's attention and keep them from hearing *anything*. Because I guarantee, after *that* little stunt, they're all paying attention on the other side of the two-way mirror.

Her eyes instantly change back into those of Alanna in disguise. "Fine," she snaps, sounding much like a two-year-old. *Thank goodness.* "But I'm not *leaving*. I'll be out there." She points at the two-way mirror, and I breathe a sigh of relief. "And I am *not* happy with you!" she shrieks as the door opens for her.

"Nice," Benson says, his voice pure acid. "Good choice, *Dad.*"

I see Thomas's jaw tighten, his instinct to defend Alanna— to let Benson know that whole thing was a sham. A facade. But after a second he calms down.

"Sammi never said your name," Thomas says, sounding angry but in control. "Maybe she didn't know it. But she didn't think you were important until you and Tavia *ran away* together, and then she just kept referring to you as the library boy." I realize Thomas is starting with stuff it *probably* doesn't hurt for the Curatoria to know. He takes a seat and gestures to me to make more chairs.

That's right; they don't know he's a Creator.

"You ran away with him?" Logan asks, his eyes flashing as he turns to me now.

"It wasn't like that." I protest, but at a pained noise from Benson I amend, "Okay, it was kind of like that."

"Tave!"

"Just sit!" I command, making a chair for him.

"I can't believe that was *you*," Thomas is still saying. "You're working for *them*?"

"He's not," I say, turning away from Logan's accusing eyes. "Not anymore."

"You expect me to believe that?" Thomas scoffs.

"And what was I supposed to do when you abandoned us and Mom went *psycho*?" Benson snaps. "Do you have any idea what happened after you left us?"

"Wait, did you know he was a Reduciate when you *ran off with him*?" Logan asks, more than a little caustically.

I shoot my eyes toward the two-way mirror, hoping Alanna is doing her job. This is not the kind of stuff I need spread all over the Curatoria headquarters. "No, I *didn't* know," I say between clenched teeth, "and he's not really. And to be honest, it kind of *is* Thomas's fault!"

Finally everyone stops talking and just looks at me. "Okay, thirty-second story, and then we *move on*." I point at Thomas. "*You* left your family, Benson's mom went crazy and moved them all in with the Reduciates. Benson traded helping them get me for his freedom. When he realized he . . . he just couldn't do it, it was too late, and everyone *died*. Okay?" I turn to Logan and add, almost pleading, "Then he was at the Reduciata prison with us and told the Curatoriates about the painting that gave *you* your memories back, just like I said before.

"And now he's here and brought a whole lot of attention to me and may have ruined everything because he's still as

242

hot-tempered as he was when he was eight," Thomas finishes for me, but now it's in a whisper, and our heads are all close together.

"Wonder where I get *that* from," Benson mutters.

Thomas glares but says nothing.

Fabulous. How am I going to confess that I arranged for everyone to meet here because I *trust* Benson?

And that they're all going to have to trust him too?

"That's *enough*," I snap as quietly as I can. "With luck Alanna is throwing a huge fit behind that mirror and covering up everything we're saying. But even she can't hold them off for long. So listen to me, all of you. We are working on something big here. Something that may literally mean saving the entire world from destruction. I don't care what kind of drama is in *all* of our pasts." I swallow hard, knowing everything I'm saying applies to me as well. "We *have* to put it to the side. Everything," I say, glaring at Benson specifically now. "Finding a cure for this virus—particularly having now seen the destruction that occurs when it kills an Earthbound—is more important than anything any of us are feeling." My chin shakes, and I clamp my jaw down on it. "Myself included."

The room is silent as Logan glares at me, Thomas glares at Benson, and Benson? Well, he glares at everyone. I realize he's truly the loser here. He has no one. He's not aware that Logan and I are having issues; all he knows is his estranged father is here, happy with his new wife, and I'm here, happy with my old lover.

I clear my throat, needing to end this awful tension.

"Thomas, Benson actually brought me some intelligence from the Reduciates. That's why we're here—because he needs to be a part of this. I believe we can trust him."

Thomas's eyes dart to me, the temptation of something new pulling his attention away from the son he hasn't seen in over ten years.

Oh please, please, please let Alanna be screeching at the top of her lungs right at this moment, I think to myself. Then finally I get it out. "I'm immune."

Thomas almost chokes in his surprise. "But . . . how . . . you're sure?"

"I've tested it, and it's true." I explain what I did in the lab. "I feel like the thing with my blood should help," I tell him. "But I don't know how to *use* it."

Thomas steeples his fingers and sways back and forth a few times.

"You've been looking for ways to directly disable the RNA?" he asks. When I nod he says, "Well, what if you isolated the proteins in your blood that repel the virus and then replicated them and inserted them into the former vaccine?"

"Would that work?"

"It's the theory behind the new advances against AIDS. Scientists are making strides with that approach. I think it's worth a shot."

I worry my lip with my teeth for a few seconds before I say, "Should I tell Daniel?"

The silence again.

"I recommend no. He was the one who brought that girl to

my practice forty years ago and then had me killed. I can't believe that after that he would do *anything* good with this kind of information. Plus, if you don't tell him, only *you* will be able to replicate your work."

"That's what I was thinking too." It won't be easy hiding it, but maybe . . . "Benson, is there anything else you overheard?"

"I wish. If there were I would tell you. Marianna just kept saying that you were immune and that they needed you and that they were going to start testing you immediately."

"It's something," I say with a little smile. Enough to make him feel useful, not enough to make Logan feel spurned. It's not an easy balance. "Okay, tell me what to look for," I say to Thomas. I conjure up a notebook and pen, and Thomas begins drawing and explaining chemistry terms I barely understand.

"When you see it," he says, pointing to his drawing, "you'll recognize it."

I shove the notebook into my pocket and take a deep breath. "I better get back. I told Daniel I'd work late tonight." I didn't eat much, but my stomach is roiling now, and I don't think I could if I wanted to. Besides, the plate's full of Benson's favorite foods. I'll leave it for him.

They open the cell door, and though one of the men looks askance at the food I left in there, I promise him it's safe and ask them to leave it for Benson. Meanwhile, Thomas is doing a good job of pretending to pacify a grumpy Alanna, and Alanna is doing a damn good job of pretending to still be angry.

I do wonder what's going through her head right now, after suddenly meeting her husband's human child. The look in her eyes before Benson chewed her out suggests to me that she'd like the opportunity to get to know him. I'm not sure that will happen though.

Logan and I are about ten feet from the main entrance to the security wing when the doors burst open behind us and Alanna emerges in a huff, Thomas close behind. "That was terrifying," she whispers the second the doors slam shut. "One second of silence at the wrong time . . ." Her voice trails off, and she shakes her head.

"Thanks for doing it," I tell her. "Do you think they bought the charade?"

"Oh please, everyone in this place will believe *anything* I do as long as it's repulsive or immature," she says wearily. "It didn't look like they were recording anything, just listening. And I refused to pipe down despite repeated requests to do so."

"It'll be over soon." *One way or another.* "I have to get back to the lab. Thomas gave me some good ideas to work on. Thomas," I look up at him, my voice barely audible, "if this works, we'll have a vaccine *soon*. Maybe tomorrow, or the next day. And once we have it, I *have* to leave this place—Logan and I both. Will . . . will you be coming with us?"

"Absolutely," Thomas says with fervor.

"Alanna?"

"I wish I could have left months ago."

So simple. So easy. One in mind and purpose. I wish my life were that way.

"When the time comes to leave, I think it will be fast," I warn. "And dangerous. I don't believe that Daniel has any intention of actually letting me go. We may have to fight our way out. Still want in?"

"Of course. We've always had escape plans in place—we'll just broaden one."

"Thank you." I chance a quick glance at Logan. "I'll be bringing Benson with me. I got him into this—it's only fair that I pull him out as well."

"That does seem the decent thing to do," Thomas says tightly, and at least Logan doesn't voice a protest.

"I expect you to do everything you can to protect him as you would me."

"He's my son, Tavia."

"That hasn't mattered for the last ten years, has it?"

His silence tells me my words are justified.

"You have to accept that you bear some responsibility for whom he was forced to become," I say softly.

"I know," is all he says, as Alanna holds tightly to his arm.

"He almost let them kill me because you left him with no explanation," I press. "Because you just took off and never looked back. If you had kept tabs on him, the Reduciates could never have done this."

"I didn't think I needed to," Thomas says weakly. "Perhaps the greatest mistake we gods have always made is underestimating humans."

"Thomas . . . how could you just walk away?" I know this isn't the time, but I need to understand.

"How can you even ask?" he says, looking almost offended now. "You know how it feels."

"No I don't," I reply, and I don't dare look at Logan as I say it—don't want to see his eyes. "I have little more than a normal human brain now. I don't know even a *fraction* of what you take for granted."

"Tavia, you can't think of yourself that way. You—"

But I don't give him a chance to finish. "Spare me your empty words, Thomas. I'm *broken*. But even broken, there is no Earthbound in the world who can truly face me. Not Daniel, not Marianna, and certainly not you."

"Are you threatening me?" Thomas asks, his eyes wary.

Am I? The truth is, I'm not sure exactly where all this nerve comes from. But something inside me wonders if it's Sonya. Standing up for the chance to live that she never got. Not that I'll ever really know her—not in this life anyway. "No. Not really. But I will protect Benson, Thomas. I will *not* underestimate him. All I'm saying is don't underestimate *me* if you let him die."

Thomas is still and silent for several seconds before he nods. "With my life then."

I fix them all with a hard gaze. Even Logan. "Then we are five," I whisper. "And when I finish this, we all get the hell out of here."

"Tavia, wait a second," Alanna says, stopping me. "We have something for you." She pulls a slightly crumpled bit of paper from her pocket with two names written on it, followed by two long numbers.

"Greta Heindlund and Elysa Meyer?" I ask, the name *Greta* setting off veritable explosions of hope in my mind. Sonya thought Greta was the key. Could it be the same Greta? Surely.

"You," Alanna confirms. "In your past lives. I may have done a bit of hacking in the process of spying, and, well, they have files on them here. And *artifacts* in the vault. The vault is so powerful but irreplaceable that Daniel has to give permission personally to let anyone in. I don't know if you can get around that but . . ." She shrugs helplessly. "It's *something*. Maybe— maybe after all you've done he'll do you this one favor."

But we both know how unlikely that is.

Still.

My fingers grip the paper, and I can hardly breathe. Two more lives I have a chance to get back. Clues to my past—why I am the way I am. Once more I curse the loss of Sonya's braid in my backpack, but this is amazing. "It's worth a try," I say, my breath heavy. "Thank you." I throw my arms around her and hug her tightly. "Thank you so much." I wipe away sudden tears of gratitude and take a ragged breath. "I have to go." I let out a little bark of laughter. "Thank you." And I spin and hurry down the hall.

Logan trails alongside me, and I know he has questions. There's no avoiding them. We've only just turned the corner before he asks, "Did you actually run off with him?"

"People were trying to kill me, Logan," I say irritably. "We didn't run off, we ran *away*. There's a difference."

"Tavia," he says, one hand wrapping carefully around my upper arm, pulling me back. "Please, it's killing me inside. First you said he wasn't your boyfriend and then that he was in love with you, but a Reduciate. And now I find out you two ran away together? What was he to you? Really. The *whole* truth."

I stop and look at him, and I simply don't have the emotional will to tell one more lie. My shoulders slump, and I lean back against the wall for help staying upright. "He was everything to me," I whisper.

"And now?" He doesn't meet my eyes anymore.

"I still don't know," I admit.

Logan's hand drops from my arm, and I expect him to argue—to make a case for himself—but he looks beaten. "I wish . . . I wish—"

"Logan," I interrupt, and finally he looks up. "Can't we just save the world first?"

"My world's not worth saving without you," he replies. Then he turns and walks away.

CHAPTER TWENTY-EIGHT

I round the final corner before the lab and run into something. Some*one*.

"Sorry," I say. "Going too fast." But my jaw drops and I suck in a loud breath before I can stop myself. It's the same guy I caught looking at me before. I'm sure of it. Those blond eyelashes, the rust-red hair.

I try to hide my reaction as he mumbles a similar apology, and I don't look back as I duck into the lab.

"Daniel?" I say as I walk through the air locks. "Do you have someone watching me?"

He looks up at me, his face completely blank. "Someone watching you?" he repeats as if he's confused by the question.

"Seriously, I need to know."

He hesitates, then says slowly, "I don't have anyone *specifically* watching you, but all of my staff are keeping a basic eye on you. It's for your own protection."

"You don't have a guy assigned to tail me?" I press.

His eyes are instantly alert. "*Is* there someone specific following you?"

I say nothing, but I know my silence speaks volumes.

He seems nervous now—no, a cross between nervous and excited. "Could you point him out if you saw him again?"

"Probably." Can the word "probably" really be a total lie? I slip onto my stool feeling super uncomfortable, and I have the strange feeling I've just given Daniel information I don't want him to have. But I can't see how. Everything is moving too quickly. I've got instructions in my pocket for what to try next with my blood, but I can't just whip them out in front of Daniel.

What I really need is time alone in the lab.

Maybe I can get two birds with one stone. "Daniel, after we're through tonight can I go down to the vault?"

He blinks at me like he doesn't understand.

"I've remembered two of my names," I explain. "And I heard you keep our old belongings in a vault here. If you have stuff for these two, I could get some of my memories back." I hold my breath.

"Out of the question."

Despite everything, I confess, I didn't expect him to just flat-out refuse me with no explanation. "W-what?"

But there's been no mistake. He's shaking his head. "No. I can't allow it."

Fury bubbles at the top of my throat. "Why the hell not? It isn't your life. Your things. They're my *memories*!" I don't realize I'm shouting until I see the techs from the other sections of the laboratory peering through the windows at me.

At us. It's okay. The angrier I seem, the better. Though really, I'm not pretending much. If I had those artifacts—the memories—surely *everything* would make so much more sense.

"Calm down," Daniel says, his eyes darting back and forth.

"I don't care if they hear," I lash out, my voice still loud.

"I *do*. I don't want them to misunderstand me the way you obviously have."

I cross my arms over my chest and shoot a simmering glare at him, waiting for him to explain.

"Tavia, this is monotonous work, but exceptionally *precise* work as well. Look at how weary you were all day after having a fight with Logan. When you get emotionally riled up it's harder for you to give requisite attention to your task." He takes a few calming breaths. "I shouldn't have spoken quite so strongly. I'm not saying *never*; I'm saying not right now. Not *today*. I don't know what happened in your lives in the past, but getting an entire lifetime of memories back is not only going to exhaust you, it'll throw your concentration out the window. But we can't have that because . . . because I need you, Tavia. I need you one hundred percent here for one more day." He straightens. "And so does everyone else in the world." He swallows hard and says, almost to himself, "We're running out of time. I was counting on you being faster."

His words reach my ears, and I feel like I've been slapped. He was counting on me being *faster*? "And so, what? You're holding my memories like some kind of carrot on a stick? You think *that* will keep me calmer?"

My heart pounds so loudly I can hardly hear anything else.

He puts a hand on my shoulder, and I jerk away, too steeped in indignation.

"Tavia, as soon as we're done, I will escort you down *personally* and help you find everything we have on your past lives. I'll talk to our specialist, cross-reference any possibilities. I will do *whatever you want*. But I need you to be here with me, fully, until we crack this thing."

I know it makes sense. I just watched our group almost fall apart with the revelations that Thomas is Benson's father and that Benson and I had a relationship. Daniel's entire argument is sound, but knowing that doesn't stop me from being furious.

"Please, Tavia." He gestures at my stool. "Please come back to work. Every minute—every *moment*—gets us closer."

With my hands still shaking, I take the two steps to my stool and drop down onto it. I raise my hand to the counter, ready to accept another slide, but my hands are shaking too much. I try to keep my head clear—to remember that I figured he wouldn't let me visit the vault. That he wouldn't trust me to get my memories back.

That I brought it up *now* for a reason.

Finally I manage to simmer down, and I grasp for an icy calm as I set the next step of my plan in motion. "Have you eaten?" I ask quietly.

"Excuse me?" Daniel asks.

"Maybe you should go eat," I say, keeping my voice level.

He stands, his eyes very slightly narrowed, looking at me in question. Wondering if I'm really saying what he thinks I'm saying.

I meet his eyes, for once unafraid. "I'll calm down faster if *you're not here*," I explain, and hope he doesn't see my other reason shining out of my eyes.

He looks like he wants to argue, but after a few seconds he sighs, and his entire body either slumps or relaxes—I'm not sure which. "I suppose I owe you that much," he says quietly. "And I *should* eat anyway. I'll be back in an hour." He pauses just before pushing the button that will let him leave. "I'm sorry," he whispers. But I don't believe it. Not after what Thomas told me, not after his refusal, not after the way he accused me of not being fast enough. I have to work with him—after the disaster in the Pacific I can't refuse. But I don't have to like it.

I watch his back all the way through the double air locks, then I transform the thick plastic over my jeans into a long slit. If I were normal, this would put me at great risk for catching the virus, but I'm immune, so I don't care. Putting on the hazmat suit is nothing more than a ruse to keep Daniel from knowing the truth.

Especially now.

I pull the notes Thomas drew for me out of my pocket and put them on the far side of my microscope where even the techs who sometimes peer through the single thick glass window between the labs wouldn't be able to see them. I don't have much time, and I can't afford to waste a second.

I dot several slides with my blood and prep them all to save time later. As I zoom in, I look for the landmarks that Thomas drew.

He's right, the proteins are pretty distinctive. However,

there are some subtle differences in mine, and I wonder if I'm literally *seeing* the result of my immunity. And probably that unknown element that allows me to transform. To never grow weaker.

In a moment of insight I wonder if this is how we all used to be. Back when we were Earthmakers. When we were immortal. I wonder if when we were cursed, this strange chemical I'm seeing was simply taken away.

But I can't chase that train of thought. I'll be lucky if I can get through all of this before Daniel gets back. I follow the directions provided—isolating different strands of proteins—and begin testing them in much the same way that Daniel and I have been doing with the DNA strands. Only there are *far* fewer possibilities. Within about twenty minutes I've found a protein that seems to repel the virus—or at least prevent the replication within the nuclei.

I force my breathing to remain calm as I slowly test all of my samples against one another. I'm just finishing my comparisons when I hear the first air lock hiss to announce Daniel's return. I shove Thomas's notes into my pocket and seal up the hole in my hazmat suit.

I didn't expect to have such positive results so quickly. I'm not sure what to do. The sad fact is, Daniel's got the lab, and I *need* the lab to make this vaccine happen. I'm going to have to tell him something.

Won't I?

My other option is to run off with Thomas and find another lab somewhere and do this on our own. But how many hundreds of thousands of people will die during the time that will take? Millions, if one of the victims is an Earthbound.

There's simply no time. I'm going to have to tell Daniel part of the truth so I can keep working in his lab.

But which part?

I have ten seconds to decide if I need to destroy all my samples or not.

The million-dollar question is, does Daniel know enough science to realize what I'm doing simply by seeing the display on my microscope? Or has he only learned the barest sliver needed to do his work like I have? I close my eyes, send a plea out to the universe that he's more on the sliver side of things, and continue to work with my blood sample.

I'm not sure what I expect Daniel to do. To say. But apparently he doesn't know either. He just slides onto his stool in silence. He hardly even glances at my display. Maybe he just trusts me so implicitly it doesn't matter.

Trusts my ignorance, I assume.

It's a full fifteen minutes before he asks, "Any progress?" in a scratchy voice.

"Maybe," I say slowly, dragging the word out. I think a half lie will keep him from questioning me too hard. Keep him working with me. Ultimately, we're both trying to get a vaccine out of this. As long as our end-goals are the same, I'll have to deal with not knowing his other motives.

He sit bolt upright. "What do you mean?"

"I . . . I . . . ." *How to explain this?* "I kind of stumbled on a protein that I think is repelling the virus."

I hear him suck in a quick breath and then the squeak of wheels as he draws closer. "Show me." I start a new slide, taking the isolated protein and pairing it with the virus sample. The nucleus attempts to create new viral DNA, but when the mitochondria begin to build it into the proteins, the proteins simply resist. We watch as the tide turns slowly, very slowly, but soon the message returns to the nucleus that the foreign RNA is broken, and the cell reverts to creating its usual, uninfected DNA.

"Blessing of the gods," Daniel says, his voice barely more than a hushed whisper. "Do it again."

For an hour we test the isolated protein on three different samples. Daniel's right, this simple protein won't be enough to *fight* an already infected host—it simply acts too slowly—but it will work as a vaccine for those still untouched.

"Here, here," Daniel says, his excitement bubbling over as he removes a tray of slides from a drawer beside him. Even though I'm not sure what to think of him, I can't help but catch his enthusiasm. We really are making progress! "These are the other samples we have of the virus. Different mutations. We have to test them all. We can't lose our heads over this." His words attempt to be somber, but I can hear the nerves in his voice.

It's after midnight before we finish testing all the samples, and I can barely see straight when Daniel flips off my microscope.

"We need sleep," he says, rubbing his hands together. "This is step one—and it's a big step—but we still have more to do. We have to figure out which proteins in the vaccine to transform into this new one, and then we need to find out how you can replicate it and what dose we'll need and—" He stops talking and takes a shaky breath. "But this is the first step. Probably the biggest step. It's the breakthrough we needed," he adds softly, and for a moment it sounds like he's talking to someone else. "This will keep her safe until I can find her. I know it. It has to be." Then he looks into my eyes. "You've done wonderfully. I knew you could do it," he says, although in my heart of hearts, I'm not sure he did.

But I keep my doubts to myself.

I keep one crucial discovery to myself too.

When I first started testing blood in the lab, I used a tiny drop of infected blood. And even though the isolated protein can repel the virus, when it has finished its job, it leaves the tissue sample unchanged—immune to further outbreaks, but not different.

But when I tried a drop of my blood, it *changed* the sample. The strange but subtle differences between my blood proteins and Thomas's drawing? When I put my blood into the sample, it gets that extra . . . I don't even know what it is.

But instinctively, I know what it *must* be: the chemical that makes me a Transformist, that makes me so powerful, that makes me immune. All of them wrapped up in that tiny something I can only see on the world's most powerful microscope.

When I use my blood, the whole sample *changes* to produce that altered substance. The sample literally becomes *just like my blood*.

Logically, even a *human* could become like me with one injection. I understand Rebecca now in a way that I never have before. This is something I can't tell *anyone*. A secret so dangerous it can't be set free. Not even to Logan or Benson.

If I'm right—and if the Reduciata ever found out—they would kill the entire world just to get my blood.

CHAPTER TWENTY-NINE

I'm too tired to talk to Logan—to keep yet another secret from him—so even though I know he'll be hoping I'm coming back to our room, I don't. I need another night to myself. In my old room. In my own space. A place that belongs to *me*, me and not Rebecca.

Again, I wish I'd never decorated the room Logan and I shared that way. Because I'm not Rebecca. Over the last few days that has become so clear. I *was* Rebecca. I know that. But I'm not her anymore. I'm different. And Logan's going to have to accept that.

I reach a line in the carpet and start counting steps to where the room I created is sitting behind a very plain wall—hidden from sight. I've counted my ninth step and am about to transform the wall back into a door when Daniel's voice yanks me out of my stupor.

"Tavia, what are you doing here? I thought you were going to bed. You need your rest."

My brain is moving so slowly that I can't come up with an immediate response. "I-I-I just want to go"—and then I realize where else this hallway leads to—"check on Benson real quick. Look in on him. Make sure he's okay."

Daniel nods shortly, but he seems nervous. "Just be fast. Get to sleep. We have a big day tomorrow."

"Yeah." I walk past where my comfy bed is waiting for me with more than a little regret. Now I *have* to go see Benson.

As I walk I can't help but wonder, what was *Daniel* doing there? Of course, that's not something I could ask. Hopefully he'll be gone when I come back in five minutes.

Fact is, I don't even have to talk to Benson. He doesn't have to know I'm there. A quick glance into the two-way mirror and then I'll go.

And I won't have been completely lying.

I push through the familiar doors to the prison area, but rather than finding the serene, tired environment I expect, I discover three security people waiting inside. All now familiar, if not friendly, faces.

"Perfect," the woman says. "We were just trying to decide whether or not we should attempt to fetch you." She rolls her eyes. "He's been asking for you for hours."

"Why?" I ask as she begins to unlock the door.

"He won't say," the woman says with a dismissive wave of her hand.

"I'm shocked," I mutter. I glance through the window and

see Benson pacing—more like stalking—from one end of the tiny room to the other.

I walk in, and the door closes behind me, but I just stand there, silent.

Benson stops and sighs in relief. "Thank you for coming. I wasn't sure if you would be . . . sleeping." He shrugs. "I swear I don't even know if it's day or night anymore."

I don't tell him that it's two in the morning. That I didn't respond to his request. That I didn't want to see him at all. That seeing him makes every emotion in my body rage like a swollen river.

Each time I've come to see him he seems more like himself. His library self. The self I was so in love with.

Maybe am still in love with.

Seeing him like this breaks my heart all over again. I stand with my arms crossed over my chest as much to keep my fingers from reaching for him as anything.

"Did you finish your project?"

I close my eyes. "Not quite. But we've passed the biggest hurdle."

"Thomas—my dad—I hate calling him that. Anyway, after you left he came back to talk with me. He told me that . . ." His voice trails off, and he just stands there. Silent and helpless.

"What, Benson?" I say, too harshly. I don't mean it. My exhaustion is getting the better of me.

"So, you know how you got rid of your scar?"

I don't know what I was expecting, but that wasn't it. My

chest spasms, and I'm sucking in loud breaths, trying to stay in control as I consider everything that lead to that decision.

He raises his arms—clearly wanting to comfort me—but I hold up a hand and he stops. Stands back until I'm in control again. "Yes, I did," I say finally, ignoring the fact that I was freaking out only seconds earlier. "We've discussed this."

"Could you . . . could you do it for me?"

My eyebrows lower. I don't understand.

"My—my mark," he clarifies. "Could you take it away?"

I think of the bone-deep weariness that even my abilities can't ease. "Tonight?" I ask in a small voice.

He steps so close I have to steel myself against moving away.

Or closing the tiny gap.

"Thomas says you've decided to take me with you when you run," he whispers, always wary for listeners. "The truth is, my chances of dying tomorrow are pretty damn high," he says, his voice gravelly. "I don't have the protections you do."

"I won't let anyone—"

"I know," he interrupts, then reins in his temper. "But do you really think you can just walk out of here? That they're going to simply let you go?"

I'm silent. I can't count how many times I've asked myself that. I know we're not going to simply be leaving—we'll be escaping. Part of me is glad he knows it too. He'll be prepared.

"I just . . . I just don't want to die as a Reduciate. Surely you can understand that."

I can. And he knows how much his mark has meant to me—irrational or not.

"It's got to be a small thing for you, isn't it?" he asks, his eyes pleading with me. "Please?"

"Of course I will, Ben," I whisper.

He looks like he's about to cry for a second before he nods stoically and turns to the side.

I was too distracted to realize what would inevitably come next.

He reaches for his shirt, and I can't pry my eyes away as he peels it off, revealing his chest, bare from the waist up. He looks up at me after setting his shirt on the bed, and we're both still as a veritable lightning bolt travels between us. His eyes darken with wanting, and I know he felt it too.

"Turn around," I whisper, everything in my body shouting at me to go to him—to throw myself against his skin and soak up that tangible warmth only he has ever been able to provide. He turns, and I'm eye level with his black mark.

It looks ugly on his skin. Not for what it actually looks like, but for what it *means*. It's not simply that he spent most of his life living in a Reduciate compound, it's that he was a thrashing twelve-year-old boy, abandoned by everyone he loved. The lines are thick, but not crisp, and where the circle of the ankh curls out into the shepherd's crook, I see a wave where the needle must have slipped, just a fraction of an inch. In my head I can hear Benson screaming, both from pain and from outrage. The scene is so clear in my imagination that I want to pull my hand back from the dark ink, as though it had a life of its own.

"Kneel," I say, but I have to clear my throat and repeat myself before the word is understandable. He drops to his knees, and I pull up a chair. I sit close to him, my thighs on either side of his hips, barely brushing him, even though the brief contact feels like touching a hot iron.

I look at his shoulder and picture what his skin would look like without the mark. Then, with two fingers, I reach out to touch it.

And stop a hair's breadth away.

Can I touch him without losing control? After such a long day, can I be strong for five more minutes?

I brace myself, but the feel of his soft skin under my fingertips still makes a shudder of ecstasy travel down my spine.

Focus, I tell myself. *Just paint*.

I make little brushing motions with my fingers, and like a gummy eraser, the black mark slowly smudges and then disappears.

It can't have taken more than a minute or so, but the sensations that jolt through my body each time I touch him make it feel like an hour.

"It's done," I say, and my voice shakes even uttering those two tiny words.

"Is it gone?" Benson asks, and in his hesitation, I know he can hardly believe such a thing could be true.

"Completely."

He drops all the way to the floor now, his chin almost touching his chest. "Thank you," he says, and it's whispered like a prayer.

He turns to look at me and seems to realize for the first time what an intimate position we're in—his torso nestled between my thighs. I know I should stand, walk away, put distance between us, but his eyes paralyze me as he turns all the way around. His fingers tremble as he runs his hands very slowly up my legs as though he can't help himself.

My thighs, my hips, my waist, then his fingers are gripping my ribs and his breathing is shallow and fast.

I can't move. I can't think. No, I can think one thing. Only one. How much I want him. How much my body needs to be next to his.

How long it's been since I held him and called him mine.

My will is splintering, cracking, and I know in seconds there'll be nothing left and I'll be standing in a room with Benson, with his shirt already gone.

I'm on my feet before I can let myself regret my decision. I almost shove him over getting away. I can't be feeling this, not now. Not tonight. My lungs are on fire as I back away, my hands held up in front of me.

"I can't . . . I . . . I just—" But I can't speak coherently. I fumble for the doorknob behind me and fling the door open, nearly barreling over the woman who unlocked it. I cross through the doorway, and though I hear Benson call my name, I slam the door against it.

And I run.

CHAPTER THIRTY

I shove the heavy door closed and press my back against it as though I were barring something out.

"Tavia?" Logan rises from the chair he was apparently lounging in, his feet bare, his belt off.

Where am I? I ran to Logan. I fled to our shared room. Our shared world.

That realization hits me like a boulder. I escaped to *Logan*.

"I—I—" Now that I'm here, I'm not sure how to explain why I came.

What I wanted. What the hell I was doing.

But on some level, it makes sense. For as long as I can remember, Logan—in so many lives—has meant safety to me. But what kind of safety is it tonight? Safety from Benson? Safety from myself?

"I came home," I whisper. And even though the words feel

strange coming from my lips, they feel so true. I *know* that this is where I belong. This is where Fate intends me to be. Not just in this room—with Logan. With my eternal lover.

I slide into his arms with an intrinsic naturalness that comes from thousands of lifetimes of doing this exact thing.

We fit like puzzle pieces.

A tremor of guilt ripples through me because I know that I might fight this fated joining another day. Assert my independence and insist that I *do* have a choice—that I can change my destiny. But today I'm out of energy to fight.

Today I will be precisely what the universe wants me to be.

And the universe wants me in Logan's arms.

Tonight I hold nothing back. I always have before. Even that first night after his memories came back—so full of bliss and delight—I held back. Because even though the feelings were all there, Logan was a stranger. And I knew it.

Since then there have been doubts, worries. They were always present, gnawing at the edges of my subconscious.

They aren't gone. If anything, they've multiplied.

But tonight I make believe.

Tonight I *pretend* they're not there.

Tonight I give him everything.

The red numbers on the clock read 5:27 when I slip out of bed early and transform Logan's shirt into my own clothes.

I'm silent.

Because I'm sneaking away.

It's easy to think your reasons are good enough in the dim,

seductive darkness of the night. But even underground, without the sun, sunrise is illuminating, laying bare my secrets, fears, and justifications.

I look at Logan, still sleeping heavily, his profile barely visible in the murky darkness. I feel like I've used him. And even though I know he wouldn't mind—he's as bad as Benson at taking whatever he can get—I don't want him to look me in the eye. To see that I'm unsure again.

To know that even as I lay in his arms last night, I dreamed of Benson.

So I make myself soft socks, pick up my worn Chucks, and slink away before he can wake up and catch me.

I descend the wide stairs to the atrium, where a couple of people are working on creating what looks like a huge Viking ship on one wall, and, without pausing to check it out, I go directly to hallway that will take me to the replica of my Michigan room.

I can't face Daniel yet.

Can't face anyone.

I drop into my twin bed fully clothed and sleep fitfully for a few more hours, plagued by nightmares. Shapeless forms chase me, their skin mottled with pox, like the diseases of the past. Right before I wake they catch me. They surround me, their reddened skin breaking and oozing, fingernails raking my arms, my face. They gather closer, closer, suffocating me, more and more of them, piling on top of me until I can't breathe. Until the weight of them crushes the air from my lungs, breaks my bones, presses my insides.

I gasp for air as I sit up. Every part of my body is tingling.

I'm not sure what time it is now, but there's no way I'm going to get back to sleep. My shirt is soaked with sweat, and my sheets are clammy.

I can't go back to Logan. Not just *now*—not ever. And not because of our differences or his lack of understanding about humans. Oddly, it seems like none of that matters anymore.

It's because of Benson.

I don't have that universe of love to return to Logan. I'm not convinced I'm even *capable* of it without the eternity of memories that Logan has. That I'm *supposed* to have. The love I have for him has the same finite limits of any human.

And with so little to give to begin with, it's not fair to offer him only a fraction of that sparse portion. Even if I had all of my heart to give, it would feel paltry in comparison.

But to offer him only the half of my heart that's truly his would be downright insulting.

And only one half belongs to him.

The other still belongs to Benson. I know that now.

I lean my head against the mirror and feel the soothing cold spread from my forehead to my cheeks, slowly cooling away the fear from my nightmare.

Although it's almost as terrifying to admit to myself that I still love Benson. Love the boy who betrayed me and got my guardians killed. But I can't deny this feeling. Or the way my heart wants to beat out of my chest when I see him, the sympathy I can't keep myself from feeling.

The want I felt deep in my belly when I saw him without his shirt on last night. This morning?

271

It's like the whole confrontation in Camden never happened.

I'm so quick to forgive him. Is that a good thing or not? Does it make me more goddess-like?

Or more human?

And which do I want to be?

I glance at my clock. 6:54. Somewhat early morning, but not extreme. I don't want to go to the lab yet, but suddenly this room feels too small. Claustrophobic. Not enough space for the explosion of my emotions.

I decide I need a kitchen.

I transform the back wall into air to make sure I don't run into anything important, then I carefully transform a few more beams, hoping I'm not about to really disturb the architecture.

One final beam lets in a streak of light, and I realize I've hit another room. I guess I should have expected that. People don't just build enormous walls full of empty space. I'm about to fill in the hole before anyone notices what I've done, but curiosity gets the better of me.

I stoop down and peer through.

It takes a second for my eyes to focus. Then I'm on my feet, my hands tearing at the wall for a few seconds before I remember my powers. The hole becomes Tavia-sized, and I step through into the battered remains of a familiar prison, the faint scent of smoke lingering in the air.

"Benson," I breathe, rushing forward. But his cell is empty. No, no, it's the *wrong* cell. In *way* the wrong part of this building. I look around and realize that although it looks a lot like Benson's prison—has nearly the same layout—it's not the same.

A second security wing, maybe? Hidden in the walls of the Curatoria? But . . . it's been destroyed. Like something exploded.

All over the shiny white tile.

Oh gods.

I can't breathe as I stare around me, turning in a circle to take in the scene. The space where the walls of a prison used to be, three white squares of floor, each smaller than the next, three matching two-way mirrors.

I know what I'm going to find even as I look over my shoulder at the wall behind me, but still my heart pounds at the sight of the huge black Reduciata symbol.

This isn't Benson's prison, it was *mine*.

As soon as the realization washes over me it feels so obvious. To my right I can see the path of destruction I made during my escape. And though that wall has been made whole again, I'm pretty sure if I were to walk over and make it disappear I would find the open space the helicopter took off from.

I remember something from the previous night, and everything snaps into place. Daniel got nervous when he saw me hanging around here. He was worried I'd find this place. That's why he sent me on my way!

He must know about it. Know that's where we were held. Of course he knows—he's spent the last three days convincing me that he knows *everything* that happens here. But . . . but it doesn't make any sense. Why would they *pretend* I was in a Reduciata prison?

But in an instant I understand. Benson said they were going to test me. *This* was the test. *Creating* the sledgehammer didn't work. *Creating* the bomb didn't work. What finally got me out of there was when I *transformed* the prison bars and walls.

That perfectly timed rescue wasn't timed.

It wasn't a rescue.

It was a sign that I had passed.

The painting. Now I know what was bothering me about it. The painting was waiting for me in our room when we arrived at the headquarters. But Benson said he arrived in a helicopter *after* us. That's what was bugging me when I talked about the painting with Daniel. The painting shouldn't have been able to make it to the headquarters ahead of us.

Unless someone could simply walk it down the hallway while we hovered pointlessly in the air.

I hate that I didn't see it before. But even if I had, how could I jump from that to all *this*? But it's proof that Daniel knew.

My whole body sags in despair as I stare around the destroyed cell. This changes everything.

Everything.

And yet . . .

I breathe in and out, trying to catch the tail of a stream of thought that's making me nervous. Finally, as the adrenaline begins to settle, it solidifies in my head.

If it was all just a Curatoriate test, then why was Benson there? And Sunglasses Guy?

There were *actual* Reduciates there. There's no way to fake that.

Is there?

I mean, I can change my face into my mom's. Were they all in disguise? Was that *all* part of the test?

Except that the *Benson* who was there really was Benson. Inside and out.

Then is this all just a Reduciate facade? The whole Curatoria headquarters? Everything?

No, that's not possible either. Because Alanna and Thomas are here. And I know they're who they say they are because Benson knew Thomas instantly. And Thomas and Alanna knew about Sammi and Mark.

No, there are definitely Reduciates *and* Curatoriates involved here.

Somehow—in some form—the Reduciata and Curatoria are working together.

CHAPTER THIRTY-ONE

I catch sight of something red under a piece of a splintered wall, and my heart speeds up as I run to it. I want to cry with joy when my hands grasp the ragged canvas of my backpack. It's been opened, its contents strewn across the floor. But it's *mine*. I start to riffle through it; the files are gone, though they didn't bother to take the bag of gold. And the journal is gone too.

Inwardly I thank the gods for Rebecca's foresight to not write her secret down, no matter how much frustration it's brought me. I frantically unzip pockets trying to remember which one I kept it—there!

I collapse on the floor in relief as I hold up the plastic zip-locked bag containing the braid from Sonya's life. I can't *believe* I got it back! I try to swallow the lump in my throat, but I can't. Everything, even this terrible, awful discovery, is worth this moment.

I want to take the whole backpack with me, but I realize

that, even though this place looks abandoned, if anyone were to come back and see it was gone, they'd know.

Besides, nothing else in there is nearly as important as this artifact from Sonya's life.

A pounding on my door makes me nearly shriek in surprise. It's not the cell door—it's the door in my secret bedroom. But how? I apparently forgot to get rid of the door when I stumbled in half-asleep this morning, but even so, I didn't think anyone knew I was here. Or that anyone would question a random door among thousands in the headquarters.

I stuff the braid into my pocket and creep back through the hole, closing it behind me, reminding myself that I can come back any time.

I open the door to Logan, his face a tableau of despair, his clothes rumpled, hair tousled. "Logan." I don't know what else to say. "How . . . how . . . ?"

"I followed you. I know, I know, intruding on privacy and all of that, but I couldn't sleep without knowing you were safe. I had—I had to know *where* you were." He pauses, his jaw tight. "I didn't even care if you were with . . . if you weren't alone. As long as I knew where you were."

"Logan—"

"It happened again."

I don't understand.

"Like the thing in the South Pacific. It happened *again*."

"No." Everything I just discovered falls from my mind, and I follow Logan as he sprints down the hallway—grateful that after having my leg healed, I can easily keep up.

The main atrium is full of people when we burst out of

the hallway. Most of them are clustered around the giant flat-screen television, which has been moved to the center of the room. For easy viewing, probably. The hulking Viking ship I saw earlier is still mounted on one wall, but it's only half-finished and makes the whole place look abandoned despite the hundreds of milling people.

The news story is eerily similar to the one three days ago except that last time the news started reporting hours after the disaster. It seems to only be minutes now. The reporter is stumbling over his words, in a near panic, the camera shaky.

"The Andes Mountains, for as far as anyone can see, are simply gone. There's no logical explanation. They just disappeared. There's no way science can even begin to . . ." His face crumples, and he loses his professionalism for just a moment. "Sarah, people *fell out of the sky*. Mountain villages, bodies just crashed into the ground. The devastation, the sheer carnage. It's . . . it's unspeakable."

The camera pans, and I'm not the only one in the atrium who claps their hand over their mouth at the red splashes of blood amid splintered remains of houses and shacks, scattered in mounds for—as the reporter said—as far as the camera will allow anyone to see.

The scene goes back to some reporter in the United States, safe inside a network studio. Sarah, I assume. "Again, we have only the barest reports of this disaster, and we are still trying to sort through fact and fiction. Scientists are already at work to determine if this incident could have anything to do with the devastation we saw in the South Pacific only days ago, but that connection has not yet been confirmed. We urge our viewers not to panic—to stay tuned as we get more updates."

The Andes Mountains. Another Earthbound. It must be.

This is my fault.

Maybe I should have told Daniel the truth—the whole truth. Maybe we should have guzzled Red Bull and worked all night to close that final gap between the isolated protein and an actual working vaccine.

But would that have helped an unknown Earthbound who was already sick? I don't think it could have.

And if Daniel is working with the Reduciates, would it have mattered at all? Am I simply helping him make a vaccine he's going to keep for himself?

Is *anything* I'm doing making any difference? Or am I as helpless as everybody else?

I try to tell myself that it doesn't matter. That the what-ifs and maybes can't affect me. It's the past. I can't change it. I have to let go and look forward and keep doing the only thing I can: making that vaccine.

But that thought doesn't ease the sickness in my belly. Doesn't stop the tears that flow as I press my face into Logan's shoulder, sobbing as he bears almost my entire weight. Crushing me to him like *I'm* going to disappear next.

I don't care if he takes it wrong. All I know is I need someone to hold me. To have the strength I don't have. To love the flawed person I am. To be my lifeline when I'm not sure I can bear to ask my broken heart to beat one more time.

CHAPTER THIRTY-TWO

"Curatoriates."

The shock of real human speech is almost enough to make me lift my head from Logan's shoulder. But I recognize Daniel's voice and push even harder against Logan. I can't bear to look at him. To be reminded of the work I've been too slow with. Of the fact that I'm working with a man I can't trust. Of the possibility that maybe he *wants* all this to happen.

"Listen to me, please. We cannot lose ourselves to fear."

A motivational speech, I should have known. I don't care to hear anymore. I want to *leave* the headquarters entirely, and if I thought it would help anything, I would. But when Daniel is finished I'll have to find the will to live again and drag myself upstairs and resume my work with the hope that not only will I succeed, but that somehow I can get the vaccine into the right hands.

Because even though we have again lost literally millions

of lives—not to mention the mountains I've always considered some of the most beautiful land in the entire world—there's still more to save. So much more. And as long as there's someone, something, to save, I have to try.

In a moment.

Another.

The sound of my name makes my head jerk up.

"In our time of such great need Tavia Michaels has not only come to us, but after last night, I promise you, we are on the cusp of finding the answer. The vaccine that will keep us all safe. That will keep the entire world safe. The gods, the same gods who cursed us to roam this earth forever, have not forgotten us. They've sent Tavia, even as we teeter on the brink of literal extinction. And we are so close to succeeding."

His expression is open, honest, pleading with his people to keep faith in him. But my tear-ravaged face heats beneath my skin, and I wish I could curl into a ball and disappear into a puff of humiliation.

What the hell is he doing? Is he *trying* to paralyze me under the weight of expectation? I know him too well to believe he's just trying to make his people feel better.

He's trying to accomplish *something* with these trite words. He must be. He never does anything accidentally.

I hear his continued speech as though through a long tunnel, the words barely making sense as they reach my ears. What is his true purpose? I've got to figure it out. If I don't . . .

"And once she does, we will go out into the world. We'll find everyone possible and distribute this vaccine. We are literally poised to be the saviors of the entire earth. And if there is any way for us to fully make up for the mistakes of our past, this is it. Tavia, come to me."

I shoot a look of death at him, but it's too late. He's staring at me, holding his hand out. The crowd parts like the Red Sea, and fingers reach for me, touching my shoulders, pulling me forward.

But I don't feel adored. I don't feel appreciated. I feel used and cheap. They're tearing me from Logan, pushing me toward Daniel, and I don't like the metaphorical significance. Or what it says about my own decisions.

But they are too many and I am just me. In about a minute I've been thrust forward, up the stairs, where Daniel takes my hand and raises it, joined with his, over his head. He turns, and though no one can see how tightly he grips my fingers, I know—even as I look back at Logan—that I have no choice but to go with him. Even if he has to drag me up those stairs, he will.

A mournful cheer follows us, and I know that every hope—every desperate spark of possibility that exists in the hearts of the Curatoriates—is fully invested in me.

"What the hell was that?" I demand as soon as the door to the science wing closes behind us.

"It was necessary," Daniel says. His entire demeanor has changed now that everyone isn't looking at him. Looking at *us*.

"You didn't have to drag *me* into it," I hiss. "What if we can't do it? What if *I* can't? Do you think they're going to blame you? It's not even safe for me here anymore. You've ruined everything."

"It was *necessary*," Daniel repeats, his voice hard with an edge I've only heard a time or two before. He looks at me, his gaze drilling into mine for several seconds before he says slowly, deliberately, "You're not the only one with secret plans, Tavia Michaels."

I clamp my jaw shut.

He knows.

I'm not sure what precisely he knows. But *something*. I shouldn't be surprised. I was kidding myself to think I could keep secrets from him in his own territory. His own domain.

But how much does he think *I* know?

"Are you ready?" Daniel asks, gesturing toward the detoxification room.

I breathe deeply. Am I ready? Am I ready to work *for him*? Now that I know he's somehow connected to the Reduciata? That he killed Thomas in another life to keep him quiet? He admitted he has his own secret plan that revolves around me. Can I justify being complicit in that?

But what choice do I have? The vaccine is more important than anything else. Can keeping it out of Reduciata hands really mean more than getting it *into* human hospitals?

Earthbound I can handle later; humans have to be saved *now*.

Once the vaccine is complete I can retrieve my artifacts from the vault and leave. Or, at least, that's what he once told me. Now, with my heart half-breaking, I realize that I may have to leave without my belongings. If I want to escape with my life.

I finger the braid in my pocket. I wish I could use it now. But what excuse would I be able to offer now that he's dragged me right into the lab itself?

First things first. We have a world to save. No matter what, it always comes back to that.

I let my head fall. I surrender. This is my job, like it or not. I've just pulled my fingers out of my pocket when a crash sounds behind me and someone I don't recognize rushes in.

"Daniel! Daniel! You were right. We have him. And undeniable evidence. We've got him."

A smile curls across Daniel's face, and my stomach feels like a storm of bees at the sight.

"Excellent. Have him brought to the stairs."

The man blanches. "In front of everyone?"

"In front of *everyone*," Daniel says softly, and suddenly I'm afraid. "Come on," he says, beckoning to me almost as an afterthought. "Our work will have to wait for a few minutes."

I'm confused, but there's nothing to do but follow Daniel right back down the steps we just climbed.

Back to the people he just declared me to be the hero of.

I feel so sick.

Logan meets me halfway down the stairs. "What's happening?" he asks as he threads his fingers through mine. I don't protest; I want something to hold on to too.

I shake my head, my eyes fixed on Daniel's back. I don't like what I heard in his tone. Saw in his eyes. There's a sound from behind the nervous crowd—many with tears still streaming down their faces—even as the noise from the televisions becomes oddly irrelevant. The people part, making way for a man held tightly by two others and surrounded by a group of people dressed in plain, cream-colored clothing. Security. So innocent-looking. So *not* innocent.

As soon as he gets close enough for me to see that rust-red hair, I realize who he is. "No," I whisper, my stomach twisting and wrenching within me.

"Is this him? The man who's been following you?" Daniel asks.

I can't speak. I won't speak. The man looks up at me pleadingly through those soft blond eyelashes. I can't. I don't care what Daniel thinks this guy has done—or worse, what he's simply going to convince *everyone else* this guy did—I can't condemn him to death with one word.

But clearly the look on my face shouts louder than my will.

A woman hands a tablet computer over to Daniel.

Daniel stares at it. Then he clears his throat. The audience hushes instantly.

"It has come to my attention that the details of my work with Tavia have not been as secret as I had hoped. Specifically, from the Reduciata."

A ripple goes through the crowd at the name that is practically blasphemy in this Curatoria world. It just makes me angrier that Daniel continues to play them.

"Our own security forces have been closing in on this man, and now I have the proof I was waiting for. The spy's computer," he says. "With an unsent e-mail that reads: *They're close. Reports say on the cusp. They have the girl. Should I destroy everything or just kill her?*" Daniel looks up at the crowd, then turns the tablet around so the gathered Curatoriates can see.

They're not close enough to actually read it. But the gesture is all the proof they need. Exclamations of fury explode below me, people shouting insults and suggestions for how to punish him. It feels like a fight in junior high, with the bullies ganging up on one kid. I'm sick to my stomach, and I wish I could leave, even if it would look cowardly.

"A Reduciata spy," Daniel says. Loud, clear, but calm. "A man—not even an Earthbound, just a man—who would damn the entire world for what? Reduciata favors. Make no mistake: we fight for the life of the world." He turns to glare at the hapless man, who looks too terrified to be a traitor.

And I wonder . . .

"And we fight against people *like this*." With his final word, Daniel thrusts out his hand and clenches it in a fist.

Then the man is choking. His face turns red, and he gags and retches. Blood pours from his mouth, splattering to the floor seconds before he falls to his knees, his hands slipping in the wetness and smearing the dark stain across the beige tile. The crowd is alive with buzzing again, but no one rushes forward to help.

I try.

I step away from Logan, release his hand. But his arms snake around me, and he pulls me back, gripping me tightly against his chest. "There's nothing you can do," he whispers. "It's already over."

As if hearing Logan's words, the man crumples to the ground. His chest spasms once, twice.

And then he is still.

Everything is still.

"I will not let this world die," Daniel says, his voice quiet, yet it *echoes*. "Not if I have to kill a thousand traitors like him. I will right my wrongs."

Silence.

I know one of two things will happen now. The Curatoriates will rise up against Daniel.

Or *for* him.

The silence stretches on for ten seconds. Twenty. It verges on a minute when a slow clapping starts.

One set of hands is joined by another. Another. A dozen more. A hundred. Everyone claps, a few shout out Latin phrases I ought to understand. But I know what they *mean*.

In an instant they are utterly loyal to Daniel again. Their suspicions, their questions, even much of their fear at the disaster in South America: all gone. Replaced with godlike awe and reverence for a killer. *That* was the purpose of the speech earlier. Of that little *demonstration*. Daniel used me. He used me to catch this spy—assuming he wasn't actually a pawn; I don't even know anymore—and then manipulated us both in a show of power to draw all of the Curatoriates closer. To regain their absolute loyalty.

If this all goes wrong, they will still side *with him*. They will remember his words and trust that he did everything he could.

What will they think of me?

I stare in disbelief and horror at the man on the floor. He's dead because of me. I may as well have choked the life out of him myself.

CHAPTER THIRTY-THREE

I don't think I'm on the right side.

I'm not convinced there *is* a right side.

Trust ye the Curatoria but tenuously, and the Reduciata not at all. The words from Quinn Avery's journal run through my head in a scream.

But they're a single force now! Does the fact that none of the other Earthbounds know the brotherhoods are working together even matter?

I know, and I'm still helping Daniel.

What does that say about me?

Daniel turns to me and, after a moment, holds out his hand.

To escort me up the stairs?

I shake my head and hold tight to Logan. Daniel's face darkens just a little. That wasn't what he wanted, but I can't simply act like this completely unjustified slaughter didn't happen.

He continues to hold out his hand, pushing it closer. At the same time he pins me with his eyes—daring me to defy him.

I dare.

I duck around Logan and flee. When I look back Logan is standing frozen in indecision.

When did I stop being the one who hung back because of fear? I don't know, but now I run, tearing up the stairs and weaving around corners until I'm almost lost.

But not quite.

I'm around the corner from the security wing.

I don't think. I don't consider. I just shove through those doors.

"Let me in," I demand of the two security people sitting at the desk. "Now!" I shout when they don't move fast enough. They unlock the doors, and I don't wait for them to close behind me.

I run to Benson.

His arms wrap around me, holding me tight to his chest, his mouth close to my ear, and the ragged sound of his breathing echoes so loudly it becomes the only sound in my world.

"I can't go back," I say, my breath coming so fast, my throat spasming; it feels like sobs are coming, threatening to overwhelm me, but I'm talking too quickly to let them truly take over. "I can't. Daniel he—he just killed a man. No trial, no jury, he didn't even get to speak up in his own defense, and then he—he—and then he was dead. Dear gods, Benson, he just killed him."

"It's okay," Benson says softly, soothingly, his hands

clenched around my arms so tightly I'm not sure if he thinks he's comforting me or holding me for comfort. But it seems to work both ways, and I don't care that his grip makes my arms throb. I need it.

"It's not okay. Benson, it's never going to be okay. What the hell am I doing helping someone like this?"

"You're saving billions of people in the world," he whispers. "And then we're all leaving."

His words finally get through. This isn't our home; this isn't our life. We were never going to stay.

I just needed to be reminded.

"Leaving," I repeat numbly.

"Together," he whispers. And I latch onto that word. "Daniel's a cruel bastard, and Sammi and Mark had good reason not to trust him," Benson murmurs. "But that doesn't change the fact that he's the one who has what you need to save everyone." His eyes dart to the two-way mirror before he whispers, "Do you think you can finish today?"

The mirror. I forgot. I didn't think of anything except Benson. They probably heard everything.

But how much could it possibly matter? What the hell could they tell Daniel that would have any effect? We're almost out of time; Daniel said so yesterday. Twenty-four hours, the end of today. And then we have to leave. There may as well be bright red numbers counting down on the huge screen in the atrium.

I follow Benson's line of sight to the mirror, but I shake my head and turn back. It's too late. I don't care what they hear anymore.

"I have to, or Daniel will evacuate us. He says the Reduciates are going to attack but . . ." I hesitate. If the Curatoria and Reduciata are working together, why would Reduciates be attacking? They wouldn't. It's yet another lie. Why is Daniel *really* in such a hurry?

I push that thought away—it's not important enough to reach the top of my priority list at the moment. I'll probably be analyzing Daniel's motives until the end of my days. However many—or few—I have left. For now, I have to focus. "Thomas was right, about the protein thing," I whisper to Benson. "But we—I still have to put it into the old vaccine. Transform it so it can use the vehicle of the last one." I scrunch my fists against my eyelids. "I don't even know what that means, and I have to figure out a way to do it in less than eight hours." I slump against him, my forehead resting on his chin. "I'm just so tired."

His arms rise to envelop me, and I feel small.

Not bad small. Small enough to disappear into Benson's arms. To hide from the world.

Small like an ant, I think, and a tiny smile touches my lips.

Like *two* ants.

Two ants who are just big enough to be each others' worlds.

It's so hard to even comprehend that it has literally been only a month since I discovered I could *make* things. Since the first time Benson and I kissed. Two weeks since the *last* time Benson and I kissed. Now I rub my nose against his warm neck and breathe against his skin, needing the comfort that emanates from it.

From his mouth.

"Benson," I say, and somehow our lips are mere millimeters apart.

And I lean forward.

A tiny whimper escapes me before I sink against his mouth. Searching, taking, grabbing his shoulders and pulling him closer. His arms tighten around me as he kisses me back. "Harder," I say. "Hold me tighter." Already I can barely breathe, but I need to feel him even more. To know that he's *here*. That he's one thing the world, the Curatoriates—*Daniel*—cannot take from me.

His teeth scrape at my bottom lip because I won't pull back, not even to give him a breath of air, but it doesn't hurt. Not really. Maybe a little, but in that way that reminds me I can feel. That I'm not numb. And that's what I want.

Only when my forehead is damp from clenching every muscle in my body so hard—trying to hold him tighter—do I slowly relax. "I have to go back, don't I?"

"No," he says. And for a moment I dream that maybe that's the truth. "You don't *have* to. But I know you, Tave. And I know that you won't be able to live with yourself if you don't finish what you started."

I know he's right. But I steal one more kiss before I pull in a shuddering breath and swipe my arms across my face, removing any traces of kissing or tears. I cling to Benson's hand like a little child. It's too much for one person to bear, but he seems willing to share the load. "Be ready," I whisper.

Then I let my fingers fall away from his.

I walk to the door. It opens. And though every cell in my body is screaming at me not to, I walk away. He's right; I have to.

I leave the security wing and nearly run into Thomas. He's alone, strangely, and it makes me wonder where Alanna is. His face is panicked, and he calms considerably when he sees me.

"Oh good. Can we talk? Quickly?"

In a moment everything from this morning—from before the horrific broadcast, the terrible killing—comes back. "Yes. Yes! Go down to the atrium, find Logan." *Oh dear gods, Logan. He's going to hate me.* "Tell him we need to meet in my special room. He knows where it is."

Thomas hesitates.

"You *need* to see something," I say. I have to show him the hidden Reduciata prison. If nothing else, to assuage the irrational fear that I imagined the whole thing. I give him quick directions. "It's a very private place where we can talk."

He finally nods. "I'll go get him."

"Thank you," I breathe.

We part ways, and as I enter my secret room, I realize I still haven't eaten breakfast. No wonder I'm so tired. I create a large container of trail mix and nervously eat handfuls as I count the seconds waiting for Thomas and Logan to show up.

Finally a tiny knock on the door. I turn the knob and the two slip in, clicking the door quietly closed behind them.

"Are you okay?" Logan asks. It seems like a strange question. Even if it were possible to be *okay* after that display, in the face of everything else, would it matter?

"No," I answer honestly. "But I don't think I'm going to be anything approaching *okay* until I leave this place."

"You and me both," Logan murmurs.

Thomas nods, his eyes closing for a few seconds. "Believe

293

me, I understand." I remember how many years—lifetimes—he and Alanna have spent in hiding.

"Where's Alanna?" I ask.

"Keeping watch. Making sure no one comes down this hallway. I'll tell her everything later." He hesitates. "Are you going back to the lab?"

"I have to."

He pauses. "What's your next step?"

"Transferring the isolated protein into the vaccine. Something about dosage."

Thomas waves those words away. "Do you think you'll get that far today?"

"Maybe, but you know we have to test it."

"You don't think he'll just test it on the humans here?" Logan asks.

"After this morning they'd line up to volunteer, wouldn't they?" I can't hide the cynicism in my voice.

"After this morning half of them would walk in front of a gun for him," Thomas says. "He's . . . he's brilliant."

I nod, my voice catching in my throat. "He's also made it so they won't just let me leave until I'm done."

"Not out the front gates anyway," Thomas agrees. "At this point you'll not only need to escape but find a away to do it right under his nose."

"He must know I can."

"Certainly." Thomas hesitates, then moves closer and puts his hands on my shoulders. "But I'm not sure if he knows that *you* know that. You hide your independence well around him."

"I'm not hiding; he makes me feel useless," I confess, not

sure just when I realized it. Daniel is the one who has told me time and time again that I'm *necessary*, but only for my transforming ability. The insinuation is that the rest of me is interchangeable. I'm certain now that he's done it on purpose. Brilliant is the least of what he is. A long-term strategist with his own best interests in mind.

But what else could you expect from the leader of a millennia-old brotherhood of gods?

"We all need to be prepared," Thomas says with a sweeping glance that includes Logan. "But you especially, Tavia. Remember that in all this, *you* have the upper hand. Don't let him forget that. And for all our sakes, do *not* let him convince you otherwise. Because I have no doubt he'll try. Subtly."

"Like a snake," I whisper.

"Tavia, despite his talk, make no mistake, there's nothing more important to Daniel than *Daniel*. That, above anything else, is what our research into him has uncovered. This morning he risked throwing you to the wolves to re-win the loyalty of his people in case things don't work out. Make certain he remembers how much he needs you, how he needs you *much* more than you need him. That alone may end up being your ticket to staying alive."

I nod, accepting these vile things about Daniel as truth now. I don't try to justify or romanticize. There's no time for that anymore. Today is the day for facing cold, hard facts, and I brace myself to do just that. Thomas seems to be through talking, but I haven't shown them my discovery yet.

"There's more." My voice is choked, but I make myself speak. "It's worse than you could possibly imagine."

Thomas stares at me, but there's a trust there. He believes it *can* be so bad. Logan doesn't look as convinced.

I walk to the back of my small room—to the plain wall that was going to be the back of my kitchenette—and press my ear to it, just in case someone has decided to go in there since this morning.

Then I make a hole.

I turn to beckon the two to follow me, but Thomas's face is chalky white and he's staring, not at the hole but at me.

"How did you do that?"

I didn't think. I've never told him. Or Alanna. Haven't told anyone except Daniel and Logan. And technically, Daniel told *us*.

"You're a Creator," Thomas says warily. "I've seen you work."

"I'm both," I say, figuring that's the easiest explanation. "That's why Daniel needs me."

Thomas shakes his head. "He'll *never* let you go. Daniel will never, *never* let something so valuable slip through his fingers."

"I know." But a part of me cheers that Thomas believed me with almost no explanation whatsoever.

Thomas's hand is shaking as he lays it on my shoulder. "When everything breaks loose, I'll get you out. I swear. I will *not* leave something so valuable with him."

"Especially not after you see this." My voice sounds hollow, dull. Like I've reached a level where I can't actually get any lower.

We duck through, and I watch Logan carefully, ready for . . .

whatever he's going to think. Do. He almost recoils when he sees our old prison, and I want to run to him and hold him, comfort him. But I can't now. Not after kissing Benson.

After *choosing* Benson.

"I don't understand," Thomas says, looking around.

I turn him so he can see the huge Reduciata ankh painted on the wall. "This is where Logan, Benson, and I were held. Where were *rescued* from."

"But . . ."

"I made the walls disappear, and we tried to escape that way," I say, pointing. "But then when we were trapped, Curatoriates burst in and took us away. They knocked us out once we were in the helicopter."

"But not for secrecy, like they said," Logan fills in, his mind processing everything so quickly, "only so we wouldn't know that all we did was go up, make a circle, and come right back down."

"Exactly. Benson told me the Reduciates said I would have to be put through tests, and that was it."

"Just a test," Thomas echoes, still sounding shocked.

"Except that there were *Reduciates* involved. Benson—" I spare a glance up at Logan. I haven't told him yet. That I want to be with Benson. I can't. Not now. It would be too much for him. "Benson was here too. In that cell." I point. "And other Reduciates I recognized from Portsmouth." I look at Thomas and wait until he meets my eyes. "We simply have to come to terms with the fact that on some level, the Reduciata and the Curatoria are working *together*."

His nod is small but determined.

"At the very least, Daniel knows. He found me in the hall-way just outside last night and got nervous and sent me—" I can't tell Logan where he sent me. "Away," I finish lamely.

"But . . ." Logan's voice trails off as we turn to him. He concentrates, gelling his thought, and then asks, "Why was *Daniel* here?" He sweeps his arm out, taking in the dilapidated room. "It doesn't look like anyone has been in here since we left." He arches an eyebrow. "They certainly haven't cleaned it."

He's catching on fast—dealing with the shock. Better than I would have in his place. But then, he is a millennia-old god. Perhaps I shouldn't be so surprised when he demonstrates a sliver of wisdom and maturity.

But he's right. Why would Daniel be here? And so late at night. His getting nervous about me is easily explained by not wanting me to figure it out. But why would *he* be hanging about? My heart falls to my stomach. "There must be more to all of this."

"Anything that direction except the dead end?" Thomas asks, pointing down one end of the hallway.

"No. Behind the wall is just the space where the helicopter took off. I was conscious long enough to see that much."

"This way then," Thomas says, and I'm happy to let him take the lead as we stride down the messy hallway together toward a door.

"It might be locked," I say.

"Only if they really took the time to make this a true pris-on. People who think they can't possibly get caught tend to be sloppy."

Sure enough, Thomas's hand closes around the doorknob, and when he pulls, it opens.

He peers around the door through a narrow crack. Then he turns and puts a finger to his lips. We slip through into another prison-esque space nearly identical to the last one—except, of course, that it isn't destroyed.

And it doesn't look quite like a prison. It takes me a few seconds to realize what it *does* look like.

A hospital.

CHAPTER THIRTY-FOUR

There is a patient in two of the three cells, each hooked up to a bunch of machines. Instead of one door—like in the Curatoria cells as well as the cell Logan and I were held in—there are two, just like in the lab.

They're air-locked, I realize.

"This is a quarantine," I say breathlessly. "These two—they have the virus. They've got to." They both have the gray pallor and sagging skin that I remember Mark having the last time I saw him. "Maybe . . . maybe Daniel's hoping to save them?"

But we all know it's too optimistic to hope Daniel has something positive in store for the pair before us.

"We'd better find out what we can and get out of here," Logan says grimly. "This area looks like it gets frequented much more often than the other." He's right, everything smells clean and disinfected. But on top of that, there's a half-empty coffee cup on the counter, and the trash beside me is partly filled with food paraphernalia like paper plates and plastic forks.

"Let's try to be gone in ten minutes," I suggest, and they all nod, faces as bleak as I'm sure mine is. Hopefully Alanna can continue to keep everyone away for the time being. I go to some files sitting at what looks like the central desk and begin flipping through them. "It looks like this is a set of Earthbounds named Nima and Bedrick?" I say, stumbling on the odd names.

"Earthmaker names, I bet," Thomas says. "We almost never use them because they're extremely helpful as passcodes and in verifying intentions, et cetera."

"Oh," I say, and despite everything else, I feel a little disappointed that I don't remember mine. "There are also files on Shinla, Harnon, Elsa, and Regini. But there are only the two patients here. Where do you think the others are?"

"Wait, what were those names?" Logan asks, standing in front of a map full of pins and strings that's hanging on the wall. I repeat the strange names. "And the first two?" he asks, and I can hear the strain in his voice. It's so quiet and tense that my heart pounds in fear of what he's discovered. "They're all on here," Logan whispers. "Shinla and Harnon are pinned on in France, but they have a thread that goes to the coast of Russia and the South Pacific." He takes a breath, turns, and glances at me, but I can't meet his eyes. "Elsa and Regini are pinned in California, and their threads go to the north and south ends of the Andes Mountains."

Silence settles around us with the weight of wet sand—or perhaps more accurately, the dry sand the headquarters is currently buried in.

"What about the two in there who are sick?" I ask, but I can't make my voice rise above a whisper.

Logan shakes his head, looking more confused than worried. "They're pinned in South Africa, and their threads go to the sand dunes in California and Death Valley. That doesn't seem so bad."

"No!" Thomas's haggard whisper makes us both jerk around to face him. "You two don't know. That's where *we* are."

"But . . . that means in the next day or two . . ." Logan's words fade away.

I remember Daniel's angry words from yesterday: *We're running out of time. I was counting on you.* The twenty-four hours, the lies about Reduciate attacks. This is why he's so insistent we have to evacuate *tonight*. "He knows. He knows this is coming." I study the map.

"How did he know which Earthbounds were infected?" Thomas asks. "It kills so quickly."

"Unless . . ." Daniel's words pound through my thoughts. *I was counting on you. Counting on you.* Why would he be counting on me? I put my hand to my stomach at the suspicion that's forming. He was certain I could work more quickly. So confident, he must have gone ahead and started the clock. "Unless he infected them himself." But I can tell from the looks on Thomas's and Logan's faces that they had the same thought. I just said it first.

"He's got to have tracked them down and infected them. I don't see what else this map could possibly mean," I say.

"But why would he choose to destroy his own headquarters?" Logan asks.

"To cover up evidence?" I count the days. "He probably infected them the day he confirmed I could transform. He must have been so confident I could just magically crack the code to a new vaccine, so he could take what he wanted and leave. No one would make the connection if the entire desert disappeared only hours later. Assuming anyone survived at all. And then he would be in control of the vaccine. He would be untouchable." I look at them both, my eyes going from one face to the other. "We can't just leave. Not when we're so close to a real vaccine."

"How long do you think we have?" Logan asks, turning to look at the patients.

"I don't know. But the time limit Daniel gave me is up in less than eight hours. I don't know how much leeway he gave himself, but I would guess we don't have more than a day."

A gasp from Thomas brings us both back around.

"This is me," he says, pointing to two pieces of paper that say *Sacha* and *Ren*. "And this is Alanna."

My heart pounds so loud I'm shocked no one else can hear it. "What did you create?"

"Half of Asia and most of Africa," he says in despair. "As a mixed pair we were incredibly efficient."

I think of what percentage of the population that must be. A full fourth. Maybe more? Depending on which parts of Asia, it could be *half*. "Half of the world's population gone in one swoop," I murmur in a tiny voice.

"It's worse than that," Thomas says. "Because of what's happened in the South Pacific and now South America, I've been thinking about what the consequences would be if Alanna and I caught the virus. If an entire continent dis-appeared, the resulting tsunami alone would devastate the entire earth. A handful of survivors at best." He shakes his head and swallows hard. "The Earthbounds who knew it was coming would be prepared. They could survive. But beyond that . . ."

He doesn't have to say.

"The headquarters seems so safe," Thomas says, and his forehead is damp with perspiration. I've never seen him so close to unraveling. "It's been entirely virus-free. But if Daniel wants us to catch it, I don't see how we can stop him."

"You two need to go without me then," I say, my throat tight. Knowing I'm signing my own death warrant by sending my best allies away. "Hide in the desert until you hear—*from me*—that the vaccine is ready. We can't risk you two."

"No," Thomas says sharply. "I will *not* leave you. You are too powerful to just hand to Daniel."

"Then you have to hide," I protest, desperate tears build-ing up in my eyes. "Go to Alanna, tell her, and then stay out of sight. Not your room—somewhere no one would expect."

"I'll do my best," Thomas promises. "For now, we have to get out of here. And we have to get *you* back to the lab."

We leave the medical cell and pass through the destroyed area where Logan and I were held and back into my faux-Michigan bedroom. I close the wall behind us, and it feels like putting the lid on a container of toxic waste. Still there, still dangerous, but at least out of sight.

"Isn't there any way to . . . spread the word that people need to evacuate?" I ask.

"Not after this morning," Thomas says. "Who would believe me?"

We stand in somber silence for long seconds before Logan says, "Maybe we should just kill them."

"The patients?" I ask in horror.

"If they don't die *from the virus*, then nothing gets destroyed, right?"

"I think so," I say, hating the cold logic.

"But we don't *know* so," Thomas says, and I grasp onto his words like a rescue rope. "There may be some kind of tipping point where the virus takes over enough to do the damage. We can't risk bringing the entire desert down on us too early. And we also can't take the chance that Daniel will discover that we know his plans."

"So we leave them like that?" Logan asks, his voice hollow.

Thomas nods. "For now."

"What do we do?" Logan asks.

Thomas looks at me steadily. "Can you handle going back to the lab?"

"Yes, I'm ready." My voice is strong. No matter how badly I'm quaking with fear on the inside, I have to do this. And I will. "First," I dig into my pocket and produce the bagged piece of twine, "this is an artifact from my last life, as a girl named Sonya. It was in my backpack in the fake prison."

"Is that what was really so important from your backpack?" Logan asks.

I look at him askance before remembering the conversation we had the first time we met Daniel. Back when we thought he was a *good* guy.

"I could tell you weren't telling the whole truth, but I didn't say anything at the time, and with everything that's happened . . ." He shrugs. "I kinda forgot."

Logan knew I was lying. Of course he did—he's known me forever. I shove back yet another wave of guilt and nod. "After Daniel said they didn't retrieve my backpack I figured I'd never see it again. All I know about her is that she had a secret, the Reduciata hunted her for it, and she killed herself rather than give it up." I choke on the last words a little as I remember the excruciating pain of my heart turning to stone inside my chest. I glance up at Logan. "It's a secret that goes back over two hundred years. Despite everything I've discovered, I'm still not sure I know *exactly* what that secret is. But I do know they still want it. Want to keep it quiet." I don't even know who *they* are anymore. Reduciates? Curatoriates? Is there really any difference? "I think it's tied up in all of this. My powers, my immunity, my . . . my strength," I add, although we haven't discussed that yet. Still, it seems like the time for holding back information is over. "And the virus. They're all connected."

"So you just touch it and your memories come back? Like a mini-awakening?" Thomas asks.

I bite hard on my bottom lip and consider lying. But that can only be counterproductive at this point; he and Alanna are two of the only people in the entire world who are on my side. "The last time it happened I . . . well, there was a lot of screaming involved and Benson—" *Did I seriously just say his name in front of Logan?* I'm too distracted. "He was afraid it would kill me," I finish in a murmur, purposely not meeting Logan's eyes. "That's why I didn't use it before resurging with

Logan. I couldn't risk damaging myself and leaving Logan to die forever."

Thomas stares hard at the bag for a long time.

"Do you think," he says slowly, "that you will learn anything from that lifetime that will help you develop the vaccine faster *right now*?"

I consider everything I've ever heard and known about Sonya, the brief, often cryptic entries in her file, the dreams of her death, and then the one from yesterday about Greta. Could discovering more about *Greta* help? I already know I'm immune, and I've gotten what I need from that knowledge: the protein. Will finding out the source of my immunity assist me in finishing the vaccine? Enough that I can risk being completely depleted of energy? I'm running on sheer force of will already. Sonya knows secrets, yes, but related directly to stopping the virus? "I don't think so."

"And you think unlocking the memory will weaken you?"

"At the very least," I whisper.

"Then I suggest we wait."

I close my mouth and clench my jaw, even though I know it's the most logical answer.

"We already know that Daniel is completely corrupt and the Curatoria itself only slightly less so. Will more confirmation of that really help anyone?" He points in the general direction of the secret rooms. "We have a clock now. We have literally hours to save the world. I don't think we can afford to waste any time doing anything but doggedly pursuing this vaccine."

I nod, the truth of his words sinking in deep. "Okay." But

I'm not taking any chances of losing this precious artifact again. I shove the bag with the braid of twine deep into my pocket so I know exactly where it is at every moment. I suck in a deep breath through my nose. "Let's do this."

As we leave I transform the entire room back into a hollow space of nothingness. My heart aches as my haven goes away, but with as close as it is to the secret rooms, it's too big a risk that somehow Daniel will find it and know it belongs to me.

Still, I feel the sting of my parents' deaths all over again.

Logan walks me to the lab—lets me squeeze his fingers so tightly my whole hand aches by the time we reach the double doors. I feel guilty—like I'm using him—but I *need* the feel of his hand against mine to help me make this dreaded walk.

It's almost noon. *Hours* of my regular workday are already gone. And yet, I still want to stall. I don't know what comes after this, and part of me doesn't want to find out.

Logan turns enough to grasp both of my hands in his. "I'm not going to tell you to be strong," he whispers, "because you don't need any help with that. But make sure that he *knows* how strong you are."

I press my forehead against his, drawing in his confidence until I feel like what I am: the most powerful Earthbound in the world.

And Daniel will know it.

"I'll wait here for you," Logan says.

"You don't need to," I reply, giving him an out. Every moment I don't tell him about Benson makes me feel terrible. But I can't. Not now. Not in the face of everything.

"What could possibly be more important that sitting here

in this hallway waiting for you to save humanity?" he asks with such sincerity I can't help but smile.

But there actually *are* more important things. Especially now that we have a clock. "Could you . . .?" I hesitate, not wanting to ask him to do anything for me when I know in my heart I can't do—can't *be*—the only thing he really wants from me. "Could you go to the vault? Maybe take Alanna. She might be able to help you break in. Find the artifacts from my other lives. They . . . they might be all I have. All I'll *ever* have."

Lines form on his forehead, but he doesn't hesitate. "Of course."

"Don't get caught," I warn.

He backs up a few steps and grins—a perfect, boyish half grin that makes my heart race and tear apart all at the same time. "Like I would," he says. Then he spins and walks away.

CHAPTER THIRTY-FIVE

I expect Daniel to be waiting for me in the lab's lobby. Pacing even. Worrying that I might not come. But when I stand on my tip-toes to peer through the windows, he's in the lab already, meandering around in his hazmat suit.

Yesterday that would have made me nervous. Today I understand what he's doing.

Making me feel unimportant. Hardly worth his worries.

And predictable. Under his power even.

But I see through the ruse; it won't work. I know he *must* be concerned on the inside. I take my time going through the procedures involved in suiting up. I don't hurry or rush. I don't stall—my work is waiting—but I won't rush for him again. Better to stay calm. Collected. I have a job to do.

He straightens when the air locks announce my arrival. Relief crosses his face for the barest of instants, but because I'm watching, I see it.

"Tavia, I—"

"I can't talk about it," I interrupt, trying my best to sound sad instead of mad. Today I am not the Tavia he knows, who has to be spoon-fed science so she can complete her task. I am the goddess with powers he will *never* have. Who went around his back to create the vaccine he wants.

Who sees now what he truly is.

But I can't let him know that. He has to think that he succeeded, that I'm still subservient.

"I just can't," I repeat, letting my voice quaver as I power up my microscope.

"You can't feel guilty, Tavia," Daniel says in his most fatherly voice. It makes me want to grind my teeth. "He was following you. Spying on you. He deserved it."

Deserved to die in agony with no trial? Bowing before the almighty Daniel playing judge, jury, and executioner? No one deserves that.

I turn to look him in the face, our eyes meeting as I realize we're nearly the same height. Why did I always feel small? "I know. It's just hard," I say, looking down, so he can't catch the rebellion in my eyes. "Can we get to work? I think that's the best thing for me right now."

"Of course. Whatever it takes for you to feel comfortable." The falseness rolls off him now, and I can't believe I didn't appreciate it before. I curse myself for seeing what I *wanted* to see.

"I think that's best." This time my voice is strong and steady, and I thank the gods that I found Thomas before I came up here to face Daniel. That he prepared me—reminded me of my advantage.

And it's not a big advantage. Daniel is utterly brilliant, and on top of that he knows more about me than I know about myself. The one thing I cannot do is allow him to use that against me.

He needs you so *much more than you need him*, I remind myself, letting Thomas's words play through my head on repeat.

Daniel's gloved hand touches my plastic-draped shoulder in a comforting gesture, but even though there are so many layers between us, his touch seems to burn down to the bone. Then he slips onto his stool and begins to rattle off an explanation of the slides of vaccine he's prepared and how he thinks we should integrate the virus-fighting protein.

The one he still doesn't know came from my blood.

It's almost six hours later when I catch movement out of the corner of my eye. Behind the small window that looks into the lab from the foyer I can see Audra, standing on her tip-toes and waving her arms.

She apparently missed the buzzer.

Annoyance crosses Daniel's face for just a second before he walks over to the window and presses the intercom button. "What is it, Audra?"

"I need to read Tavia's TB test." Audra's voice sounds tinny over the intercom. There was no TB test. What is she pulling? "She was supposed to come in at lunch, but I guess she forgot." Audra is staring hard at me. "The test has a narrow window of time to be read," she says, looking back at Daniel. "I can't wait until morning or I'll have to do the whole thing over again."

"How long will it take?" Daniel says with obvious exasperation.

"Oh, just a few minutes," Audra says with a smile that makes her look even younger than her fifteen years.

Daniel stands, looking at neither of us for a few seconds, hands on hips. "Better go, I guess," he says to me, and I know he's just trying to keep up appearances.

I wonder what I'm getting into, but I trust Audra a hell of a lot more than I trust Daniel, so I go with it.

"You know," Daniel says as I rise, "take your time. Maybe get something to eat. I'll prepare the test slides, and then they'll have to sit for maybe twenty minutes before we can see the results. Back in half an hour?" he asks.

"Sure," I reply, barely paying attention. It's the first time I've stood up from my stool since entering the lab at noon, and every part of my body feels sore.

But we've done it.

We think.

Daniel's right though. We can't do anything else *right* at this moment. What we need now is for our tests to incubate. Right before Audra got here we took blood samples from every tech and scientist in the lab and set up Petri dishes in a warm bath to keep the cells alive. All Daniel will have to do while I'm with Audra is expose the samples to the vaccine.

The new one.

Not the one I made under my microscope, but the one I created with my powers. Because it doesn't matter if I can do it on the cellular level with a micropipette and my transformative powers; it's simply too slow. I need to be able to *create* the serum en masse with only my abilities. My first three attempts earlier today failed.

I finally manage to create a good batch on my fourth try.

Then Daniel made me do it again.

And again.

And again.

Until I did it ten times in a row without flubbing it.

I'm exhausted, but if today has shown me one thing, it's that I truly am the only Earthbound in the world who could do this. The vaccine is so complex it would be impossible for anyone of lesser strength to create. Even after months of study.

But it's done, and all that's left to do is test it. So in half an hour I'll come back and we'll see if I'm as good as I hope.

It has to work. I *have* to believe that. I can't afford the tiniest ripple in my confidence. Not anymore. I've put myself in a very dangerous position with Daniel.

And I hope I can get out of it.

I try to shake the fuzz from my head as I go through each step of the decontamination process twice before leaving the lab—it would be just my luck to cause an epidemic when we're this close.

I wish . . .

I wish I could go tell Benson. But I don't dare.

Now I realize what a big risk I took by running to him this morning. Letting the security people see us kiss. Overhear my comments about Daniel.

Because if Daniel knew what Benson means to me, he would use him as a weapon.

And it would work.

I swallow hard and push that thought away. A few seconds later I'm standing in the lab's lobby with Audra, who's dressed in soft green scrubs.

"Thank you for coming. Why don't we go out this way," she says, gesturing to the lobby doors. But that pause, that hesitation—I recognize the look in her eyes.

From myself.

Something's wrong.

I nod in agreement, and she leads me to a small, quiet alcove just around the corner from the lab. "Obviously there's no TB test," she says after we each take a seat across a small circular table, her voice a shade above a whisper. "I didn't know how else to get you away from Daniel. Do you . . . do you trust him?" My head jerks up, and I peer at her face. Unfortunately, her expression doesn't give anything away.

So now we do the tightrope walk. If I say yes, whatever she has to say will be taken off the table—literally.

But if I say no . . . there's so much risk. Audra is still a sworn Curatoriate. They found her at thirteen, re-awakened her memories, and took her in. And they've told her they're looking for her *diligo*, whether that's true or not. She has many valid reasons to be *very* loyal to them.

Worse—I realize, every muscle in my body clenching up—she's a doctor. She was on the helicopter when Logan and I were "rescued." She knows we didn't go anywhere.

She might even be the one treating those Earthbounds with the virus in the secret room.

She could be as embroiled in this as anyone.

CHAPTER THIRTY-SIX

"The hesitation is enough," Audra says, and I have to remind myself that she's so wise beyond her years. "There are whispers just beginning to take root in the medical department. Dark, dark whispers," she says, turning her light brown eyes to me now, and the depth of sorrow I see there takes me by surprise. No, not even sorrow—despair.

Betrayal.

What in the world has happened?

"You saw what Daniel did to that Reduciate this morning."

"*Everyone* saw," I whisper in a vicious hiss, still angry at the whole thing.

She nods passively. "Sometimes we need a reminder that Daniel is exceptionally powerful. At least that seems to be what he thinks. Do you understand what he did to that man? Physically, I mean?"

"Only in the vaguest terms," I admit, my voice shaky.

"Let me show you," Audra says, and a pen and notebook appear in her hands, newly created. "I've heard of him doing it before. And not just in this life. It's his preferred method of execution because any Destroyer can do it before or after resurgence. So it's always been possible for him."

She's sketching now, with long fingers, and though her lines lack the grace and beauty that a drawing by an artist like me would have had, I can appreciate the precision and control that allow her to wield a scalpel. It's easy to see the angle of a chin, the curve of a neck, the long tubes that make up the inside of a human throat.

"Pretty basic—this is the esophagus," Audra says, pointing with her pen. "Windpipe, same thing. The food we eat goes down it and also the air we breathe. It's ever so simple," Audra continues, and she draws two straight lines across the esophagus, an inch or so apart from each other. "Daniel simply removed this small section of the esophagus. Not his entire neck—that would be messy and bloody and all of the Curatoriates would be horrified. But," she says, pointing with her pen again, "keep the job inside the skin and you get all of the drama with none of the gore. A show of *power* rather than ruthlessness."

It had all seemed pretty ruthless to me, but I remember my discussion with Thomas and see that this was the perfect way to accomplish everything Daniel wanted. Including his attempt to paralyze me with guilt, to keep me even tighter under his thumb. I'm so glad that part failed.

Audra looks up at me, her pen unmoving between her limp fingers. "Death is fast," she says calmly, almost blandly. "With no air to the lungs, all of the muscles in the esophagus seize up, trying to prevent the unpreventable. Blood pours from the mouth as the victim coughs and sputters and tries to suck in oxygen, but it's impossible. If you do it right," she says, gripping her pen again and artfully filling in a few more landmarks, "you remove the vocal chords as well. Then there's no screaming to frighten your followers."

No screaming. More strategizing on Daniel's part. It's almost worse than if he'd hacked the man to bloody pieces.

"I apologize for the gratuitous physical descriptions, but this is the kind of thing we med-folk are into," Audra says, misreading my white face; I'm not grossed out—I'm devastated by Daniel's horrific cunning. "A stark bundle of facts that help us find logic in this world."

"It's okay," I say, trying to push my imagination away from the thought of dying in such a way, should everything go wrong in the lab tonight. "But I don't understand why this is a problem." Other than the fact that Daniel executed a man without any semblance of a trial, that is. And is strategically infecting Earthbounds. And is somehow working with the Reduciata.

Audra glances around, and the hollow fear I saw before is back. "The body was sent to medical, of course," she says, whispering now. "Daniel told us he wanted it cremated immediately. That he couldn't stand the thought of even the lifeless remains of someone so traitorous in his headquarters. If he hadn't needed to head right up to work with you, he probably would have watched us dispose of his remains personally. But he didn't. And so of course we didn't listen," she adds so calmly, as if saying the sky was blue.

"What did you do?" I ask, admiring her guts.

"We autopsied. You can learn so much from cadavers that you simply cannot learn any other way." She folds her hands in front of her, the ostensible epitome of calm. But I see a tiny tremor in her fingertips. Fingers that are so conditioned to remain steady. "So they started heating the cremator, just in case they needed to dispose of the evidence quickly. And then six doctors gathered for the initial Y-incision."

I attempt to follow her explanation, but I'm still not sure why she feels the need to tell me all of this. Why it was worth risking Daniel catching her in a lie.

"We were in the midst of giving dictation on the internal cut across the esophagus, the blood that filled the cavity of the lungs, the near-complete absence of the vocal chords, when we realized what had happened." She stops and stares hard at me.

"I don't understand," I say after a long few seconds.

"We didn't see it right away either," she whispers, and then she looks down at her drawing, the pen lying across it.

A few seconds later they both pop out of existence.

That's right. Audra has her memories, but she hasn't resurged. Her creations don't last.

"His throat was *still* cut?" I ask as realization fills my brain in an avalanche of terrifying truths—the section of my plane that returned to normal after the crash, everything I created that was gone in five minutes before I reconnected with Logan. "It should have been whole," I say as my stomach writhes and twists. At that second it occurs to me that Daniel never helped with any of the destroying work in the lab.

"The blood in the lungs, the food contents spilled into the

abdominal cavity from the collapsed tube, those were expected. The removal of the piece of esophagus still *happened* with all of its consequences. Including death, of course. But after all was said and done, the windpipe should have reverted." She looks up at me and, for once, looks like the teenager her body says she is. "Daniel has found his *diligo*. And he's keeping her a secret. Why would he do that, Tavia?"

I want to blithely respond that it's because he's a lying liar who lies—but it goes deeper than that. I remember the first day Logan and I met him, the despair in his eyes as he used his desperate search for his partner to justify questionable choices. The sorrow I've seen in his expressions since. I *believed* those emotions absolutely, even when I couldn't believe anything else. Believed that in his twisted way he was justifying so much because of his need to find her.

But it was completely false.

If he wasn't looking for *her*, why would he have done those things? Especially in light of our discovery that he has ties to the Reduciata. What could he need to work so hard to hide if he can draw from both brotherhoods? And who is this person, this partner he keeps hidden away?

"Who knows about this?" I say in a whisper so low even Audra can barely hear me.

"Almost no one."

"What about the body?"

"As soon as we realized the implications, we destroyed it. Cremated it immediately." She leans forward on her elbows. "Sometimes the truth is too dangerous to keep around."

I nod, feeling the veracity of that statement down to my toes.

"We're trying to keep it quiet," Audra says. "But a good chunk of the medical wing knows, and they have partners and friends in other areas of the Curatoria whom they have to think about. They're afraid, and when people are afraid, they talk." She shrugs and laughs in a sad, self-deprecating way. "I suppose that's what I'm doing right now."

I don't speak as I try to comprehend how deep this well of lies goes.

And I thought it was pretty damn deep already.

"I'm not ashamed to confess that I'm terrified. I felt I had to tell you because you're working so closely with him," Audra says.

"Thank you," I say, my own voice sounding very far away.

"There's more," she says, and she clasps her bottom lip between her teeth. "When you came here, on the helicopter, I didn't—I don't—know where you came *from*. But when the chopper landed and our med team was ushered on, you and Logan were already there. Unconscious," she adds. It's darkly humorous to me that she wants me to know she didn't drug me.

"We were told only that we would simply be going up and down and that we were not to tell you anything about where we had all come from. I didn't question it at the time," she says with a single-shoulder shrug. "The secret of our location is one of our greatest safeties. But now, after everything, I wonder." She leans toward me, our noses only inches apart. "Tavia, I think you were brought here under false pretenses, that you've been lied to every moment since you arrived. And I—I'm sorry I was a part of that."

She reaches out and clasps my hand. "I'm not telling you to stop working on the cure," she says, her voice fierce, "because the gods know we *need* it. But be careful. I—I get the impression that you're a victim in all of this as much as anyone . . . although I would have said the same thing about *Daniel* before this morning. Point is, you should be aware that the man you're working with is hiding something. Something big."

"Obviously," I say quietly.

"I don't know how fast the rumors are going to spread—but it can't take long. And when word gets out that Daniel's not who he says he is, the mistrust and chaos will destroy the entire Curatoria faster than any virus could. And then there will be nothing and no one to stand up to the Reduciates." She rises to her feet, a medical kit she never even opened clasped in her hand.

She turns to go, but just before she's out of arm's length I reach out and grab the corner of her scrub shirt. "Audra?" I glance both ways, but the hallway is still empty. "What am I supposed to do?"

She purses her lips and tilts her head toward me.

"Hurry."

CHAPTER THIRTY-SEVEN

Audra told me to hurry, and that's what I'm going to do. But not directly back to the lab.

I check the huge clock on the atrium wall. I don't have much time before Daniel expects me to return.

Ten minutes.

I practically run up the stairs and then down the hallway to the room I shared with Logan. I need privacy, but my Michigan bedroom is gone, and I can't risk arousing suspicion by transforming another space. Reaching the room, I close the door on the rest of the Curatoriates and glance around the apartment, curious if Logan has changed anything.

He hasn't.

The room is still a perfect replica of when Quinn and Rebecca were together. I feel a sinking in my stomach. Benson was right. Logan wants me to be who I used to be. Who I would be if I hadn't sustained so much brain damage.

But that's not who I am now.

I sit on the bed and wedge myself into a corner so I'm stable. In my hand is the plastic bag containing Sonya's braid. I know I agreed with Thomas a few hours ago when he said now is not the time—but something, something about Audra's revelation about Daniel's *diligo* is pushing me forward. Before I go back up to that lab, I need to know what Sonya knew.

I'm not sure what's going to happen, but considering how bad it was last time, I need to be prepared for anything. I don't open the plastic bag right away. I stare at the simple white twist of twine. This is the object that will bring back the memories of a woman desperate enough to kill herself to protect a secret. A secret I *have* to know now. Though logically I know suicide isn't the same for Earthbounds as it is for humans, I still get a cramp in my stomach thinking about it.

Do I *want* to know this desperate person who was once me? Do I want her secrets? Or are some things better left buried?

The next time I resurge, in my next life, I won't have a choice—Audra said all of my future awakenings should be normal, with the exception of my memories of *this* life.

In this moment, I can choose. But I can't forget as easily as I can remember. I nervously rub the braid with my thumb through the plastic.

I think the doctors may be right—that even my memories of other lives are actually Rebecca's memories. And since Rebecca couldn't have known anything about Sonya, I'll never know the entire story unless I do one more memory pull. I have to take the chance.

I slowly pull open the ziplock bag with clicks that shatter

the silence of the bedroom, and a fear like icy water makes me shiver. It's going to hurt. It's going to deplete my energy. I know that. But the work in the lab is done—the part that requires Transforming, anyway.

And my need to know Sonya's secret is so much greater after Audra's revelation. Hesitation seizes me as I reach for the cream-colored twist, but I push it away, determined to discover everything.

As my fingertips make contact, colors swirl in front of my face. The same piercing headache I remember from touching the necklace surges into my skull, filling my head with agony. I clamp my mouth shut over whimpers that fight to escape my throat. Still, it's not quite as bad as before, and I manage to remain very slightly aware of my physical body.

The warm feeling of broth being poured into my skull makes me recall the memory of the little English urchin that Marianna triggered in Portsmouth. That trace of familiarity helps calm me and wars with the jagged edges of my fears. Slowly the storm begins to calm as I spread a net around Sonya's life, rein it in and let it seep into my brain. Into *my* life.

Then the pictures are flying past—the exhilarating but manic montage that I know will take days to sort through. I try to pay attention, but the images are so fast, so blurry, and the deluge of them makes my breathing go faster and faster until my head feels like it's going to float away.

And then everything goes black.

I'm not sure how long I slump on the floor passed out, but eventually my eyes flutter open. With no windows I don't know if it's the middle of the night or early morning.

But I'm not tired.

I remember.

Pretty clearly, in fact.

My memories of being Sonya feel so much crisper than my memories of being Rebecca. I'm surprised at first, but then I remember Audra telling me to look at the big picture when I thought about "short-term memory." Of course I would remember Sonya's life more clearly; it happened so much more recently.

Most clearly, I remember those last moments, just like in my dreams. The third one was my true death; I turned my own heart to stone. My brain really was trying to tell me things I couldn't retrieve on my own.

I can see the faces of the people surrounding me in stark detail now. Marie's face. Marianna's. So determined to hide her secret.

The secret I saw as a tiny urchin on an icy night in England, one life before I became Rebecca. When I watched Marianna meet with her partner in secret.

Her partner with his short beard and kind face.

The one that has no beard now.

The one that's waiting for me up in the lab.

Daniel.

CHAPTER THIRTY-EIGHT

I walk down the corridor as though traveling on a moving walkway going the wrong direction. It feels like it takes too long, and yet I arrive at the base of the stairs in scarcely more than a thought. My legs feel too weak to carry me, but I lift them one at a time and climb.

One, two, three, four. One, two, three, four. My mental cadence from my old physical therapist comes back to me even though my leg is now healed. *One, two, three, four. One, two, three, four.*

I feel entirely alone. There's no one I can go to. Logan is off trying to get into the vault, Thomas and Alanna *have* to stay out of sight for the sake of the entire human population, and Benson . . .

I can't go to Benson.

Even if I had time, I don't dare put him at risk. Not now when I'm so close to being able to get him out of here. Alive.

It's just me now. And Sonya.

Audra's story is spinning in my head, swirling around with my newly restored memories like a merry-go-round going just fast enough to scare you but not fast enough to throw you off.

And I want off.

But not yet. One more step. *The next time I walk out of this lab, it's going to be the last time*, I swear to myself. Then I'm going to leave. And I'm never coming back. I try not to think farther than that.

To consider that nowhere in the world is truly safe. That despite its incredible facade, the Curatoria was *never* safe. Not for anyone. It was simply a way to play both sides. To hold all the cards. All the resources.

All the power.

Thomas is right. Daniel will never let me go. We're going to have to break out. Escape. Somehow. I'm not convinced I can do it. But I owe it to the world to try.

Daniel and Marianna. Marianna and Daniel. The greatest scam in the history of the world. Splitting up to concurrently run the two supposedly warring brotherhoods of supernatural beings. It's the secret I saw on the night I was killed by Marianna as a little girl in England. The secret Rebecca was drowned for protecting. Protecting until she could get enough support to do something about it.

Do I have that yet? After this morning, I don't think I do.

And even if I did, I'm still missing a piece. One final piece to this puzzle. I still don't know what *made* me the way I am.

The elusive Greta didn't come back with Sonya's memories. Fleeting impressions, an acute sense of fear, but no information. I might be able to mine it out of my brain in the future—the way I keep getting new memories of Rebecca—but it's not going to happen before my feet reach the lab.

The truth is, I may never know. Not really. Not unless Logan can manage to get Greta's artifact. Assuming, of course, that the Greta Alanna found and the Greta Sonya mentioned are, in fact, the same person. Surrounded by so many lies, even if someone told me, would I recognize the truth?

I go through the mockery of the detoxification process—the hand washing, the chemical spray-down between the air-locked doors. Surely Daniel knows I'm immune. He's playing both sides. But now would be the worst time for Daniel to find out that *I* know. I need to catch him unawares.

I look beyond the double-paned glass to see that our samples are out of their room-temperature bath and waiting for the final step. This is where we really test my abilities. Can I truly just create something that has been altered on a level even tinier than cellular . . . and have it *work*?

The thought scares me as much as it fills me with wonder.

Assuming it works, that's what I'll spend the next several months doing. Making *more*. Millions and millions of doses for everyone who has survived Daniel and Mariana's terrible plot. And when the world has all the vaccine it needs, I'll disappear like Thomas and Alanna.

I can't wait.

When Daniel sees me, his eyes light up and he rubs his hands together excitedly, like we're about to have a hearty meal. As though this morning never happened.

It makes me sick.

Everything he does makes me sick.

"I almost started without you, but I decided you deserve to see the results for yourself."

I nod wordlessly. As though I agree.

"Ready?"

We each take half of the Petri dishes holding vaccinated samples mixed with every mutation of the disease Daniel's team was able to find.

My new vaccine has to repel *all* of them, or it'll be useless—just a tiny bump on the road for this fast-mutating sickness.

We have forty samples to test. I begin bringing them over to our worktable.

"Where are the lab techs?" I ask. Normally they would have done the menial work like this for us. Had the samples ready and waiting.

"I told them to stay away," Daniel says, and his whole body seems tense. "It's not that I think this is going to fail—I don't, I have great confidence that this is it—but *if* it does, I can't have it getting out." He smiles tightly at me. "Just the two of us."

I don't argue, but it does seem odd—and I make a note and store it away in my head.

Two hours later my chest is tight and I'm having trouble focusing on the final couple of slides. Every single one has been effective so far. Daniel's hands are trembling visibly as he clips in his last slide.

We've hardly spoken this entire time. Just one word. "Positive. Positive. Positive." The word that means the vaccine is working. That it's repelling the virus.

I rub my eyes before peering into the microscope again.

Despite the excitement, my body is tired. From hunching, from that clenching of all my muscles just before I'm sure of what I'm seeing, from holding and releasing my breath.

From not exploding with all the secrets inside me. I glance at the clock. It's only a few minutes until Daniel's countdown technically ends. But how accurately can you estimate the time of somebody's *death*?

It could happen early. The thought makes me shiver, and I force myself to focus on my slide. I've got to finish and get the hell out of here.

"Positive," I whisper, then reach for the last slide.

Daniel sits up straight and runs his gloved fingers through his hair. "Positive," he echoes. I turn to my final slide.

Last one.

I peer into the lighted field, focusing, zooming in, looking for the markers. *Check one, two, three, and four*.

Four signs.

All positive.

I lean back. *I'm done.*

Yes, this vaccine is literally going to save billions of people, but what I'm truly thankful for at this precise moment is that I don't have to work in this lab—with Daniel—ever again.

"Tavia?" I look over at him and see, for the first time ever, raw fear in his eyes. I don't understand for a second until he says, "Well?"

Oh. I didn't say it. I let a fraction of the relief I feel show in a tiny smile that barely curves the edges of my mouth. "Positive."

A sound that's half whoop, half sob comes out of Daniel's

mouth, and he strips off his gloves. I start to reprimand him, but realize that all of the diseased samples have been neutralized; it doesn't really matter. "Hurry, hurry, fill the trays!" he says. "Enough for everyone here—we'll get it right over to the medical wing." I stand, but my legs falter beneath me.

I didn't actually eat during my break.

I'm so weak already. But I don't want to stay in this lab one *second* longer than I must. I can last—I have to. I create some orange juice inside my mouth and swallow it down. I've got to get through this.

We stand in front of the trays upon trays of empty tube holders. For our tests I only made one tray's worth, but I generated the whole thing with one swish of my hands. My abilities are so powerful that even now it's hard to comprehend.

I close my eyes and picture the isolated protein transformed within the active viral vaccine that Daniel's team made. I draw my inner camera back and picture the drops of murky fluid, then tubes full of the liquid, then trays full of the tubes. I open my eyes, take a breath, grit my teeth, and wave my arm over the table.

With the quietest of clatters, the trays are full.

Thousands of doses of vaccine against the virus that's ravaging the world. That's killing Earthbounds so violently the world is being destroyed with them.

The earth's salvation. There in hundreds of tiny tubes.

I did that.

I take an unsteady step backward, not from weariness but the sheer enormity of what I've just done.

"So . . . so that's it? There? Just like last time?"

I nod, staring.

A grin spreads slowly across Daniel's face. "At last," he whispers. "At last." He turns to me, his arms outstretched.

I do *not* want to hug him, but he doesn't give me time to protest. He draws me to him, pounding my back with his hand. I'm just lifting my arms to push him away when fire thrusts into my stomach and everything in my body clenches around the stabbing pain of a knife, jammed into my abdomen.

I yank back, my wide eyes staring at Daniel, but his hand whips up and grabs my face, squeezing my jaw and pulling me forward toward him. My skin seems to burn where his bare fingers touch my face, and distantly I realize he's never touched me. Not skin to skin.

Even the first day we met, he never proffered his hand. And until today, he's never touched me until we were both decontaminated and *gloved*.

And now I know why.

As I stare into his intense eyes, feeling the blood pouring from my stomach, soaking into my shirt, I feel a memory rushing at me and pulling all at the same time, ripping my soul away in what I now recognize as one of the ways my mind handles remembering a single moment.

By dropping me directly into it.

CHAPTER THIRTY-NINE

I'm walking down the street. Germany, 1943. My body hurts. Each step unsteady and aching. It takes a while to realize that it's because I'm old. I don't remember ever being old before.

It's raining. Not the kind that really gets you wet, the kind that just makes you miserable. My arms are full of groceries, and they're too heavy to spare a hand to swipe across my damp face.

Today I went east. Every day I walk as far as I can to a grocer—as many different ones as possible—and create new ration tickets to exchange for meager helpings of the barest necessities.

It's stealing, I know—those ration tickets are my creation; they aren't real. And since I still haven't found my Quinn, they will disappear in about five minutes. But I think of myself as a rather sadder version of Robin Hood. Stealing from the poor to give to those who have nothing.

Someday I will be caught. But it will take a while yet, I think. No one suspects the little old lady, and I do my best to look even older and more frail than I actually am every time I go out.

Perhaps I can last until this war is over. My dear friends and me. The three families that have been with me for almost two years now, and the ones who come and go.

I'm almost home.

I pretend to fumble at the lock on the door, but actually I'm giving the special knock that will warn my friends that I am coming, that it is only me. I push the door closed and lean on it for a few seconds, breathing hard.

My frailty is less and less of a pretense these days. I stand straight and get two steps before something dark comes down over my head and I scream and drop the food.

I'm shuffled out the door and loaded into a vehicle. I say nothing. There's a chance that I've been turned in to the SS, but my friends are safe. I will do nothing to endanger them if even the slightest possibility exists that they are yet alive. I hope and pray to anyone who may be out there that this is the case.

It feels like hours before the rumbling of the vehicle beneath me stops. My arms are seized again, and they march too fast for me. My feet drag, and I cannot move quickly enough to get them beneath me to walk on my own. Finally I'm shoved onto a hard surface—my hip bruising on the left side—and the dark material is yanked away from my face. I gasp at the fresh air, filling my lungs.

"Greta."

My name is spoken by a voice that freezes my soul to ice. I raise my eyes and see a young Daniel. Barely more than a teenager. And his partner. Marianna. The Ice Queen I used to call her in a long-past life. She's only about thirty, but her hair is prematurely graying—as it always is. It adds to her austere facade.

Ah, so not the SS kind of trouble. The Earthbound kind of trouble. They must be desperate if they're together again. They're never together. It's too risky. Someone might find out.

Someone like me.

They've been hunting me since I was that tiny, half-frozen child in England and I saw them together and the Ice Queen murdered me for it, not recognizing me as my child-self.

Though in that life Daniel had gotten himself so scarred I barely recognized him for who he was when I accidentally awakened my memories as Greta nearly thirty years ago.

Ironic, that all these years I've been hiding from the SS, and who catches me but Daniel and Marianna? My nemeses, who secretly formed and ran both the Curatoria and the Reduciata—bending all the Earthbounds in the world to their twisted wills.

It's a level of greed and corruption I can scarcely imagine, though I've meditated on it for almost thirty years now.

And yet, a cheerful thought comes to me: if it is they who have found me, perhaps my friends are safe. I know it's the last comforting thought I'll have in this life.

Perhaps that's why my mouthy side kicks in. "You've caught me," I say. "An old woman of seventy-three. But I have several lives left. Are you really going to spend the next few hundred years chasing me?"

"No," Marianna says, piping up from behind Daniel. She

336

has a glass syringe, and whatever is in it makes fear tremble within me as my incredible intuition kicks in. "This will be the last time. The last time you see anything, actually. But especially us. And, of course, also your diligo—Quinn, I believe his name was the last time you saw him."

That makes me fall silent. He is my weakness, and she knows it.

I'm not ashamed of that. The businesslike relationship she and Daniel have come to share is downright unnatural for a pair of Earthbounds. We should be entwined so tightly that death feels preferable to separation.

I certainly feel that way. But without the help of the Curatoria, what are my chances of ever finding my Quinn again? I've always known that the probability was small—especially when the war began—but whatever Daniel and Marianna have come up with, they obviously think they can do something of permanence. To ensure Quinn and I never meet again.

Marianna passes the syringe off to Daniel and walks to the opposite side of the room. I'm not sure if she's handing off her dirty work, or if after shooting me last time, she feels he deserves a turn. Regardless, I have no time to protest before the sting of a needle plunges into my arm.

CHAPTER FORTY

I return to reality with the ghost pain in my arm replaced by the overwhelming agony in my stomach—the shirt around the knife brilliant with the red of my own blood.

But even that can't wholly distract me from what I just saw.

That moment. *That moment* is what made me what I am. Daniel and Marianna *gave me the virus*. They expected me to die forever.

But I didn't.

Why didn't I?

I should have. Instead, the virus *changed me*. It must have mutated, even back then. I know at least one memory-less life must have passed between Greta and Sonya, but what I clearly remember from touching Sonya's twine braid is that as a newly graduated eighteen-year-old, I stumbled upon a ring in an antique jewelry store and awakened my memories.

Along with abilities so powerful—so difficult to control—they terrified me.

I have all the pieces now. Not all the answers, but the pieces: I knew about Marianna and Daniel's secret partnership; Marianna must have recognized my child-self *after* she shot me. Then they had to get rid of me. Eternally. That's why they tried the virus on me. But that ill-fated experiment turned me into a Transformist and gave me unimaginable powers along with immunity.

I knew all of those incredible things had to be tied together. I just needed more information.

But has it all come too late? I look down as I throw my hand over the pain in my stomach, forcing back a scream as that hurts even worse. The knife is still there, blood staining my shirt all around it.

Oh dear gods! Leave it? Pull it out? I clench my fist around the bloody handle, but I'm frozen with indecision. All I can think of is Inigo Montoya in *The Princess Bride*, and a bubble of laughter builds up in my throat. I gasp against it, knowing that I'm lost if I let the hysteria take over.

I have to breathe.

I have to talk.

"You don't want to save the world," I say, my mind fuzzy from the pain as I pretend to be far more ignorant than I am. "You're going . . . you're going to let them all die." And he might succeed. I only made maybe a hundred thousand doses of the vaccine. Not enough for even the barest fraction of the human race. And now he's going to kill me.

Leaving over six billion people without a cure.

"Oh, I wouldn't say that," he says softly, his face close to mine. "I want to save the world for the *important* people. But you're right; there aren't very many of those." He shoves me from him, and I stagger, falling against the table where the electron microscope sits. The one I've been hunched in front of for four days. "And *you* are not one of them."

He reaches out a hand, and in the same motion he used with the red-haired Reduciate pawn this morning, he clenches his fist.

Suddenly, I can't breathe. My body tightens, spasms, searching for air. I slide to the ground as I fight the urge to cough, remembering the conversation I had with Audra. *No air to the lungs, all of the muscles in the esophagus seize up, trying to prevent the unpreventable.*

The drawing. Audra's drawing!

I picture it in my mind and continue to fight. I close my eyes, grip the hilt of the knife in my stomach even tighter, and force myself to concentrate on each individual part of my throat, willing it back together, transforming destruction into wholeness. The esophagus, the tubes that connect to the lungs, the vocal chords. It feels like it takes hours, even though I know it can't be much longer than a single second.

The pain recedes; I suck a cautious, silent breath in through my nose.

And my lungs calm.

I did it!

I open my eyes the tiniest crack. Daniel's watching me, but it's not with suspicion—he's watching me die. He *thinks* he's watching me die. There are few Earthbounds powerful enough to heal themselves from the inside out with no medical knowledge whatsoever.

But then, he's always underestimated me.

Audra's voice sounds so loudly in my head that it's like she's there screaming it in my ear: *Blood pours from the mouth as the victim coughs and sputters and tries to suck in oxygen, but the connection to the lungs is gone.*

I have to make it look good. I let myself cough, forcing it out of my new throat as I collapse onto the floor. Shaking away the gross-factor, I use my powers to fill my mouth with my own blood, and the next time I cough it splatters everywhere.

Daniel jerks back and away from the splash of red, and in the split second that his eyes leave me I suck in a deep breath, fall fully to the floor, and hold it, willing my entire body to be completely still. I have to convince him I'm dead.

One, two, three, four, five, six.

I want to cry when I hear Daniel move, but it's not away; he moves *closer*. I don't understand until I feel something small and cool against my lips. For a second I think he's trying to feed me something, but a tiny peek from under my lashes shows me a test tube with a small amount of blood in it.

Finally Daniel walks away. My lungs are burning, but I force myself to suck in air slowly and silently.

Why did he take my blood?

The answer makes my body rigid with fear even as I chide myself. Of course he knows I'm immune. He's Marianna's *diligo*. He knows *everything* the Reduciata knows. Has *always* known. But now that he's not in such a hurry, of course he'll want to study my blood.

But no one, *no one* except me, knows the truth. That my blood is more than immune. That it's a *cure*. More than a cure. That it can turn Earthbounds into . . . into whatever I am now.

He can't have it.

Marianna can*not* have it.

The sheer enormity of the depth these two have gone to fills me with a rage that momentarily numbs the pain in my stomach.

How long? Everybody talks about Daniel as though he's been the leader of the Curatoria for as long as it's been in existence. They must have been scamming everyone the entire time. . . .

From the beginning of the existence of the brotherhoods, just like Greta thought.

I glare at Daniel's back. My acting job has bought me a few minutes, max. If I were at a hospital I'd probably leave the knife in, but it's so sharp, surely it's just going to do more damage. I brace myself and then make the knife disappear with a thought. It's much less violent than actually pulling it out, but the moment it goes away I feel my life ebbing out of me through that void—sucking my energy.

I create a tight strip of bandaging across my abdomen. I debate closing the skin, but all that will do is make me bleed internally. And make it more difficult for a doctor to get inside again to patch me up. Bandaging will have to do. I consider trying to heal myself the way I did my throat, but dismiss the idea almost immediately. I was only able to restore my esophagus because Audra took me through step-by-step. And even so, I know I'm going to have to have her look at it later. Fix my shoddy work.

Right now I just need to get out of this lab!

Keeping a close eye on Daniel's back, I force my aching body to rise from the floor. He's on the phone. And after seeing Sonya's last moments I'm betting I can guess with whom.

"She's dead," he says softly. "We'll have to fight her again in her next life—with her immunity we might be fighting her forever—but at least she can't interfere anymore right now."

I stare at the tiny vial of my blood hanging from Daniel's fingers.

Part of me wants to transform it into infected blood.

But if Daniel and Marianna caught the virus it would kill them forever. And what landforms would they take with them? How many more millions of people would I condemn to death for my own vengeance?

With a heart-rending pang of regret, I ripple my fingers and transform the red liquid in the tube to simple water with food coloring. Then I take a deep breath and change all of the new serum into the old, useless vaccine. I remind myself that the cure exists within *me*—that the blueprint is in my head. I'll just have to find another way to get it to the world.

"I'll tell them a Reduciate assassin killed her," Daniel says. "It works every time."

Of course it does.

I inch toward the air locks. The timing will have to be perfect.

"Absolutely. Worked on every sample and every mutation. I have her blood and the vaccine; I'll be on a chopper within the hour. We're cutting it close—I don't know how much longer they'll live."

They. The two Earthbounds dying in the secret room, I assume.

I stretch my hand out toward the button that will activate the air locks, but his next words shock me into stillness.

"I'll pick up the mixed pair on my way out. They'll come easily enough, and I'll infect them in the air. One more week for the virus to kill them while we get to the safe house and this will all be over."

My lungs freeze. One week. Not only do I have to get out of here, I have to make sure that *he* doesn't.

And that he doesn't lay one finger on Thomas and Alanna.

Daniel's starting to turn. With one hand I push the air-lock switch, and with the other I transform the floor into air, plunging all of its contents down to whatever lies beneath.

I wish I knew the layout of the headquarters better—I'd take out layers and layers of ceilings and floors. Maybe create an endless void. But even as strong as I am, I'm not all-powerful, and I can't change what I'm not familiar with. What I can't see.

But some of it is visible *now*, so before I go I transform one more floor, dumping Daniel and the debris another ten feet.

Daniel's face as he falls would be satisfying if I wasn't far, far too late. If he hadn't already killed so many people—destroyed so many lives. But as I stand in the air-lock doorway, I can't help but feel a pang of regret as the beautiful microscopes shatter on the concrete floor two stories down from the lab, and debris piles on top of it all. On top of Daniel.

CHAPTER FORTY-ONE

There's no time for reveries—and no guarantee that the fall killed Daniel. If there's one thing I've learned since becoming an Earthbound, it's that it is *hard* to kill a god.

I know I should have done something more extreme—cut off his life directly—but I just couldn't. I can't become what he is.

Too late, as I stare at the destruction of the lab, I realize what I've done—I've exposed samples of the virus into the Curatoria headquarters. If the destruction of Death Valley doesn't kill them, the virus will. Forever. I have to tell everyone to get out!

Doing what I can, I create a huge plastic dome around the rubble, then stagger into the hallway and toward the grand staircase that looks like it's a million miles away. Pain shoots through my abdomen, and blackness crowds in on my vision. I force it away. Once I get to the stairs it'll be easier.

Or so I think. The first step down jars my body, and renewed agony ripples through me. My head spins and my knees tremble. "Help." But my brand-new vocal chords don't want to work quite right. "Help! Help me!" I finally manage to yell in a voice that only just sounds like my own.

Faces turn to me. And shock and gasps ripple through the crowd. The last time they saw me Daniel was declaring me to be their salvation. What am I now? I remember how I look, my mouth caked in my own blood, my clothes spattered and ripped. I must appear completely crazy.

The conspiracy theories pouring from my lips certainly don't help my image. "Daniel has betrayed you all. He's . . . he's . . . a Reduciate." *No, it's worse than that; he's manipulated their entire organization and thrust the world into infinite peril. But that's the only word they'll understand*—Reduciate. "He did this." My head swirls. I'm not sure if I'm talking or whispering now. "Help." I get that last plea out before my knees collapse from under me.

And I fall against something warm and solid.

"Tavia." *Thomas. Thank you, gods.* I don't even mind that he and Alanna were supposed to stay in hiding. Maybe now we all really can leave together.

"We have to escape." I try to open my eyes, but they won't obey.

"Drink this." Alanna's voice pushing a straw into my mouth. Something sugary sweet. I don't like it, but a tiny sliver of my consciousness reminds me that I need it if I'm going to survive. If anyone is going to survive. I *am* the vaccine now.

"Where is he?" Thomas whispers, but not to me. I don't know who he's talking about.

"I don't know. I told him not to go far, but he said he had something to do."

No. *Logan.* They don't know where he is. And it's because I sent him after my artifacts.

"Tavia," Thomas repeats, bending down so I can see his face without opening my eyes too much. "We're a hundred miles away from anything. You're hurt—I'm going to take you to medical. We need to get you fixed up, then we'll leave. Just like we talked about earlier."

"No, Thomas, listen to me." I reach out and grab his sleeve, hanging on like that's all that's keeping me here in this world. "Daniel knows about you and Alanna. Knows *everything*. If he's not dead, he's coming after you next. But . . . but . . ." My brain is swimming me toward unconsciousness. But there's something—something I have to tell him. "The virus," I finally remember. "It might be loose."

Thomas hesitates, staring at me in horror.

"Thomas, please," I beg. "I destroyed the lab. I may have let the virus out. Everyone has to leave—especially you."

He stares. An infinity passes. "Logan or Benson?"

Now? Seriously?

"I can't save them both. There's no time. We can look for Logan, or we can break Benson out. We can't do both."

The crowd around me yells, grumbles, calls out questions, but it's like all sound has been muted. Time slows, stills, stops.

Which one?

Which one?

Of course.

"Benson," I breathe.

Then my legs are swept out from under me, and I'm crushed against Thomas's huge chest. He's holding me, running down the stairs so quickly that each step jolts my entire body and I have to bite down on screams of pain.

At the bottom of the stairs he doesn't pause but heads for the western staircase that will lead us to the security wing. To Benson. *Thank you*, I think, my eyes trying to close on their own again.

"Stop them!" Daniel's voice reverberates through the hallway. Tears of pure and utter hopelessness well up in my eyes as Thomas jerks to a stop and turns just enough that I can see Daniel. He looks terribly powerful, standing there, straight and tall, though his sleeve is torn and dusty and blood pours down several gashes—the most obvious across his forehead, blood striping his face like a macabre mask. He points a finger at us. "She has the vaccine, and they're taking it to the Reduciates!"

The Curatoriates hear his lie, and unlike how they reacted when I made a similar declaration while equally bloody, they *listen* to him. And then they turn as one, the fear and anger in their eyes shooting directly at us.

Daniel raises his fist, and I know whatever he is about to do will look like it's attacking Thomas, but it'll kill *me*. There's no way Daniel is going to let me live now. Especially if he saved a few vials of what he thinks is the new vaccine.

And if he managed to protect himself, then he probably did.

"Run," I whisper.

But I didn't have to. Thomas is already fleeing, shoving people out of his way as he leaps up the stairs two at a time.

I expect something—the floor to collapse beneath us, the roof to suddenly lose its supports and rain down on us, but when I peek back, I see someone on top of Daniel taking care of him in the oldest human way—with his fists.

Someone blond.

Logan.

But there's only that tiny second before the screams and crashing begin. A panicked crowd of humans can kill; I don't want to know what a panicked crowd of gods can do.

I keep my eyes scrunched shut against tears, but it doesn't take much imagination to picture the walls of the Curatoria prison falling away before Alanna's destructive power.

The security doors shut some of the noise out, and I'm surrounded by voices, protests.

Then silence.

"Benson, take her. No questions. We have to get her out of here. To a hospital."

I'm tossed roughly to Benson, and I shriek in pain, but as soon as I settle in his arms, I know I'm safe. Not what I once thought of as *safe*—protected from bodily harm—but safe in the knowledge that even if I die, I'm in the right place.

"She's bleeding!" Benson says.

"Worse than that—she's half-dead," Thomas says, his voice farther away now.

"You're going to help her, aren't you?"

"I'm going to do my damndest."

"Please, Dad—" Benson's voice breaks off. "Show me how to save her. I'll do anything."

"Benson, I would lay down my own life for this girl of yours. I only gave her to you because I think you would too. Now *run*."

"This way." Alanna's voice now. My eyes are scrunched closed. It's all I can do to even stay conscious as I bounce around in Benson's arms.

I'm trying.

Trying.

Logan. We left him. I don't think Thomas even saw him. I try to speak. To tell them to go back. But nothing in my body is obeying me. My eyes won't stay open. It hurts to breathe.

They're taking me in a small space. A tunnel, I think. "We made this about a year ago," Thomas explains as they jog. I wonder if he's talking to cover up the sounds behind us. Sounds of destruction I can't bear to think very hard about, despite the rumbling of the earth beneath us. "Took ages to get around all the pipes and footings and crap that go into a structure this big."

"What do we do when we get out?" Benson asks, his breath heavy from carrying me. I want to help, but I can't.

Can't.

"Making dune buggies is one of my specialties," Thomas says, but now, with my eyes closed and listening closely, I can hear the fear and panic in his voice too. I remember how

Benson used to get very quiet when he was afraid. My tired, weary brain finds it humorous that his father is the opposite.

"How long before we can get her to a hospital?"

Thomas doesn't answer right away.

"We've never had reason to time it," Alanna says softly. "But at least an hour, maybe two. Once we get going I'll help you staunch the bleeding. It's all we can do."

"Hold on," Benson whispers, and it takes me a second to realize he's talking to me.

And that I was letting go.

How did he know?

Warm air hits my face, and I cling to consciousness as Benson slides into something that must be the thing Thomas talked about. Dune buggy?

"Hold her tight," Thomas says. "This is *not* going to be a smooth ride."

Benson's arms tighten around me, and even though somewhere in my brain I know I'm dying, I feel safer. The weird vehicle bounces into action, and suddenly there is sand in my nose and I have to cough, but doing so sends spasms of pain through my abdomen and I can't hold back a scream.

"Cover her mouth with this," Alanna says, and cloth goes over my mouth and nose as my head lolls on Benson's shoulder.

I force my eyes to open one more time to look behind us. The last thing I see as we speed away is the entire enormous glowing triangle collapsing into the desert sand and the bright stars twinkling against a black velvet sky.

CHAPTER FORTY-TWO

It was the first glowing triangle I saw. Nothing more, nothing less. Just simple chance. I ran from my Colorado home and jumped the first train I could get on. Then, every time it stopped, I would go walking, looking for glowing triangles. The symbol of a Curatoria safe house.

It took over three months.

I'm not proud of the things I did to stay alive during that time, but here I am, and technically, no one got hurt.

I don't like going to the Curatoriates, not when I know about Daniel and Marianna. But if I'm careful, I can use their resources to help me find Quinn—whatever his name is now—before they figure out exactly who I am.

Then I'm gone.

But even having made the decision ages ago, I'm terrified to take those last few steps to the door tonight. Into the lion's den, really. But I have to find my diligo *if I want any chance of this all ending. Ending happily, I should say.*

I should have told Quinn about Daniel and Marianna. I know that now. Trying to find each other without the brotherhoods is hard enough without one member of a pair not having any idea he needs to avoid them both.

If I could go back . . .

But I can't. Maybe this house—these random Curatoriates—could be a step forward though. I lift a hand that feels like it weighs five hundred pounds and press the doorbell. I hear the chime peal beyond the thick door.

A minute passes. Two. Or maybe it's only seconds; it's impossible to tell. But finally the door opens and I'm standing before a tall man with regal, prematurely white hair, dressed in a three-piece suit. I'm glad it's dusk so he probably can't see the scuffs and stains on my shabby jeans.

"Can I help you?"

Dear gods, can I even say it? "My name is Sonya," I start.

"Yes," he prompts when I'm silent.

I peer up at him, channeling every ounce of courage I have within me. "Sum Terrobligatus."

His eyes widen, but he covers it quickly. "I suppose so, if you can be quick about it," he says just a touch too loud. "Come in."

I resist the urge to glance in both directions before hurrying through the doorway. Because, really, what good would that do anyway?

I walk into a nice parlor that—though dim because no

one has turned the lamps on yet—looks both elegant and comfortable.

"Please have a seat," the man says, more anxious to please now that the front door is closed and locked with—I notice gratefully—two bolts plus a chain.

We sit in armchairs on opposite sides of a carved coffee table, and I'm trying to figure out which of us is supposed to speak first when I startle at a movement in the doorway.

The man's eyes follow mine, and he smiles. "Don't worry. This is my daughter, Samantha. She's a Curatoriate as well. Young, but initiated."

Sammi stands there, long blond hair curling around her shoulders, staring at me with excitement, but still that inner strength I always sensed in her later in her life. Even at seventeen years old, she has it.

And although I know this isn't how the first meeting with Sammi and her father actually ended, I rise from my armchair and rush over and throw my arms around her, overjoyed to see her again, even though I know it's only a dream.

Her arms lift and wrap around me, hugging me back, and for the first time in so very long, I feel at peace.

CHAPTER FORTY-THREE

I awake to the sound of a machine pinging out the beating of a heart. *My* heart, I assume. It's so reminiscent of the way I awoke from the plane wreck that for a moment I wonder—really wonder—if everything, every terrible and wonderful thing, could have been a dream.

The most awful, wonderful dream of my life.

But the throbbing I feel is only in my stomach—not my leg and head and chest and throat, the way it was when my poor, barely alive body came back to life after the crash.

I blink, and my eyes obey me—another difference.

The light is piercing but bearable. I look around at a small but clean hospital room. At first I think it's empty, but then I see Benson curled up in the gray recliner, his dingy white T-shirt almost blending in.

"Benson?" My voice sounds different. Not a lot, but enough that I know these are *not* the vocal chords I was born with.

He's instantly awake. "Tave!" He vaults up out of the chair, trips on his shoes, and sprawls on the floor. Maybe not quite instantly.

I smile weakly as he gets to his feet and comes to sit beside me, reaching for my hand. The one without an IV. "How do you feel?"

I have to consider his question. "I've felt worse," I settle on. *Oh, that is the truth*. I confess the pathos that being stabbed in the stomach only rates *minor inconvenience* in my life.

"Is . . ." I hate to ask Benson, but it's the most important question. "Do you know if Logan got out?"

Benson shakes his head. "Not *no*," he corrects quickly. "We *don't* know." He shrugs helplessly. "We don't know anything beyond the four of us."

Oh gods. Logan.

And the loss feels somehow worse having woken up in a hospital bed for the second time in my life. I hate hospitals now. *Hate* is too tame a word. I want to jump up and run screaming from the room rather than lie here at the mercy of a team of doctors and nurses as I fight to make my body obey me. Tears are pricking at my eyes, and panic and regret and a sharp mourning are sweeping through me. "Benson," I whisper, "hold me."

He hesitates for a moment, but I know it's not *me* per se—he's worried about hurting me. Again. I scoot over a bit, and he slips into the bed, his body warm against mine. I curl against his shoulder, and his hands rub up and down my back as I wait for the terror to fade.

"I left him." My heart aches at the thought. "I saw him. At the last second."

"Dad said we had to," Benson whispers.

"No." My lips tremble. "There was a moment when I had a choice. I chose you. Instead of him. *I* left him." The sight of the triangle collapsing in on itself. It would have killed all the humans. Or—at the very least—those not close enough for an Earthbound to save them.

What about Audra?

Daniel?

Logan?

Logan.

Logan.

My heart wants to cry, but my body has no tears left. "I would know, wouldn't I?" I ask. "If he was dead?"

Benson is quiet for long seconds, his fingers rubbing lightly over my arms. "Maybe," he finally says. "You often seem to just *know* things."

It's not a yes. But it's not a no either. "Thank you for bringing me here," I say into his shirt.

"Thank you for holding on," he whispers.

After a few minutes I feel calm enough to raise my face from his shoulder and look at him.

"I hope he's alive, Ben. But I can't go back to him."

He's silent, and I know I've put him in an awkward position, listening to me talk about the guy I should be in love with. Who might be dead.

I'm not sure just how to explain this, but it has to be said.

"Benson, have you ever been to the top of a really tall build-ing and looked down and gotten that weird feeling in your stomach?"

"Sure."

I hesitate. "That's how I feel when I look into Logan's eyes. The way he feels about me—the love he has for me—it's so vast and deep it makes me dizzy to see it."

He shifts uncomfortably but doesn't pull away.

"But I can't spend the rest of my life trying to be good enough for someone. I can't love someone just because I'm supposed to. I just . . . I can't be with him." I lay my cheek against his chest again. "Especially when I want so badly to be with you." I chuckle sadly. "I guess I really am an ant."

"An ant?" Benson asks, clearly beyond confused.

"I'll explain another time." I force myself to sit up. To look him squarely in the face. "Benson, I'm at war with the Earthbound. Maybe some of them will believe me and be on my side, but I don't think there will be very many. It's literally going to be me against nearly the entirety of *both* brotherhoods." I grip his arms with my hands. "Will you stand with me?"

"To the death," Benson whispers with zero hesitation.

"Thank you." The words feel so paltry. I lift a hand to his face, and when my fingertips make contact, my whole body seems to sag in relief. As I pull him forward with the slightest pressure against his cheek, I feel an almost audible click, as though my life was on the wrong course and only now is going back to its true destiny. My lips touch his, and a warmth spreads through me that's more than wanting and desire—although it's that as well—it's comfort and pleasure and something beautiful that I can't describe.

I push nearer, press closer, and a pain shoots up from my abdomen, making me gasp.

"I'm so sorry," Benson says, looking me up and down, not sure what he did.

"It's my stomach," I say, gingerly fingering the surface of my hospital gown. "It hurts."

"Do you want to look at it?"

"Yeah," I say, not understanding why he's even asking.

"Well I . . . I have no idea what you're wearing under . . . there."

I snort at his reddened face. "Like that really matters," I say. I pull the bottom of my hospital gown up, leaving only the blanket to cover the barest of essentials, and reveal my stomach.

"Oh gods," I breathe. I must seriously be under the influence of more pain meds than I thought because there's a line of staples from just below my belly button to right between my breasts.

Benson is staring in horror. "I didn't see it while you were still out," he says, his face having gone from red to white in a matter of seconds. "They only described it."

"What happened?" I ask. I am *quite* sure this is more than what Daniel did to me.

Benson sits back down on the edge of the bed, and it's probably a good thing he did so before *falling* over. "Here's what the doctors told me; maybe you can make sense of it. I told them we were at a party last night and that I didn't know what had happened to you, just that you told me to take you to a hospital. When they came out, they told me you'd been stabbed."

"Daniel stabbed me," I confirm.

He nods. "But that wasn't the weird part. They said they had to extend the incision because your entire abdominal cavity was filled with blood and . . . and stuff. They used bigger words. But basically, they said it looked like you had been stabbed multiple times, but that there was only one entry wound, and they had to go all over cleaning everything out."

"Oh, thank goodness," I say, and Benson looks at me funny. I explain as well as I can what Audra told me about what would have happened in my body when Daniel severed my throat from the inside. And the resulting mess it would have created. "I would have had to go to someone else and have it fixed, but they were smart enough to take care of it. So now everything's okay."

"You made yourself a new throat?" Benson asks, amazed. I remember that he's been around Earthbounds his whole life, and instead of that making me mad, this time I'm proud that I could impress someone who has seen everything he's seen. "That's why you sound different."

I kinda love that he noticed.

He looks somberly down at the incision my belly. "We can't stay here waiting for your stomach to heal," he says. "We took a risk checking you in and letting them take you into surgery. I am so sorry to do this to you, but how soon do you think you can leave?"

"Benson," I start to scold.

"Tave, it's not easy to kill a god. Even after everything collapsed, they could be on their way here *right now*."

"Benson—"

"Please, please, Tave, don't make me watch them take you again." His eyes shine with tears, and I reach out a hand for his.

"Just look," I whisper, then turn my attention to my stomach. Slowly, carefully, an inch at a time, I transform the staples into unbroken skin. In less than a minute Benson is sucking in fast breaths and staring at my unmarked abdomen.

"I didn't think of that," he says after a long silence.

"It's not perfect," I say, cringing as I push up to sitting. "The stitches are still there on the inside. I don't know enough about anatomy to heal it all the way down, not to mention muscle walls and organs and . . . stuff like that." I transform the air around me into underwear and loose cotton pants as I slide from beneath the blankets, and another thought gives me a cotton T-shirt and bra instead of the short hospital gown. I smile painfully at him as a jolt sears through my abdomen. "I'm going to be very sore for a while."

Sore may be a bit of an understatement; it's difficult to even stand up straight. But I have very little pride left, so I let myself hunch, leaning on him. Another thought takes away the IV, the little chest sensors, and the heartbeat thing on my finger. "What do we do now?" I ask, trying to be brave.

"Thomas and Alanna are getting us a car."

"Dare I ask exactly what that means?" I ask, rolling my eyes.

"I'm not sure, actually," Benson says. "Before he left us—my mom and brother and me, I mean—my father was an automotive engineer. For all I know he's *creating* us the best car

ever made. But he could be acquiring it the other way too."
His phone chimes and he pulls it out and looks at the screen.
"We're about to find out. He's ready and wants instructions."
He looks up at me in question.

I take in a slow breath and run my fingers through my hair,
turning it jet-black. "Tell him to drive around to the front door,
that we'll be there in a few minutes." While Benson's tapping
away I add smudgy black eyeliner and several pieces of silver
jewelry as well as shoes. I take stock of myself and quickly
conjure up a purse just before a nurse pokes her head through
the door.

"Oh, excuse me," she says, and ducks out again only to
return a few seconds later. "Are you Jane Simmons?"

"No," I say honestly, though I imagine that's the name
Benson came up with for me.

"But . . ." Her eyes return to the chart open in her hands.
"You shouldn't be out of bed."

"What?" I say, letting false indignation hang heavy in my
tone. "But I was just released. My mom and dad are getting the
car. This is my brother, Bud," I add when the silence stretches
out a little too long. I smack Benson on the shoulder in what I
hope is a sisterly fashion. "He drove me here last night."

"You just got out of surgery," the nurse says, still befuddled.

"What? Whoa, no," I say, holding both hands up in front
of me. "I was in for food poisoning. And cramps," I tack on,
and I lift the bottom of my shirt enough to show my unmarked
stomach and pat it gently. "Bad combination," I say. "But I'm
good now. The doctor said I could go."

The woman stares at my stomach, then at the chart, then my stomach again. "I'll be right back," she says.

"We better get out of here," I tell Benson, turning toward the door. "She's going to call security or something stupid in a second, I'm sure."

Benson nods and takes my hand in his. It feels right, our hands joined as we head out to fight a world that would prefer us dead.

We manage to skirt around the corner without seeing the nurse, and I hope she doesn't get in trouble for the stunt we just pulled. Alanna and Thomas are waiting for us right at the front doors, and though they give my new look a double take, Alanna hurries around to help me into the sedan. It's a very fancy-looking car and I don't quite recognize the make, so I suspect it's newly created rather than newly stolen.

"She sealed her skin on the outside," Benson explains under his breath, "but she's still sore." He sits behind the driver's seat, and I lay down carefully with my head on his lap, my hidden incision throbbing from the fast walk.

"Where are we going, Tave?" Thomas asks, pulling away from the hospital.

Anywhere but here, I think. But I have a plan. "Phoenix," I say. "There's a Mayo Clinic there." I remember seeing it from the Greyhound two weeks ago. It's perfect. Close, in a huge city, and no one would expect me to go back there after the attack on Logan's family.

"Well, the news is just trickling in," Thomas says over his shoulder. "The two people we saw in the secret hospital room must have managed to live maybe an hour after the Earthbound panic led to the collapse of the headquarters—which is what we saw as we drove away."

Despite the flat tone of his words, I can't help but believe that if the initial collapse didn't kill *those two*—helpless and unconscious—maybe Logan survived too. They make earthquake-proof buildings; maybe the headquarters was designed to stand up to a collapse.

"But they're definitely dead now. Death Valley is gone," he finishes, almost in a whisper, and my hopes sink. "Leveled. More than leveled, actually. It's a hole in the ground hundreds of miles across. There's a lake at the bottom, but they still can't tell how deep it is." He pauses. "I expect it goes down to bedrock, but that's only a guess."

"Any sign of . . . of anyone?" I ask, hearing the desperate edge in my voice and not caring.

"No, but that's not surprising. No Earthbound would let themselves get caught in the middle of this." He pauses for a long time. "There's just no way to know if Daniel *or* Logan are alive, I'm afraid. Not yet."

I nod, and then tears are leaking down my face. The rough pads of Benson's thumbs rub them away, and I smile painfully up at him.

"People are already fleeing the city," Thomas continues. "The bad news is that means it'll take us hours just to get over the bypass and into Arizona. But the good news is we have the perfect hiding place among hundreds of thousands of other terrified people. There's no way in hell anyone is going to find us."

"Good," I say softly.

"What are we going to do?" Alanna asks me.

I turn my head so I can look at her, peering at me over her seat. "The gods can't help us anymore," I say, my voice firm and confident as the plan continues to gel in my head. "It's time to go to the humans."

Acknowledgments

Every time I sit down to write these, I know I'm going to forget about six people, so to begin with, thank you to the six people I'm about to forget.

Gillian Levinson is the absolute champion of this series, and half the good stuff in here is directly because of her. No, really. To my awesome Razorbill and Penguin team including but absolutely not limited to Ben Schrank, Marisa Russell, Tara Shanahan, Anna Jarzab, Erin Dempsey, Courtney Wood, Shanta Newlin, Lisa Kelly, Erin Gallagher, and all the other hard-working folks who have had their fingers in the proverbial *Earthquake* pot. You all rock!

No Earthbound series book is complete without a thank you to Scott and Ashley, who are always so supportive but also let me ask a million questions of Scott regarding his brain injury, which, coincidentally (no, it actually was!), mirrors Tavia's. To Kali, whose volunteer babysitting days made the first draft of this book possible. Oh, Saundra, you make my continuing sanity possible . . . and some days I'm sure it's at the expense of yours.

My husband, Kenny, was truly a knight in glittering, dazzling, shining armor on this book, which really didn't want to be written. Thank you for making sure I got twice as many hours of writing time as I usually need. My amazing children, who are the joys of my life: Aud, Bren, Gid, and Gwen, I love you all! And to my masses of extended family who all help in various ways, thank you, thank you, thank you.